J. CAROL NEMETH

Discovering Elena

J. Carol Nemeth

Dedication

Most every author will at some point dedicate one of their books to "the best mother in world." I've already dedicated a whole series to both of my parents, but since this book is written about the mother of my heroine, I'd like to dedicate *Discovering Elena: My Mother's Secret* to my mother, Mary Sue Amick Pruitt. To say she was the best mother in the world is the truth. At least in my world.

Mama wasn't perfect by any stretch of the imagination, but one thing I recall about her was when she grew upset with us kids, she never yelled at us. Even when she raised her voice, she didn't truly raise her voice. You might ask how that's possible, but you have to understand, my mother was a soft-spoken woman with a gentle nature. She just spoke slower to emphasize her words. She used to tell us that as the youngest of two until she was twelve, she was a hoodlum when she was a child. Then along came a younger brother. It's hard for me to imagine that, considering her adult nature, but I'm also fully aware how God can change a person when they give their lives to Him.

Mama was the wife of an old-fashioned Baptist preacher, and she supported his ministry while raising three children wide-spread in ages. She was always there for us as well as my father. She was always easy to talk to, and always wanted to know how our school days went. Since I was not particularly good at higher levels of math, and she was, she dragged me through Algebra and geometry. Bless her heart, I couldn't have made it without her.

My mother passed away in 2020 just before covid-19 hit the US. She was in the last stages of Alzheimer's, but the doctors found she had stage four Multiple Myeloma just four months before she passed. In reality, it likely was a blessing. She already didn't know who we were. Yet just days before she passed, I was with her, and told her I loved her. Her eyes were clear, and she told me she loved me too. That night she went into a coma. Four days later she left us. I believe with all my heart that was a gift from the Lord, the ability for us to share our love one more time. Her legacy as an amazing mother lives on. I'm thankful that one day I'll see her again and that she's whole and perfect.

This is for you, Mama. I love you.

Prologue

National Theater on Max-Joseph-Platz
Munich, Germany
April 20, 1944

The last haunting notes of Johannes Brahms *"Schwesterlein, Schwesterlein"* echoed through the vast theater as the orchestra's instruments ended their notes, and Elena Jäger's soprano voice faded away. She moved the microphone stand to the side and took a slow, graceful bow. Her white silk, figure-hugging evening gown pooled around her ankles. The audience surged to their feet, filling the hall with thunderous applause. Elena lifted her head and straightened her spine. She blew a kiss to the orchestra conductor and another to the orchestra in general. Lifting her eyes to the audience once again, she smiled and blew kisses in every direction before bowing again.

As she straightened, a young man in a tuxedo hurried onto the stage and handed her a bouquet of the finest red roses. Before making a hasty retreat, he pulled a second dozen from behind his back and handed them to her. The applause continued as Elena lifted the delicate blooms to her nose and smelled their sweet fragrance. As the lead soprano, she'd expected a dozen roses, but she'd never received a second dozen before. Warmth flowed through Elena at the audience's hearty ovation. Who could've sent

1

these beautiful flowers? Gunther? Her heart sank. Even if they were from him, it had been a thoughtful gesture.

It was time to go. She must leave. Now.

With one last blown kiss, Elena stepped sideways toward the stage right, waving to the audience as she went. Would she make her contact? She had to. There was no other option.

Once behind the side stage curtains, Elena turned to rush to her dressing room. She must change quickly. In a half hour, she had to meet her contact. Gunther would come to her dressing room. There was no way to prevent him from coming, but she'd already formed a plan. They were meeting his friends for dinner. She *must* deliver the package first before meeting Gunther and his friends at the restaurant. It wouldn't matter what happened to her once that package was delivered.

Slipping into her dressing room, Elena removed the silk evening gown and tossed it onto the couch in the corner. She yanked the navy suit from the hanger in the wardrobe along with a white silk blouse. Slipping into the suit, she pulled a felt hat from the wardrobe shelf and set it on her head at a jaunty angle, securing it with a hat pin. A touch of netting draped across her eyes. Glancing in the mirror over her dressing table, she tilted her head and viewed her reflection with a tight smile. Good enough, she supposed. There wasn't enough time to change her makeup from stage to everyday, but taking a tissue from a box on the table, she wiped at her face, smoothing the greasepaint to make it a little less dramatic. She shrugged. It would have to do.

Grabbing her clutch, Elena hurried to the door and yanked it open, only to find the German major standing in the doorway. Her heart nearly leapt from her chest. Gunther. Why had she jumped? She knew he'd come.

"Elena, my darling, where are you going in such a hurry?" Gunther's icy-blue eyes narrowed as his chin lifted.

It made his peaked officer's hat stand that much taller on his head, giving him a foreboding appearance. One she'd seen far too often. "You know we're expected for a dinner engagement with Herr Schmitt and his wife along with Herr General Guttenberg and his wife. You weren't leaving, were you?" His lips pressed into a tight, thin line.

Gunther Jäger was a handsome man, but at present he looked cold and disapproving. Elena needed to tread lightly. Giving him a sweet smile, she reached up with a steady hand and ran a finger down his smoothly-shaven cheek to his cleft chin.

"Darling, I have not forgotten our dinner plans with our friends. However, I must run home first. With having to sing this evening, I forgot the gift for Frau Schmitt. In case you forgot, this dinner is to celebrate her birthday." She leaned in to give him a kiss on his cheek. "I'll be quick. You go on to the restaurant and explain that I'll be there shortly." Elena touched his shoulders and laughed happily. His face gentled as a responding smile turned his lips upward. "And thank you for the gorgeous roses, my love." She stepped over to the dressing table to pick them up. "I was in such a hurry to get home and retrieve the gift, I almost forgot them. I'll put them in water when I arrive home."

The iciness returned to his eyes. "*I* did not send them to you. If I did not, who did?"

Elena didn't have to pretend shock. Who indeed? "You didn't send them? Then I have no idea."

Gunther stared into her eyes and must have been satisfied that she was telling the truth. "You would never betray me, would you, my love? Perhaps they are from a secret fan who comes to the theater to listen to your lovely voice." A smile lifted his lips and his features softened. "After all that's how I fell for you."

A surge of relief flowed through Elena. She turned him around and gave him a gentle push. "Indeed, it is, my darling. Now, go. You mustn't keep our friends waiting."

Gunther chuckled and turned back to her. "Ach, *nein*, my beautiful darling. Not without another kiss first." He swept her into his arms and pressed his lips on hers.

Elena pretended to accept Gunther's kiss while all the time writhing inside. She didn't love this man, but she had to keep up the charade. One day she would be free of him. Yes, one day…. She pushed him away. "Gunther, you must go. Hurry, or they'll be waiting on both of us." Elena tittered a light laugh she didn't feel.

Gunther straightened his officer's hat. "Yes, my darling. Until later."

Disgust twisted Elena's insides. If only—.

When Gunther turned right to leave through the lobby of the theater, Elena hurried out the rear stage door and into a waiting cab. It wound its way through Munich's back streets to a small row house several blocks away. Elena climbed out and asked the cabby to wait for her, then she hurried up the half-dozen stone steps to the wooden door and knocked three times.

Within moments, the door opened a few inches exposing the familiar tired face of the older woman. Eyes that had seen much in life stared at Elena but didn't show recognition. "I don't want anything from the market this evening," the woman spoke in perfect Czechoslovakian.

"Perhaps you have something for me instead." Elena responded in her native Czech tongue. "I'd be happy to purchase it from you."

A slight smile lifted one corner of the woman's lips. "*Ano*. Yes, I believe I have something you may be interested in." She swung the door wider, and Elena slipped inside.

After scanning the street in both directions, the woman closed the door behind Elena and locked it. She motioned with her hand. "Come. This way. He is here."

Elena followed her down the darkened hallway in

silence. Once in the windowless storeroom, the woman turned to Elena and gathered her in her arms. "Oh, my child, it's wonderful to see you. You are as beautiful as ever."

"Zofia, you risk so much." Tears nearly clogged Elena's throat as she held the older woman. "I don't know what I would do without you."

Zofia Beranek pulled back and held Elena's cheeks between her work-roughened hands. "Oh, my precious Elena-lamb, you and everything about this make it all worth it. It will all be over soon. You will see."

Elena shook her head. "No, not yet. There's still work to be done."

"No, Elena. Your work is over. It's time to go."

A masculine voice spoke from the door, and Elena turned to find Major Mark Scott leaning against the doorframe. The American US Army soldier was dressed in German peasant clothes, a wool cap pulled low over one blue eye. How could his eyes look so warm and friendly when Gunther's were always icy and cold? Elena shook the thought away.

He pointed at the roses in her hand. "I see you received my flowers."

"These are from you?" Elena's voice was little more than a whisper. "But...how? Why?"

"Your performance was flawless." So was his smile.

"You were there?"

He nodded. Wait. What had he said before his comment about the flowers?

"What do you mean, my work is over, and it's time to go?" Elena slipped from Zofia's touch and stepped closer to the major. "It can't be. I still have work to do here. You must take the package as planned, but I must return to continue my job."

Major Scott eased away from the doorframe, shaking his head. "No. I'm here to take you home."

Elena allowed her eyes to roam his handsome features. "I can't. I can't leave him. He'll come after me. He'll find me. He won't stop until he does."

"Elena—" Mark took a step toward her.

"No." Elena stepped back. "I won't. Gunther is one step away from finding out. He's always suspicious of me. I must continue—"

A loud banging at the front door interrupted Elena, immediately followed by a deep German voice insisting the door be opened or it would be crashed open.

"Elena," Major Scott's voice held an urgent note. "He's already found out."

Zofia sprang into action. She slid two large crates aside to reveal a hatch in the floor before retrieving a small wooden crate. "Here. Open the hatch, Major. Take this package. Hurry, child. You must go with him. There's no going back. You must leave. Now."

Elena eyed in the direction of the pounding noise. "But—"

Major Scott yanked open the hatch in the floor and turned his stern eyes on Elena. "You must come with me. If he finds you here, you know what will happen to you." He held out his hand toward her. "Elena, please, come now. This package. Help me take it to the US."

Elena stared into his eyes and identified something she'd never seen there before. Her heart hammered, and she reached her hand to clasp his. She nodded and turned to the older woman waiting impatiently. "But Zofia—"

"Go, child. There's no time. I will be fine. I will take care of everything, I promise. Including the envelope."

Elena blew her a kiss and disappeared through the hatch, hearing Zofia's voice for the last time.

"Here. Take the package, Major. I'll cover the hole. There's a lantern at the base of the steps, and you'll see a tunnel. Take it to the river. Your boat will be waiting for you as planned. Be safe, and keep my girl safe."

"I will."

After Major Scott descended the stairs, Zofia lowered the hatch door before she pushed the crates over it. She hurried to the front door and unlocked it.

"I'm sorry it took me so long to answer. I was on the third floor, and my arthritis is bad. What is this pounding about, Herr Major?" she demanded in German with a scowl on her face. "Can't an old woman get some peace? What do you want?" She scanned the street to find Elena's taxi driver had gone. Thank God.

The German major stood on her stoop peering behind her. Two German soldiers stood on the steps behind him, rifles slung over their shoulders. "Pardon the interruption of your peaceful evening, Frau; however, we suspect a young woman came here on a mission of nefarious purposes. Is this so? Are you hiding this young woman?" The officer lifted his chin and stared at Zofia with cold blue eyes.

Zofia would not be intimidated. She stood aside and held out an arm of invitation. "No, I am not, Herr Major. Please, come in. You are welcome to investigate my home and bakery. It's humble, but it's all I have."

Glaring down his nose at her, the major and his soldiers surged into Zofia's home to search.

Please, my God. Protect my humble home and protect my darling Elena, the Major Scott, and the package. They are all so important to me, to the war effort, and to You. Take them safely to America. And if You see fit, protect me. Please forgive my lie. Yes, I did hide my Elena. But it was necessary to protect her.

Zofia waited for what seemed like an interminable amount of time by the front door as she prayed. After a time, the German major returned followed by his soldiers. Had he torn her home apart? Would they haul her away?

What is my fate, Lord?

The major stopped before her and bowed slightly, clicking his shiny, black Hessian boot heels. "Danke, Frau, for indulging our—necessary search. As you said, there was nothing to find. We will take our leave. For now. Have a peaceful rest of your evening."

As the two soldiers passed her, Zofia noticed they were eating *Berliner pfannkuchen* from her bakery. These filled donut-like pastries were popular in her bakery, and the soldiers had helped themselves as the Nazi military were known to do wherever they went. Of course, the major hadn't stopped them. Who cared if it tore into her profits? Zofia released an indignant huff and closed the door behind the men. It did not matter. As long as Elena, the major and the package were safe.

My God, please make it so.

Dogwood Station, Ohio
Mid-March, 1970

Chapter One

Kate Cigler leaned her head against the window frame and stared out at the cold, pouring rain. Thank goodness it had only drizzled at Grandma Margareta's funeral that morning. How utterly miserable it would've been if it had poured like it was now. She was grateful it wasn't snowing.

"Darling Katarina, Mr. Calhoun is ready for us." A gentle arm slipped around Kate's shoulder and gave her a squeeze. The soft Czechoslovakian-accented voice spoke near her ear. "Come, sweets. It is time to meet with the lawyer."

Kate turned to find her great-aunt Anna Cigler beside her. Her grandmother's youngest sister wore a sad but tender smile on her wrinkled features, and her lips trembled. Auntie Anna's thin frame bore the burden of sorrow beneath the black funeral dress she wore, but she held her chin high. She'd arranged her gray hair in a bun at the back of her head, and gold wire-frames sat low on her aquiline nose. Her bright pink lipstick had faded since she'd applied it that morning before the funeral.

Kate returned her squeeze. "Of course. I'll be right there."

Auntie Anna patted her shoulder. "Don't be long. He's

setting up in the dining room as we speak."

As her great-aunt slipped away, Kate turned her gaze to the drenched scene out the window. How in the world would she go on without Grandma Margareta? A tightness settled in her chest as a burning grew behind her eyes, and tears slid down her cheeks. "Oh, Grandma," she whispered to the windowpanes. "What am I going to do without you?"

Kate suspected what Mr. Calhoun would tell her, her aunts, and her great-uncle. Although the bakery was thriving, and she and her elderly loved ones could continue to make it work, it could be bought out from under them if they didn't come up with the money to purchase the property first. It wasn't that they couldn't make the lease payments; it was the fact that Andrew Hawthorn, property developer, wanted to add it to his properties in town. She couldn't allow that to happen. It was prime real estate and the perfect place for the bakery. They had built a phenomenal business at its current location. If Hawthorn took the property and they had to move, they would lose loyal customers.

It wasn't that Grandma Margareta had such a great business head, but she did have wisdom that Kate depended on. Far above that, Grandma was a great prayer warrior, someone Kate would definitely miss. *I know, Lord. I can pray too. But, Grandma—she had that certain something special with You, didn't she?*

"Katarina, Mr. Calhoun is waiting." A different accented voice spoke from the doorway. This time it was Auntie Genevieve, her voice strident. "Come. Now."

Kate straightened and turned from the window. "Coming, Auntie Genny." She wiped her eyes with the tissue in her hand.

With hesitant feet, she followed her great-aunt into the dining room where a balding man in his late fifties sat at the dining room table tamping papers into a pile, his open briefcase set beside him. A row of dining room chairs stood across the worn carpet in front of the table. Auntie Anna sat beside her husband, Rudolf. Kate called him Uncle Rudy. Rotund and bald except for a gray fringe around the edges, Rudolf Cigler wrapped an arm around his Anna and tugged her close to comfort her.

Kate took the chair between Auntie Anna and Auntie Genevieve, an avowed old maid. Auntie Genevieve wore her dyed-brown hair piled on top of her head. Coiffed perfectly at the beauty parlor weekly, Auntie Genevieve made sure there was never a hair out of place nor a gray hair on display. The spitfire of the family, she wasn't ashamed to taste-test all the recipes in the bakery. Her figure showed it.

Mr. Calhoun, the family lawyer, raised his eyes to the small assembly and viewed them with a sad smile. "My condolences for the loss in your family, my friends. Margareta Vitu Cigler was an amazing woman. When we lost her husband—Rudy, your brother, Jakub—it was hard on your family. Now, losing Margareta, it's another hard loss. She was an amazing sister and grandmother. You, Kate, for being such a young woman, have had too much loss in your life, what with your mother, your grandfather, and now your grandmother."

He eyed the papers in front of him. "I have Margareta's will. There isn't much to go over, but here it is:

"'I Margareta Vitu Cigler, being of sound mind do leave—'"

Mr. Calhoun read Margareta's will through to the end. She had only the bakery which she left to Kate. The house, having no lien, was also left to Kate with life rights to her two sisters and Rudy. The proceeds from the bakery were to be used for business expenses and for the usual salaries of the family who worked in the bakery.

The attorney informed Kate a safe-deposit box sat at the bank with some good pieces of jewelry and several savings bonds in her name. Mr. Calhoun handed her the key to the box and indicated she was free to check it out whenever she liked.

Kate held the key in her palm. *Why didn't Grandmother ever tell me about this?*

"I know what you're thinking." Mr. Calhoun clasped his hands on top of the papers on the table. "Margareta didn't feel there was a need to tell you until after her death. She knew you would need them after she was gone."

Kate's throat tightened, and tears slipped from her eyes. The desire to toss the key across the room nearly overwhelmed her. She'd rather have her grandmother back than whatever lay in that safe-deposit box, but her grandmother had prepared for Kate's future as best she could. Kate must accept that and appreciate her efforts, not squander them or be ungrateful. *Forgive me, Lord. Help me be wise with what she left me.* Wrapping her fingers around the key, she lifted tear-filled eyes to the lawyer. "Thank you. I'll check it out soon."

"Good. Carry on her legacy with the bakery, my dear. It's what she would've wanted." He cleared his throat and added, "You are well aware that Andrew Hawthorn, the big developer in the area, is buying up properties in town. He has his eye on your bakery. Fight for it. Don't let your grandmother's bakery fade away. Fight for what she left you for her sake."

"The bakery will carry on, Mr. Calhoun." Auntie Genevieve spoke up, her chin lifted, her accent strong. "We will see that it does. Margareta worked hard to build her business in this community, and no property developer will take it away." She pointed a finger at her own large bosom, emphatically stabbing at it several times. "I, Genevieve Vitu, will fight alongside my niece, my sister, Anna, and Rudy to make sure that does not happen."

On the other side of Kate, Auntie Anna gave a vehement nod, clasping her hands together on her thin lap.

"Indeed."

Kate wrapped her arms around her great-aunts' shoulders. "I love you both so much. Thanks for your support. We'll make Grandma proud."

Kate lay on her bed later that afternoon, but sleep eluded her. All she could do was ponder how she'd carry on Grandma Margareta's legacy when Andrew Hawthorn wanted the bakery property. When asked, Mr. Calhoun explained he didn't deal with property law much, but he would do the best he could if it came down to it. He highly recommended finding a lawyer who dealt solely with property law. He had always been their family lawyer. How in the world could they afford a property lawyer as well?

Kate rolled to her side and tucked her hand beneath her pillow just as a knock sounded on her bedroom door.

"Come in."

Glancing toward the door, she found both of her aunt's entering. Auntie Anna held a small wooden chest in her hands. Kate sat up and swung her legs over the side of the bed.

"Oh, my darling, were you sleeping?" Auntie Genevieve halted at the foot of the bed.

With a quirk to her lips, Kate shook her head. "I tried napping, but sleep wouldn't come."

The aunts sat on the bed, one on either side of her. Auntie Anna reached up and pushed a stray tendril of hair behind her ear. "Ah, sweets, I am sorry. You have much on your mind, and you're missing your dear grandma, God rest her soul."

"Yes, but so are you, Auntie."

"True, but my darling Rudy comforts me. You and Genny have no one."

"Bah." Genevieve waved a dismissive hand. "We have

one another, and we have God."

"That's right." Kate wrapped an arm around both of their shoulders and tugged them close. "We have each other, and we have God. Now what do you have there?" She indicated the wooden chest in Auntie Anna's hands.

"Well, you see, this is something else your Grandma Margareta wanted you to have. It's not from Mr. Calhoun. She asked Genevieve and me to hold it for you until after her death. If one of us passed, then the other would give to you."

"What's in it, and why would she keep it until she died?"

Auntie Anna ran a wrinkled hand tenderly across the embossed lid of the chest. Tiny carved flowers and leaves decorated the aged patina of the wood. Embedded in the center of the lid was a small, beautiful oval painting featuring a man and a woman in baroque dress surrounded by flowers and greenery.

"Isn't this lovely?" Auntie Anna ran a finger along the carved flowers. "Tell me what you remember of your mother, Katarina?"

Kate thought of how her mother always lifted her spirits. "Mother had a heart of gold, and she was beautiful. She was kind to everyone she met. Mother loved working in the bakery alongside Grandmother and both of you. The three of you came up with the most delectable pastries and desserts anyone could imagine. And Mother loved her family. She loved me. When I was a child, we built forts under the dining-room table and sat beneath reading books all evening after the bakery closed. That was my fondest memory of her. She taught me to read in Czech and in English. Both she and Grandmother taught me to bake." Kate released a soft laugh. "Imagine that. The daughter and granddaughter of bakers."

"You are a well-rounded young woman, Katarina," Genevieve huffed. "Don't take it for granted. Those women taught you everything they knew."

Kate patted her great-aunt's hand. "I know that. I'm blessed to have such strong women in my life. You two as well as them." She patted Auntie Anna's hand. "I'm so glad I still have you both. Now the suspense is killing me. What's in that chest?"

Auntie Anna lifted the carved lid. "Clues to secrets from your mother's past. We can't tell you those secrets. They are not ours to tell. You must find them for yourself, my sweets. We promised. On our hearts." Crossing her finger over her heart, she pressed her fingers to her lips. "You must discover who you are. Those secrets are not in this chest, but there are clues here that may help you find those secrets."

"Auntie, you aren't making sense." Kate glanced into the chest. "What's in there?"

Auntie Anna handed her the small chest. "Take a look and see what you can discover."

Kate stared into her great-aunt's faded brown eyes and spotted a challenge there. What—? She accepted the chest and lifted out the first item, a folded pink baby hat. Kate unfolded it, turning it over and over and rubbing the soft, silky fabric between her fingers. She lifted her eyes to her aunts'. "Mine?"

They shrugged and kept their lips clamped shut. Laying it in Auntie Genny's lap, Kate reached for the next item. Several black and white photographs, faded and yellowed. Holding them close she discovered one of her mother standing beside an American army officer in uniform. Both were smiling. Beautiful as ever, Mother looked happy. The next photo was also of Mother, but this time she stood next to a German officer. Her smile appeared forced. Why in the world was Mother standing beside a German officer? In the third picture two babies lay on a blanket beside a little girl. This was all so confusing. 'Secrets,' Auntie Anna had said. What secrets had Mother held? She'd died of leukemia when Kate was eighteen. Why hadn't she told Kate about her secrets before she died? Why now? Why had Grandmother waited until after her death for this chest to come to Kate?

One final item lay in the bottom of the chest. A metal medallion. Kate retrieved it from the chest and turned it over and over in her fingers. It wasn't complete. The medallion was half of a heart with words embossed into the medal. Holding it close, Kate turned it toward the light. What did it say? The words were written in Czech, and she had the right half. Translated into English her half read:

> shall be
> reunited

She peered at her aunts again and wasn't in the least surprised when their eyes evaded hers.

"Neither of you are going to make this easy for me, are you?"

They remained silent.

Kate turned the metal medallion over again, but there were no more clues. Looking inside the chest, nothing remained. She returned the medallion inside, and took another view at the confusing photographs before returning them to the chest. Taking the baby cap from Auntie Genny's lap, she held it, glancing at her great-aunt's. "Are you sure you won't give me a simple hint as to who this belonged to?"

They shook their heads, crossed their hands over their hearts and kissed their fingertips.

Kate blew out a breath, refolded the tiny cap, returned it to the chest and closed the lid. "Will you at least tell me *where* I'm supposed to start looking for Mother's secrets? I don't see anything here that indicates where I should begin."

Auntie Anna reached into her sweater pocket and

withdrew a small piece of paper. She handed it to Kate. "Here is an address. You must go there to begin your search."

Kate accepted the scrap of paper and read the address. "Wyoming. Wyoming? This is not a good time to head to Wyoming. Let's straighten out the bakery situation first, and ensure Mr. Hawthorn can't take our property. Afterward, I'll pursue this. Mother's secrets have been hidden for a long time. They can wait a little longer."

"No, Katarina. You must pursue this now. It's what Margareta wanted." Auntie Genevieve's voice rose causing Kate to jerk her head around and stare at her.

"But…but why? What's the rush?"

"Darling, Margareta knew the importance of you beginning this search. It was something she wanted you to do with great urgency."

Kate turned toward Auntie Anna. "Why not begin while she was still living? I don't understand."

"It was her wish, child. All we can do is follow her wish."

Kate ran her hand over the lid of the chest. "But, what if Mr. Hawthorn attempts to take the bakery while I'm gone?"

"Bah! What can he do? Nothing. You are the legal lessee, and until your lease is up, he can do nothing. Your lease states the owner cannot sell the property out from under you." Auntie Genevieve waved a dismissive hand. "Besides, God is on the side of right, and we are right." She crossed her arms over her chest and harumphed.

Kate chuckled. "He won't succeed with you two and God working against him."

"Indeed." Auntie Anna nodded. "So, go. Search out your mother's secrets and discover what you need to know. It was Margareta's wish as much as the bakery's legacy."

Kate was torn between staying to ensure the bakery survived and the need to find out what was in her mother's past. She'd always thought her mother was a simple baker. Apparently, there was more. So much more. She slapped the scrap of paper with the address against her palm. "All right. I'll go. But I'll stay in touch by phone to see how things are going here, okay?"

"But of course." Auntie Genevieve threw up a hand. "I wouldn't expect anything less."

As her aunts left the room, Kate sent up a prayer. *Abba Father, I have no idea what I'm getting myself into. All I have are a few items and an address. I'm almost afraid to find out more about Mother. If she wasn't simply a baker from Ohio, who was she? Lead me, Father. Guide my footsteps as I go into unknown territory. Please don't allow Mr. Hawthorn to take our bakery while I'm gone.*

The next morning Kate knocked on the open door of the bank president of the Dogwood Station Bank and Trust. He peeked from beneath his black-framed glasses then shoved them onto the bridge of his nose. Standing, he urged Kate inside and proffered his hand toward her.

"Ah, Miss Cigler. Please, come in."

Kate entered the luxurious banker's office, her feet sinking into the thick carpet. "Thank you, Mr. Kendrick." She shook his outstretched hand.

"Please, have a seat." He indicated one of the chairs arranged in front of his polished mahogany desk. "I'd like to extend my condolences on the loss of your grandmother. Margareta Cigler was an amazing woman and a long-time customer of our bank. I must say I've been expecting you."

Kate lifted her chin and met the banker's eyes. "I'm sure you have, sir. You probably also know I'm here to open my grandmother's safe-deposit box."

Steepling his fingers on the shiny surface of the desk, he tilted his head in acknowledgment, giving the impression of a bow. "Of course. You have the key, I presume."

"Yes, I do." Kate held the key for the banker to see.

He leaned toward an intercom on the side of his desk and pressed a button. "Miss Agnew, I have a customer that would like to open her safe-deposit box. If you'd be so kind as to accompany her to the vault, please?"

"Yes, sir," the feminine response sounded through the speaker.

"Thank you." Mr. Kendrick released the button. "Miss Agnew will take you to your box. She will assist you in opening it if you find it necessary, then she'll leave you to explore the contents. If you decide you wish to remove those contents, just push the intercom button on the wall in the vault to request a bag."

Kate held one up in her hand. "That won't be necessary. I brought my own."

"Of course. Please leave the safe-deposit box and key on the table, then stop by and let me know whether you've emptied it. I'll let Miss Agnew know to close out the account and return the box to its place."

"Certainly. Thank you."

A young woman arrived to accompany Kate to the vault. There she found Kate's box, placed it on the table, and ensured Kate's key worked. When the box was open, the woman left Kate to search the contents.

As Mr. Calhoun had stated, there were several lovely old pieces of jewelry. Kate placed them in the little bag she'd brought. Searching further, she found seventeen savings bonds, five at $1000, six at $2500, and six at $5000 each. Fifty-thousand dollars.

Kate's knees nearly buckled. She grabbed the side of the table to steady herself. This wouldn't be enough to save the bakery, but it would certainly help. That is, if they were mature bonds. She would have to check with Mr. Kendrick to find out. She laid them aside and searched further. A bank book was the last item in the box. Kate flipped through the pages of the small, thin booklet until she reached the last entry. It was marked a week before Grandma's death. Thirty-five thousand dollars. That was to be used for upkeep of the bakery and of the house. There were repairs that needed to be made on both. She'd wondered where that money would come from. This would certainly help on that front, and she was the one who would have to take care of those things now. Grandma had squirreled away money knowing she wouldn't always be around. *Thank you, Lord, for her wise foresight.*

As Kate stuffed everything into the bag, she prayed she could fill the shoes that Grandma had left behind. It was her burden to bear, but there was One Who would help her bear it. Thank goodness she wouldn't bear it alone.

Uncle Rudy pulled his 1969 Lincoln Continental to the curb in front of the airport terminal and slipped it into park. Exiting, he walked around to help Auntie Anna out of the passenger seat. As he passed the shiny cream-colored hood, he removed his handkerchief from his pants pocket and rubbed a couple of spots. Kate doubted there was actually anything there. Her great-uncle babied his one-year-old car. He kept it waxed to a glossy shine, and if a fly dared land on it, it would slide right off.

Kate and Auntie Genevieve climbed from the back seat and walked to the humungous trunk where Kate's suitcase and carry-on case awaited. They'd left Dogwood Station a couple hours early in order to make Kate's flight on time. As Uncle Rudy rounded the car to open the trunk, she scanned the façade of the Cleveland Hopkins Terminal. Kate had never flown before.

A plane lifted off the ground to her left sending her heart into her throat. Goodness. Perhaps this wasn't a good idea after all. The train may have been a better idea, and she could've departed right from Dogwood Station. But riding all the way to Gillette, Wyoming, by train would take a couple of days and far more money than she was willing to spend. Kate had, thus, booked a flight, looking forward to a new experience. Now she wasn't so sure.

"It will be fine, holčička. Do not worry." Uncle Rudy wrapped a firm, reassuring arm around Kate's shoulder, the Czech word for 'little girl' he used as an endearment for her always brought warmth to her heart. He laid a kiss on her temple.

Kate wrapped an arm around his waist. "Thanks. I'll try not to."

He opened the trunk and withdrew her luggage. "Let's get you checked in. You don't have much time before your flight."

The foursome made their way toward ticketing where Kate purchased a ticket to Casper, Wyoming, and another for a puddle jumper to Gillette. Puddle jumper? It sounded atrocious. Once they'd checked in, their little group ambled toward the gate and took seats to await the flight to be called.

"Well, I'm not waiting until the last minute to give you this, sweets." Auntie Anna tugged a paper bag from her over-sized purse and handed it to Kate. "I emptied almost everything from my handbag, so I could bring this for your trip."

"What is it?" Kate reached for the proffered bag.

"Sweets for the sweet, my sweets." Auntie Anna laughed at her own joke. "From the bakery. You must have something delicious to eat on the plane. Not that cardboard stuff they feed you." She wrinkled her nose and sniffed.

"Bah." Auntie Genevieve waved a dismissive hand and frowned. "What they feed you will be unhealthy. Believe me."

Kate laughed. "How do either of you know? You've

never flown before?"

Uncle Rudy rolled his eyes. "They don't know anything. When they immigrated from Czechoslovakia, they came aboard a ship."

"We just know. Don't ask." Auntie Genevieve gave her brother-in-law a stink-eye before patting Kate on the arm. "We're your elders. Trust us."

Kate stifled a laugh as she opened the bag. "Goodness, Auntie Anna. No matter what they serve, it won't be as good as this. Mmm. I'm tempted to take a taste now. It's smells wonderful, but did you leave anything in the bakery?"

Auntie Anna smiled. "Go ahead. There's plenty in there."

"It's the truth. You could share with half the passengers on the plane." Auntie Genevieve's brow furrowed. "We'll have to bake twice as much tomorrow before we open the bakery to ensure there's enough for the customers."

"Oh, shush, Genny." Auntie Anna frowned at her sister. "I'll do whatever it takes for my sweet niece. She deserves it. Not to mention she's leaving us for no telling how long."

Auntie Genevieve turned to Kate and pulled her toward her, planting a wet kiss on her cheek. "Don't I know it. Oh, my darling, we'll miss you so much."

Tears threatened as Kate swallowed hard. "I'll miss all of you too. More than you can know."

Uncle Rudy poked Kate with his elbow. "Don't look now, holčička, but there's a young man staring at you."

"Where?" Auntie Genevieve's eyes darted in every direction.

"Where?" Auntie Anna turned, peering at every man in their vicinity.

Kate lifted her gaze and instantly met dark gray eyes in a tanned face framed by short well-groomed, black hair.

When a grin lifted one corner of his lips, Kate yanked her eyes away. "Aunties, stop it." She hoped her harsh whisper didn't reach the man's ears. He sat only two rows over directly facing them. How embarrassing.

"Oh my, but he is handsome, Katarina." Auntie Anna's whisper was anything but quiet. "Shall I go bring him over and introduce you?"

"No. Ew. Not by a long shot. Stay right where you are." Kate grabbed her great-aunt's arm in case she jumped up and did so. "I am not interested in meeting a strange young man in an airport or anywhere else."

"Well, my darling, you may not have a choice. I believe he's coming over here." Auntie Genevieve chuckled. "Smile for the handsome man."

Kate's eyes darted from her great-aunt to the young man approaching them. Goodness, he was tall and, yes, handsome. Her heart hammered for some reason. Why in the world should it beat fast for a stranger? It made no sense. *Lord, what in the world...?*

"Excuse me. I'm sorry for interrupting, but you look familiar. Have we met before?"

That had to be the oldest line in the book for picking up a girl, but certainly strange when that girl sat with three elderly people in an airport. Kate plastered on a cool smile. "No, I don't believe so."

He held out a strong-looking hand. "Perhaps you're right. I'm Gabriel Flanagan."

Kate stared at his outstretched hand for a moment. It would be rude not to shake it. She would likely never meet this man again, so why be rude? The second she offered hers, he enveloped it in his warm hand. Their eyes met, and her heart picked up its pace again. *Lord?*

"And you are?" One brow lifted, and his grin looked genuine.

"Um, I'm Kate. Kate Cigler." She tugged her hand from his and turned to her elders. "These are my great-aunts Genevieve Vitu and Anna Cigler, and my great-uncle Rudy Cigler." Mr. Flanagan shook each of their hands, bestowing smiles on them all. "It's a pleasure to meet you." His gray eyes returned to Kate. "I'm sorry. I thought for sure we'd met before. You look so familiar." He bent to pick up his bag from where he'd set it at his feet. "Again, I'm sorry for interrupting. I hope you have a safe and enjoyable flight." Kate returned his smile. "Thank you. I hope you do as well."

The young man walked away just as her flight was called. Kate and her family stood to say their goodbyes. As Kate gave Uncle Rudy a hug, she whispered, "Take care of the aunties, Uncle. Keep them out of trouble."

"Ah, my holčička, you know I will. At least as best as I can. I'm a little outnumbered, you know." Uncle Rudy released a soggy chuckle before growing serious. "I'll pray for you while you're gone. Find your mother's secrets and come home to us. Life won't be complete without you." His voice broke on the last words as he gave her another squeeze. He released Kate and stepped back. "Go, before your flight leaves without you."

Kate walked away, her own eyes stinging with tears. She followed the line of people preparing to board the plane. At the last second before entering the door, she peered back to find the three dearest folks left in her life waving at her, watery smiles plastered on their faces. With one last smile of her own and a wave, Kate stepped through the door to an adventure she'd never dreamed she would take.

Chapter Two

With the help of the stewardess, Kate found her seat. She lifted her carry-on bag to put it in the overhead compartment.

"Here, allow me."

A familiar voice spoke from beside Kate, and she turned to find the young man from the terminal, a grin on his face. Before she could respond, he whisked the small bag from her hands and stored it above the seats. Immobile with surprise, Kate simply stared.

A brow lifted as he waited for her to sit, and the line of people behind him grew, their faces becoming more impatient by the second. Kate finally moved. "Thank you."

"My pleasure. Is one of these yours?" He pointed at the row of three seats.

"Yes." She slipped into the seat by the window. He dropped beside her into the middle seat, and the flow of passengers proceeded past them, some grumbling and shaking their heads. Kate barely noticed as she was far too aware of the man in the seat beside her.

Removing her book from her purse, she laid it on her lap and leaned forward to place her purse beneath the seat in front of her beside the bag of pastries from Auntie Anna. The aroma wafted to her even now causing her mouth to water. Once the plane was in the air, perhaps she'd retrieve one. Glancing at the man beside her, she wondered if she dared offer him one.

He crossed his long legs at the ankles and tucked his feet beneath the seat in front of him as the plane pulled away from the gate. "Do you fly with this airline often? I still can't shake the feeling I've seen you before."

Kate met his dark eyes and shook her head. "No. This is the first time." She avoided telling him it was her first time flying. Ever.

"I see. Are you stopping in Casper or heading elsewhere?"

Kate lowered her brow. "You ask a lot of questions, sir. Especially of a young woman traveling alone."

A contrite expression settled on his features, and he nodded. "You're right. I apologize. You must have a doppelgänger that I've met somewhere along the way. I'm not thinking straight. Forgive me?"

Kate eyed him. He seemed sincere, and she wouldn't share further information with him, so there shouldn't be a need for concern. "All right. I forgive you."

The plane taxied down the runway and gained speed. A gasp escaped Kate as it lifted off the ground. She grabbed the armrests and held on.

Gabriel Flanagan watched the woman's reaction as the plane lifted from the ground. He chuckled inwardly at her gasp and as she held her breath those few moments they were shoved back into their seats.

"Are you all right?"

She nodded but didn't speak. When the pilot announced they had reached their flight altitude and they could remove their seatbelts, she didn't.

"Are you sure you're all right, Miss Cigler?"

Her knuckles had turned white from gripping the arm rests.

"Not only is this your first flight with this airline, it's your first flight ever, isn't it?" Gabe turned to the terrified woman beside him. "Can you speak and at least tell me you're all right? Should I call the stewardess?"

Miss Cigler turned wide eyes toward him. "Oh no. I'm fine."

He grinned. "Okay. Maybe you should release the armrests. They'll be fine too."

She eyed her fingers gripping the arm-rests as if her life depended on it and immediately released them, clasping her fingers in her lap. The young woman sent him a tight smile. "I had no idea what a take-off involved or how it would feel."

"Strange, huh? Especially the first time you experience it. I've flown so many times now I've grown accustomed to it and don't even think about it anymore." He paused at the uncertainty in her eyes. "You should've told me. Perhaps I could've helped you through it."

"But I don't know you. Why would I have told you that?" Her eyes searched his.

"You're right. You don't know me, and you certainly have no reason to tell me anything. Especially after I've asked so many questions of you." His eyes dropped to the book in her lap. "I see you're a reader. Why don't I leave you to enjoy your book."

Gabe dropped his head against the headrest and closed his eyes. The beautiful woman at his side had rocked his world from the moment she and her three elderly companions sat down across from the row in front of him at the terminal gate. Her name wasn't familiar, but her face sure was. Why? Who did she remind him of? He wracked his brain to think who. Gabe would likely never see her again since he was disembarking in Casper. She might be as well, or she could be traveling on to who knew where. She wasn't about to tell him, and why should she? He nearly chuckled aloud. He hadn't exactly garnered her trust with his forward behavior.

Gabe stifled another chuckle at the memory of her elderly great-aunts who were more than willing to introduce Miss Cigler to him. He peeked out of the corner of his eye. She was engrossed in her book, so he took a moment to study her profile. Perfection. He'd noticed earlier that her eyes were dark brown. They'd reminded him of chocolate. She possessed a pert nose and a bow-shaped mouth that Gabe found quite delectable. Wait. What? Where had that thought come from? He snapped his eye closed. He'd never see this woman again, so he shoved the crazy thought away. It was naptime. Drawing in a deep breath, he released it slowly and blanked his mind. Or attempted to.

As she read, Kate listened to the soft snore of the man beside her. Glancing over the seats in front of her, she spotted the stewardess coming down the aisle with a cart. In spite of her great-aunts' warnings, she'd see what they had to offer before she pulled out her bag of pastries. Her aunties had never flown before and truly had no idea what was served on a plane.

When the stewardess reached her row, she asked if she would like chicken or beef. Kate chose the beef and, at the direction of the stewardess, lowered the tray table on the back of the seat in front of her. Wow. They'd thought of everything on these planes. Kate eyed Mr. Flanagan who appeared to be deep in sleep.

The stewardess passed Kate's meal over him, handed her the water she requested, served the aisle passenger, and moved on. Kate was tempted to poke him and wake him up, but it wasn't her place. After saying grace, she tucked into her meal and found it far better than she'd expected. When she returned home, she'd be happy to dispel her great-aunts' misgivings.

Later when the meal had been cleared away, Kate decided she still had room for at least a portion of one of the pastries. Glancing around, she leaned forward and lifted the bag into her lap. Unfolding the top, the fresh sugary scent made her mouth water. Hadn't she just eaten? Delving into the bag, Kate retrieved a *Koblihy*. Auntie Anna knew this Czech fried donut was one of Kate's favorites. With this donut sprinkled with powdered sugar and filled with chocolate custard, Kate would be hard pressed to eat only half. Taking a bite, she released a soft moan.

A light chuckle came from the seat beside her. Kate's head spun to the side and her eyes met the gaze of Mr. Flanagan. So much for him sleeping. His smile broadened as he tapped his lip then pointed at hers.

Kate tilted her head in question.

"You have a little…powdered sugar. Right there." He eyed her mouth and pointed again.

"Oh." Kate covered her mouth and licked her lip before grabbing the napkin she'd kept from lunch. She wiped her mouth and eyed him. "Did I get it?"

"Yeah. Not that it matters." His eyes moved to the pastry in her other hand. "You still have more to eat."

Warmth invaded Kate's cheeks as she laughed softly. "Yes, I do. Would you like one? My great-aunt handed them to me at the airport this morning. They're fresh, and there's a variety. I'm not sure what all she put in here." Kate held out the bag. "Please. Help yourself."

Mr. Flanagan's eyes moved from Kate to the paper bag before he lowered his hand inside. "Thank you. I believe I will. I obviously slept through lunch."

"Yes, you did. And it was quite tasty too."

Withdrawing a large cinnamon roll, he held it up and compared it to hers. "This looks amazing."

"We bake some Czech recipes like mine, which is a

Koblihy—a fried donut filled with custard." She held it up for him to see. "And we also bake recipes like the cinnamon roll that folks are a little more familiar with. Most people don't realize the cinnamon roll actually comes from Sweden." Kate took another bite and grinned.

He eyed his pastry. "Really? I did not know that. Interesting." He took a bite, savoring it. "Wow. This is probably the best one I've ever had."

"But of course. It came from Cigler's Bakery."

It wasn't long before the plane began its final approach to Natrona County International Airport in Casper, Wyoming. Kate tucked the pastry bag beneath the seat and her book back into her purse. Mr. Flanagan stretched his long legs before him and buckled his seatbelt.

Kate tightened hers. "Is landing better or worse than the take-off?"

Mr. Flannagan grinned. "Don't worry. They do this every day. Often a couple times a day. You'll be fine. There will be the sensation of dropping, but it's a slow drop, so don't worry."

Kate's eyes widened. "Dropping? Really?"

He chuckled. "Would you like to hold my hand?"

"N-No. Thank you." Kate sputtered, then turned her attention out the window as the ground grew closer, but in reality, the plane was lowering. It looked the other way around to her. *Breathe, Kate. Have faith. Lord, help me not to fear. I know you have this plane in the palm of Your hand. You do, right?* Kate forced her breathing to slow down as she continued to pray and watch the plane lower to the ground. Suddenly the runway lay beneath them, and the plane touched down. No skipping about. No bouncing. It was a smooth landing. *Thank you, Lord.* Kate drew in a deep breath and blew it out all at once, dropping her head against the headrest.

Mr. Flanagan nudged her elbow. "You're on the ground, safe and sound. See? No harm, no foul. Think you'll fly again?"

Kate half-smiled. Although she was unsure when she would return home, she knew she'd have to fly there eventually. "Most likely."

"Good. At least you're not ruined for flying. It gets easier every time."

The plane taxied to the gate, and once the door opened, the passengers filled the aisle to disembark. When it came time for Kate and Mr. Flanagan to leave, he lowered Kate's carry-on bag for her, and they made their way to the gate. As passengers passed them, he turned to her.

"Are you're heading to baggage claim?" He held up the palm of his hand. "Only so I can help with your bags. Nothing more, I promise."

Kate tilted her head and laughed. "Thank you, but no. I have another flight to catch."

"I see." He proffered his hand. "It was a pleasure traveling with you, Miss Cigler. Perhaps one day I'll discover who your doppelgänger is."

"Perhaps you will. Safe travels, Mr. Flanagan." Kate removed her hand from his and strode down the terminal to find her next gate, then on to discover her mother's secrets.

The puddle jumper landed at Gillette-Campbell County Airport that evening amidst a thunderstorm. Kate's umbrella was securely tucked away in her carry-on which they'd made her check with her larger suitcase, since there were no overhead compartments in the tiny plane's cabin. She, along with the other nineteen passengers, descended the seven steps to the ground and collected their luggage before hurrying to the small terminal a few hundred steps away. Lightening flashed and thunder rolled throughout this process. The passengers were soaked by the time they entered the terminal.

Dripping wet and thankful for her coat, Kate made her way to the car-rental desk to claim the car she'd reserved. Glancing at her wristwatch, she hoped they were still open. It was almost seven o'clock. It seemed several other passengers had the same idea. Stepping into line, Kate waited for her turn. With the influx of passengers and the weather, several agents stepped up to assist, and before long, Kate was on her way in a 1968 powder-blue Ford Maverick. With luggage stowed in the trunk, she pulled out the address her great-aunts had given her and a map the car-rental agent had provided. Following the route they'd suggested, she turned out of the airport and headed in that direction. Kate had no idea who resided at that address. All she knew was she needed to go there first to begin the discovery of Mother's secrets.

Mother had never indicated any secrets from her past, and that fact left Kate reeling. Her mother, grandparents, great-aunts and great-uncle had immigrated to the United States from Czechoslovakia after World War I. Mother had married a soldier who served in World War Two but had died in the war. Kate was born after his death, so he'd never been able to see her. What a hero he must have been.

Kate's childhood had been a happy one surrounded by her loved ones. They all doted on her, especially Mother, but they didn't spoil her. From childhood Kate worked with them in the bakery, and they taught her everything they knew. Although thankful she still had her three elderly loved ones, Kate sorely missed Mother and her grandparents. Especially Mother. Her eyes stung as tears threatened. It appeared she didn't know Mother as well as she thought she did. What would this trip unearth?

The two-lane road Kate drove on was paved but mostly deserted. Every once in a while, an old pickup truck would pass in the other direction. A fence line stretched as far as the eye could see on both sides of the road. Occasionally, a herd of cows grazed along the fence line. Fences separated pastures that ran perpendicular to the fence line along the road. Mama cows and their babies grazed together in separate fields. Kate was awestruck at the difference between this vast land and Ohio.

Darkness descended as Kate continued her journey down the lonely stretch of road. According to the map, it would be another hour and a half before she reached her destination. If whoever the folks were at her journey's end weren't receptive to her visit, she'd have to drive back into Gillette for the night, and she'd have to find a place to stay. How would she proceed with discovering Mother's secrets then? She had no idea.

Trust in the Lord with all thine heart and lean not unto thine own understanding. The verse from Proverb 3:5 that Kate had learned long ago popped into her head. *That was You, wasn't it, Lord? You're gently reminding me to trust You in this situation and not myself and* my *understanding of it. Which is nothing. Okay. I'll simply keep driving and wait until I arrive to find out why my great-aunts sent me here. There's a reason, isn't there?*

Kate turned the rental car left onto a dirt road and stopped. She'd become so used to driving down the long, lonely, paved road she'd almost missed it. Thankful the rain had stopped earlier, she stared at a curved, rusted iron sign that read *Scott Ranch* that hung across the road. An odd-looking symbol sat on either side of the name.

She lowered her gaze to the dirt road lit by the car's headlights, the road stretching between wooden fence rails on both sides. With a deep breath, Kate pressed the accelerator and urged the Maverick forward. In decent shape, the dirt road was wide enough for two vehicles, but she met no one as she drove for another few miles. Truly in the middle of nowhere, Kate had passed no buildings other than a barn or shed since she'd left Gillette. She was happy she'd followed the rental agent's advice and filled the car's gas tank before leaving town.

After a while Kate passed a large shed with a short driveway but kept going. Before long, a sprawling, log, ranch-style house came into view, its windows lit with a golden glow, giving the impression of a warm welcome.

At least Kate hoped so. The dirt drive gave way to a wide, paved driveway that circled beneath a timber-and-stone portico. Did she dare drive beneath it and park? No, probably not. Only expected guests would do that. Kate parked further back and walked to the few wide stone steps that led to the double, solid oak doors. She lifted the heavy iron knocker and banged it against the metal plate beneath it. As she stood waiting for someone to answer, Kate scanned the landscape around the front of the house. Hidden lighting around the grounds conveyed a fairy-tale appearance. Breathtaking. Who were these people? What kind of place was this? It was so beautiful and out in the middle of nowhere. She couldn't begin to understand—

The heavy wooden door opened behind Kate, and she turned to find an older woman standing in the soft light of the entrance, her hand grasping the doorknob.

"Yes? May I help you?" The woman's gray hair was gathered in a soft twist at the back of her head. A few bangs swept to the side of her forehead. She wore a light pink sweater set and a narrow gray skirt. Low black, comfortable-looking shoes encased her feet. Gentle but curious blue eyes took in Kate's appearance.

The sudden urge to retreat to her car and drive back the way she'd come nearly overcame Kate. No matter how gentle those eyes were, Kate wasn't sure she could explain her reason for being here. It didn't make much sense to her. Why would it make sense to this woman or anyone else here?

Drawing in a deep breath, Kate tugged the packet of

photos from her purse and held them out, her hand unsteady. "I'm sorry for disturbing your household so late this evening, but I just flew from Ohio to Gillette and then drove here. It's been a long day. My name is Katarina Cigler. My family calls me Kate. I was sent by my great-aunts who provided me with these family photos and told me it was time I discover some secrets my mother had. She passed away several years ago and never told them to me." Kate released a nervous laugh. "I'm so sorry. This probably isn't making any sense to you. It doesn't make a lot of sense to me either, but here are the photos they gave me. They told me to come to this address to seek answers. I have no idea why."

The woman's blue gaze pierced hers as her brows furrowed. She lifted a hand to accept the photos, her eyes shifting to skim through them. Kate watched for a reaction. She gave none. Once she finished looking through them, she returned the photos to Kate.

"Please, come in."

Come in? Did that mean she knew something?

When Kate stepped inside, the woman closed the door and turned to Kate. "My name is Martha Holcomb. I'm the housekeeper here at Scott Ranch. I…please, follow me."

She turned and led Kate across a wide entrance hall decorated with western-style paintings and rugs into a large, rustic living room. Straight from a magazine, it nearly took Kate's breath away. Cordovan leather and suede couches and chairs clustered around a huge river stone fireplace with a solid oak mantel. The room was decorated with pottery, old iron ranch implements and western blankets and rugs. Log beams adorned the ceiling while the walls were rustic log and chink. Kate swallowed and reminded herself not to gawk.

Mrs. Holcomb stopped next to a leather armchair near the fireplace and indicated it with an outstretched hand. A slight smile lifted the corners of her mouth. "Please, have a seat. I'll fetch Mr. Scott, and you can share your story with him."

"Thank you." Kate sat in the leather chair and sighed. She dropped her purse to the floor beside the chair and held the photos in her hand. How could a leather chair be this buttery soft? She stared into the dancing flames of the fireplace and welcomed their warmth. After a couple of minutes, Kate began to relax. If she wasn't careful, after her long and stressful day, she could easily fall asleep.

Of its own volition, her head rested against the back of the overstuffed chair. Hopefully Mr. Scott would come soon. She wanted to get this interview over with. Perhaps he could answer her questions, and she could find out quickly whatever it was she needed to know. What could it be? Auntie Anna and Auntie Genevieve wouldn't even give her a hint. Did they know all the details of Mother's secrets?

Kate closed her eyes. It had been a long day, and she was so tired. She would rest her eyes for only....

"Miss Cigler?" A deep voice spoke from a distance before fading away. "Miss...."

"Why don't I—"

"I'll take her...."

Voices faded in and out while Kate felt as if she were floating. She sank onto a cloud. Then... darkness....

Kate woke to bright sunlight streaming across her face. She clamped her eyelids tighter. Why in the world had Auntie Anna left her curtains open last night? Wait. What? Sunshine never shone through Kate's curtains. The sun always shone on the other side of the house. Kate's eyes popped open, and the sunlight she'd been avoiding instantly blinded her. Lifting a hand, she blocked the offending rays and attempted to get her bearings. That couldn't be her window since the sun didn't shine in hers. Disoriented, she took in the huge bedroom with log and chink walls. Where in the world was she?

Kate sat straight up in bed. A huge bed. Far bigger than hers at home. She shifted her eyes around the bedroom, the beautiful western décor sinking into her sleep-fogged mind. Memories of her arrival to the Scott ranch last night returned to her, but she certainly didn't remember climbing into this behemoth of a bed. Her eyes lowered to find she still wore the same clothes she'd worn all day yesterday. So, when…and how…?

A knock sounded on the pine door. Kate threw back the covers and climbed from the bed. She stood barefoot on the thick, carpeted floor running her fingers through her hair in an attempt to tame what must be a disheveled mess. "Come in," she called. She attempted to straighten the blouse she wore, but there was no hope for the wrinkles embedded in the silken fabric.

The door opened, and the woman she'd met the night before—Kate recalled her name was Martha—first peeked around the door, then shoved it open further and entered with a tray of food.

"Good morning, Miss Cigler. I hope you slept well. It would seem you were quite exhausted last night." She deposited the tray on a table between two chairs across the room. "I can understand why, mind you. It's to be expected after your long journey, but we were surprised to find you deep in sleep when I returned with Mr. Scott. Why, bless my soul, we couldn't wake you for nothing." She turned to smile at Kate, then chuckle. "Mr. Scott thought it best if you got a good night's sleep before meeting with you this morning." She peeked at her wristwatch. "Mind you, it's nearly ten o'clock."

Kate gasped and glanced at her own wristwatch. "What? Ten o'clock. How could I have slept in like this? I never sleep this late."

Mrs. Holcomb clasped her hands and strolled a few feet toward Kate. "I wouldn't worry too much, Miss. Cigler. We all have our exhausting days when we need a little more sleep to recover. You came a long way, after all."

"I suppose." Doubt filled Kate's words. "I'm truly embarrassed though. I don't make a habit of showing up at strangers' homes and falling instantly asleep in their chair."

Mrs. Holcomb chuckled. "No, I wouldn't think you would." She turned and indicated the tray she'd laid on the table. "You should eat while the food's hot. Your car wasn't locked, so I had one of the ranch hands bring in your suitcase last night, so you can shower and change your clothes. I'm sure you'd like to do that before you meet Mr. Scott." She pointed over by the door where Kate's suitcase and carry-on sat. "I'll be back in about an hour to take you to see Mr. Scott. Will that be plenty of time for you?"

"Yes. Plenty of time. Thank you for thinking of me."

"My pleasure." The housekeeper turned and left the room.

Mrs. Holcomb led Kate into the living room where a tall man stood waiting by the fireplace. A fire crackled warmly on the andirons, and he turned a log over with a long poker, sending a shower of sparks up the vast chimney.

"Mr. Scott, Miss Cigler is here to speak with you." Mrs. Holcomb stopped a few feet from her boss.

He placed the poker back on the cast-iron tool stand and turned. In his mid-fifties, Mr. Scott had salt-and-pepper hair with a little more salt than pepper. A ruggedly handsome man, he was lean and well-built. Considering he owned a ranch, Kate chalked his physique up to hard work. But who was this man, especially in relation to her mother?

Had she known him?

He stepped forward, a smile on his face and his hand held out. "Miss Cigler, it's a pleasure to meet you. Welcome to Scott Ranch. I'm Mark Scott."

Kate shook his hand. He immediately released hers. "Please, have a seat. Mrs. Holcomb indicated you have some photos that you have questions about your mother's past. Some secrets you think she had."

Kate sat in a different chair than the one she'd fallen asleep in the night before. Out of the corner of her eye, she noticed Mrs. Holcomb slip from the room. "It's nice to meet you, Mr. Scott. First let me apologize for falling asleep in your chair last night. I don't make a habit of coming in to strangers' homes and falling asleep before I have a chance to meet them first. All I can say is I was exhausted."

He waved her words away. "That was obvious. Please don't worry about it. I just hope you rested well."

"I did. I'm not used to sleeping in a bed the size of the state I live in. It was great. Thank you."

Mr. Scott chuckled. "Wonderful. Now, do you have the photos you showed Mrs. Holcomb last night? If so, perhaps I can answer some of your questions."

"I do." Kate had brought them with her and handed them to him. "I recognize my mother in two of them, but I don't recognize anyone else."

Mr. Scott accepted the photos and perused them. Kate watched for a reaction, but his face remained neutral.

After looking through the photos, he met Kate's eyes, his gaze shuttered. He held out one of the pictures. "This photo is of your mother and me. I was a major in the US Army. We met while I was stationed in Washington, D.C."

"Washington, D.C.? You met my mother there?" Shock reverberated through Kate. When had her mother gone to the US capital? "Why was she in Washington?"

"Did you know your mother could sing? That she had

an amazing voice?"

"Yes, she used to sing to me when I was a child. We would sing together as we baked in my grandmother's bakery."

His brows lifted. "Bakery?"

"My grandmother owned a bakery. She just passed away, and now I own it with my two great-aunts and my great-uncle."

A fleeting smile crossed his face before it vanished. "I'm sorry for your loss. And what about your mother? Doesn't she still work with you?"

"When I was eighteen, she passed after suffering with leukemia for five years." A hint of pain flashed in Mr. Scott's eyes before he lowered his lids.

"Again, I'm sorry for your loss." He folded his hands in his lap. "Your mother was an amazing woman when I knew her. She must have been an amazing mother."

"Oh, she was." Stinging came unbidden behind Kate's eyes, and she blinked to stave off tears.

"Your mother came to Washington to sing for the troops," Mr. Scott returned to the previous conversation.

"I never knew that." Why hadn't Mother told her?

"I worked for the War Department, or what is now called The US Department of Defense. They needed someone to infiltrate a…a certain Nazi stronghold. It had to be a woman who could sing." Mr. Scott paused, his gaze staring off, leaving Kate wondering if he was remembering the past. He leveled his eyes on hers. "She had to have a voice like a…a nightingale. A professional soprano who could bring audiences to their feet. And your mother fit the bill."

Kate's mind spun in confusion. She knew her mother could sing, but a professional soprano? Her mother certainly had secrets. "She infiltrated a Nazi stronghold? But how? You sent her to spy on them? How could you do that? I don't understand."

A cloak of patience spread over the man across from Kate. He drew in a deep breath and blew it out slowly. "My dear, we would never have sent in anyone untrained to face those Nazis. Elena went through months of rigorous training, including intensive German language education. She walked, talked, ate, and slept the language and was fluent by the time she completed her training. We only sent her in once we were confident Elena was ready."

Kate couldn't believe her ears. Mother spoke German? Who was Elena Cigler?

A gentle smile settled on Mr. Scott's face. "You were looking for secrets, and you found some, huh?"

Chapter Three

"Is it just you and Mrs. Holcomb who live here?" Kate took a helping of mashed potatoes and passed it on to Mr. Scott. He speared a piece of roast beef and passed the plate to her.

"Oh, no. My adopted son lives here, but he's out on a cattle round-up along with most of the ranch hands. They'll bring the cattle in before they drive them to market by semi-truck. It's not like they used to do in the old days when the ranchers drove them all the way to market across the territory. Number one, it doesn't take as long this way, and we don't lose as many cattle. Number two, there are a few cities and highways in the way." He chuckled. "I still have a few ranch hands working around here, so you might see some fellows around. I also have a daughter, but she lives in town."

"How wonderful. When is your son due back?" Kate took a bite of the tender beef.

"Anytime, actually. I'm anxious to hear how things went."

Kate laid down her fork. "Mr. Scott, how well did you know my mother? Well, enough to send her to Germany, obviously, but other than that, how well did you know her?"

He set down his knife and fork and clasped his hands above his plate. "Your mother was a brave woman. Once she knew the necessity of the mission, she went into enemy territory without hesitation."

"So my mother was a...a spy?"

"You could say that." He picked up his fork.

"And the German officer in the picture? Did you know him?"

"No, I didn't know him." Mr. Scott filled his fork and took a bite.

Frustration rankled at Kate. Only one step forward. She'd found out who the American military man in the photo was. She had yet to find out who any of the others in the photos were. Time. It would take time. She'd come to this address and found one piece of the puzzle yet she still needed to find more. How many? Her mother was a spy in Germany. She'd pretended to be a professional soprano singer. Where in Germany? Did Mr. Scott know more than he was telling her?

"It's difficult to grasp this side of her that you're introducing me to. These secrets that she held and never told me about are hard for me to connect with her. To me she was the mother who built forts under the dining room table and read books to me. My mother worked with my grandmother in the bakery, and they taught me everything there was to know about baking. She sang to me. That's the only thing you've said that's even familiar about the woman you've told me about. The picture of you and her. That's a connection I can visually see now that I've met you. Nothing else makes sense."

He reached over a gentle hand and laid it on hers. "I'm sorry. This has to be hard for you." He released a heavy breath. "There are...other things, but I think I have to show them to you. Before I can do that, I have to first—"

"Dad? Where are you?" A younger masculine voice came from the rear of the house drawing closer as it came. "Hey, Dad! Where are you?"

"Matt?" Mr. Scott stood and dropped his cloth napkin

beside his plate as a young brown-haired man strolled into the dining room.

Dressed in typical western cowboy-wear from bandana and suede jacket to jeans, chaps, and cowboy boots, he looked dusty and tired. With cowboy hat in hand, he made a direct line to Mr. Scott. "Hey, Dad. How's it going?"

Mr. Scott wrapped him in a hearty hug, slapping him on the back, which released a dust cloud. "It's good to see you, son. I hoped you'd make it back soon." He held him away and grinned into his son's smiling face. "You must be hungry. Is everything taken care out there? Does Clayton have it under control?"

"You know he does." The young man stripped off his jacket and tossed it on a chair by the wall, laying his hat on top of it. He started to pull out a chair when he stopped and looked up.

Kate gaped as she stared at him. What...? Who...? How...? He looked just.... No, that was impossible. He stared right back at her.

"Dad. Who is this?" He propped his hands on his hips and turned to Mr. Scott. "I feel like I'm looking in a mirror, only I'm seeing a...a...a woman. Dad? What's going on here?"

"Mr. Scott? I kind of feel the same. Only—" Kate's eyes locked on the young man— "only the opposite."

Mr. Scott sat heavily back in his chair. "I know. It's time to tell you both something."

"Twins?" Matt Scott dropped into a chair beside the dining table. "But...how? You told me my mother died during the war. How could I have a twin sister, and you never told me?"

Mark's eyes moved from the accusation in his son's eyes to the young woman who sat still at the table, her own gaze staring him down. He never thought this day would come. Not in a million years. Elena sent her daughter on a fact-finding mission to discover the secrets she'd hidden so long ago. His only recourse was to tell the truth. At least part of it. If he could hide the rest, he would. The rest would be...unbearable.

"Why don't we move into the living room where it's more comfortable." Mark rose from his chair and headed in that direction. He wasn't going to wait for them. They'd follow if they wanted to hear their story— or what he was willing to tell them.

He moved to the fireplace and retrieved the cast-iron poker giving the huge logs on the andirons a lift, stirring the flames. His mind slipped back to a night long ago in Munich, Germany, when he'd helped Elena Cigler escape an evil man. Her job as spy for the US military had ended, and Mark had accompanied her to the US to begin a normal life, if that were even possible.

Kate Cigler dropped onto the end of the couch situated before the fire. Apparently, Elena had managed to live a normal life after all. As had he. After retiring from the military after the war, Mark had returned home to his wife and daughter and newly adopted son. From the sounds of it, Elena had taken her maiden name when she'd returned home.

"Dad, we're here. Tell us what happened."

Matt's quiet words drifted to Mark's ears, and he replaced the poker on the tool stand. Turning, he shoved his hands into his jeans pockets and met the questioning eyes of the young adults before him. Whew, where to begin, and... where to stop?

Mark lifted his eyes to the wood rafters above them, drew in a deep breath, and released it slowly. "Matt, just before you came in, I was telling Kate I met your mother in Washington, D.C. during the war. She sang for the troops who shipped in and out of the capital region. Her name was

Elena, and she had an amazing voice— beautiful enough to be a professional. The War Department needed a woman to infiltrate a Nazi stronghold. The fact she had such a voice made it possible."

"Are you saying my mother was a...a spy for the US military?" Matt shoved a hand through his disheveled hair, releasing more particles of dust.

Mark stared at his son, then nodded. "Yes, and an excellent one at that."

Kate lowered her gaze to the floor. "I'm just as surprised as you, Matt. Mother died when I was eighteen, and I didn't know any of this. All I knew of her was the loving woman who read to me when I was a child and helped run the family bakery. She and my grandmother taught me everything there was to run the family bakery."

He stared at her before turning his eyes on Mark. His eyes narrowed. "Why did you tell me my real mother died?"

Mark met his gaze squarely. "She asked me to. I honored her request."

"Why? I've missed all these years without my mother and my sister. Why would she do that?"

Mark shook his head. "She had her reasons."

Matt nodded. "Reasons that she took to her grave, I'm assuming."

Mark remained silent. He knew those reasons, but he couldn't tell them. His first responsibility was to protect them.

"Please don't get me wrong—" Matt stood and crossed to stand in front of Mark. "—I appreciate everything Mom did for me, and how she treated me as her own son. She'll always be Mom to me. But—"

"Hey, you don't have to say anything, son." Mark placed a hand on Matt's shoulder. "It's only normal to want to know your real mother, especially when you find out she was living all this time. I'm sorry my hands were tied by

her request. Did I know of Kate's existence? Yes, I did."
He paused. "But I made a promise, and I'm a man of my
word."

Matt nodded, his lips clamped in a straight line. "I get
it. You're a man of integrity, and I respect you for that.
You did what you had to do." He turned to face Kate. "All I
can say, sis, is I've had a great life here. I hope you had a
great one with our mother."

"I had a wonderful life with her, her parents, two of
our grandmother's sisters and one of their husbands. All
that are left are my two great-aunts and my great uncle, and
we run the family bakery in our little town in Ohio." Kate
stood and approached Matt. She stood on tiptoes and
wrapped her arms around his neck. "It's so nice to meet
you, brother. I'm your sister, Katarina. Everyone, except
my elderly relatives, calls me Kate."

Matt's arms slipped gingerly around her. "And you,
sis. I'm Mathias. Call me Matt. Welcome to the family. I'd
love to meet the rest of—my family sometime."

Kate stood back and stared at Matt, their faces so
similar. "Something tells me my relatives already know
about you, but I know they'd love to meet you in person.
They sent me here to find out about Mother's secrets, of
which you are one. The fact she was a spy is another. How
many more secrets did she have?"

Mark would keep that knowledge to himself. For now.

"What about our dad? I always thought—" He turned
his eyes to Mark then back to Kate. "Did your mother...*our*
mother tell you anything?"

Kate clasped her hands in front of her. "Mother said he
was in the military and died during the war."

"I guess that's that."

Kate snapped her fingers. "Wait. I have a couple of
things I don't understand. Maybe you can help me find the
answers to them. I'll be right back." She hurried away.

Mark dreaded what she would ask about.

Kate returned moments later with something pastel pink in her hand. She held up a tiny baby hat. "My great-aunts gave this to me to use in my search. They wouldn't tell me anything about this baby hat. Can either of you tell me anything?"

"I've never seen anything like it." Matt shrugged.

Mark crossed an arm over his chest and ran a finger over his chin in thought. "Yeah, I have. Wait a sec. I'll be back."

Kate's gaze followed Mr. Scott out of the room. Hmm. She turned to Matt who propped his hands on his hips and met his sister's eyes with a lifted brow. "I've come a long way to seek answers to a lot of questions." Kate moved in front of the roaring fire. "There's so much about Mother I don't understand. I get one answer, and it opens up a plethora of others. She wasn't simply the hometown baker I thought she was."

"Maybe not originally, but she became that for you. I went on this cattle round-up thinking I had one sibling and one mother, only to find I have two siblings and two mothers." Matt chuckled and swiped his hand through his hair. "It's true what they say. You never know what a day will bring."

Kate released a soft laugh. "No, you don't. Your dad mentioned you had a sister."

"Yeah, I have an older sister." Matt chuckled. "I've always known I was adopted, but I just never knew about you."

Mr. Scott returned with a small wooden box in hand.

The box was similar to the small chest the great-aunts had given her, only smaller and without its embellishment.

He extended it to Kate. "Here you go. Perhaps the answers to some of your questions are inside this."

Kate accepted the box and retook her seat on the couch. "Thank you."

She opened the box and found a tiny blue silk baby hat. Removing it, she held it next to the pink one in her hand. It matched hers perfectly.

"Look at that," Matt said. "An exact match. Must have been yours and mine." He turned his gaze on Mr. Scott at the same time Kate did.

His dad nodded. "It was."

"Cute." A half-grimace imprinted on Matt's features.

Kate laid the hats aside. "I suppose it was the style during the war."

"Guess the blue one was mine." Matt tossed a thumbs up.

Kate laughed as she looked inside the box. "Oh look. This matches something else I have." She held up a half of a heart medallion before slipping her hand into her jeans pocket and withdrawing the one she'd brought from her room. "I have the right side. This is the left side. Another match." She placed the two sides together to complete a heart-shaped medallion.

Matt held out his hand. "Here. Let me see those."

Kate placed them in his hand.

He put the pieces together again. "There are words on each piece, but I can't read them. They're in another language."

Kate laid the box on the couch and stood. "Let me show you. In Czech your half reads Jednoho dne budeme and my half reads budou znovu sjednoceni. Together the translation is One day we shall be reunited." She paused. "Oh my. Mother planned for us to be reunited. Until now, apparently, because great-Auntie Anna and great-Auntie Genevieve were told not to give these clues to me until after Grandmother's death."

Kate turned to Mr. Scott. "But you didn't know anything about us being reunited, did you? You were surprised by my appearance."

"Yes, I was." The older man rocked back on his heels, his arms crossed over his broad chest. "Completely surprised."

"I don't understand why." Matt ran a hand through his hair. "Why wait until after she and your grandmother died?"

"Perhaps there's a legal reason, or something you simply haven't yet discovered."

A familiar voice spoke from the dining room door, and Kate turned to find a smiling pair of gray eyes and a broad grin on a tall figure dressed in western wear. The eyes were on her and brought warmth to her cheeks. The man from the airplane. What in the world was he doing here? She'd thought she'd never see him again.

"Gabe. It's about time you stopped galivanting around and showed up." Matt made a bee-line toward the man and gave him a bear hug, then slapped him on the back. He released Gabe and held him at arm's length. "Where have you been, brother?"

"Here and there. Not that you should've missed me. You've been on round-up." The handsome man slapped Kate's brother on the shoulder, releasing a cloud of dust. "I see you haven't long been off the trail."

"Correct. We just got back. Gabe, we could've used you. We were down a couple of hands. Had to leave a few behind to run the ranch."

"Why were you down?"

Matt scrubbed a hand behind his neck. "We had a little trouble with some of the fellows before I left. A little gambling problem. You know we don't allow that kind of thing. Had to let them go."

Gabe blew out a breath. "I see. We'll have to hire some new hands after we vet them. We'll get on it. Soon." His gaze moved across the room. "What do we have going on here?"

"You're not going to believe it." Matt moved to Kate's side. "Dad, you want to explain? You've had the most practice."

Mr. Scott smiled and held out a hand to this newcomer. Kate remembered his name as Gabriel Flanagan. With everything that had happened since she'd landed at the Casper airport, how had she remembered that? She watched the interaction with interest. Who was he to this family?

"It's good to see you, Gabe. I hope you've had success with the business you were handling for me."

"Indeed, I have, sir. Everything's going great, but we can talk about that later." He released Mr. Scott's hand and turned to Kate, a grin on his face. "The last place I expected to find you was here."

Kate tilted her head and smiled. "Ditto. When we parted at the airport, I thought you were flying to parts unknown, Mr. Flanagan."

Gabe chuckled. "Now that we've met again, don't you think we can do away with formalities? Please, call me Gabe."

"Very well. I'm Kate."

"No, I didn't fly away to parts unknown. I simply made a stopover in Casper on business." He raised a shoulder in a careless shrug. "Now I'm here."

"Gabe is part owner of the Scott ranch." Mr. Scott stepped forward. "He's a partner, and—he's our lawyer. Gabe takes care of the legal end of things. We're lucky to have him."

Matt dropped onto an armchair. "We sure are. He can wrangle cattle as well as he can deal with property and business matters. His talents are limitless."

Property? As in property law? Kate's mental ears perked up. Not that it would do her any good unless he was licensed in Ohio or had reciprocity with that state as well as Wyoming.

"You're exaggerating, Matt. Besides, no one answered

my original question. What's going on here?" Gabe turned his gaze from Matt to Kate. "Why are you here?"

"She's my twin sister. Can't you tell?" Matt quirked a finger in Kate's direction. "Come here. Let's show him."

Kate moved to Matt's arm-chair and dropped onto the over-stuffed arm. She leaned toward Matt and waited for Gabe's response, which was immediate.

His eyes widened, then he nodded. "That's why you looked so familiar to me at the airport." Gabe chuckled and shook his head. "It's uncanny. How did this happen? How did you not know you had a sister?"

"Dad?" Matt waved toward Mr. Scott who'd been standing by the fireplace. Kate watched and listened as he related the story for Gabe's sake.

When he was finished, Gabe turned to Kate. "Your mom ended up in Ohio as a baker. A good one, I presume, if she learned from the two ladies I met at the airport."

Kate lifted her chin. "Her skills were phenomenal, just as theirs are."

"The pastry I ate on the plane certainly was. Phenomenal, that is."

Kate jumped up from the arm of Matt's chair. "Well, there are still some pastries in the bag I brought. They're only a day old, but I'm sure they'll still be good. I'll go get them. Perhaps Mrs. Holcomb can warm them in the oven for a few minutes to soften them up."

She hurried to her room and retrieved the bag of pastries Auntie Anna had given her at the airport the morning before. Kate had nearly forgotten them. On her return to the living room, she found Mrs. Holcomb standing to the side waiting. Apparently, someone had thought her idea of warming the pastries a good one and had called her.

A smile on her face, Mrs. Holcomb stepped forward and held out her hand for the pastry bag. "I'll be more than happy to warm these up for you."

"Thank you. And please, make sure to warm one for

yourself. There's plenty to go around."

Surprise etched the housekeepers features before fading just as quickly. "Thank you." A gentle smile lifted her lips.

Kate thanked her and turned back to the others in the room.

"I'm looking forward to tasting something from that bakery of yours." Mr. Scott stirred the logs in the fireplace causing the fire to leap and roar, returned the poker to its resting place, and lowered himself onto the couch.

"You had a taste of the pastries, Gabe?" Matt crossed his ankles and leaned his head against the back of his chair.

"Sure did." He rubbed his stomach. "Probably the best I've ever had."

Kate lowered her eyes and suppressed a grin. There was a reason Cigler Bakery nearly sold out every day. Now to keep property developer, Andrew Hawthorn, at bay.

The men chatted about ranch matters while Kate kept to her own thoughts until a short time later when Mrs. Holcomb returned with a tray of warmed pastries, plates, napkins, mugs, and a carafe of coffee, with sugar and cream. She set the tray on the coffee table and stood.

"Would you like for me to pour the coffee for you, Mr. Scott?"

With a tilt of his head, he tossed her a grin and a wink. "No, Martha, I think Kate can take care of that. You hurry back and enjoy your own pastry. I heard what Kate said. We don't want yours to grow cold."

Pink tinged the woman's cheeks. "Thank you, sir. Enjoy your treat."

"You, too, Martha." He chuckled and turned to Kate. "Will you do the honor of pouring the coffee?"

"Certainly." Kate crossed to the couch and sat beside Mr. Scott. "It would be my pleasure."

Once everyone was served their coffee and pastry, they settled back to enjoy them.

Matt's brows lifted as he chewed the delectable sweet. When he'd swallowed and taken a sip of his coffee, he eyed his sister. "If this is what comes out of your bakery a day old, I'm sure fresh must be stellar."

Kate laughed, but before she could speak Gabe did. "What I had was fresh, bro. Stellar doesn't begin to describe it."

When their ooh's and aah's settled down, Kate nearly told them of the dilemma she faced with the property developer, but she stopped herself. It wasn't their business; nor was there anything they could do. She would simply have to deal with it on her own. So far, she'd only spent a tiny amount from the money her grandmother left her. Most of that would go toward purchasing the shop. She'd figure out the rest on her own. *And with your help, Lord. I need Your guidance and Your provision. That bakery is Your bakery. If You want it to stay open, I know You'll provide. Help me put all my trust in You alone.*

Kate left her room and headed to the dining room hoping to catch someone eating breakfast. Mrs. Holcomb had mentioned the evening before that breakfast was always served between certain times and folks came when they wanted to. She entered the room and found the sun shining through the windows giving the room a cheery appearance. Just like the rest of the house, western décor adorned this room. Kate hadn't noticed much the night before due to the intense conversation she'd had with Mr. Scott. Now in the bright light of day, she noticed and appreciated it.

The room was empty of other occupants, so Kate took a seat and began serving herself. Mrs. Holcomb strode in with a coffee carafe in hand.

"Good morning, Miss Cigler. I hope you rested well."

She halted beside Kate's chair, a cheerful smile on her face.

"I did, thank you."

"Would you like coffee with your breakfast?" Her head tilted to the side as she held up the carafe.

"Yes, please." Kate moved her cup and saucer closer to the edge of the table. "Coffee would be wonderful."

The housekeeper poured the dark brew into her cup before setting the carafe on a hot pad near the center of the table. "I'll leave this in case you'd like more. There's bacon, sausage, gravy, biscuits and pancakes in the warming dishes. Please help yourself."

Kate reached for the cover of the nearest warming dish. "Has everyone already eaten and left?"

Mrs. Holcomb folded her hands in front of her. "Well, most of—"

"Everyone but me." Gabe strolled into the dining room and dropped onto a chair across from Kate. He tossed a grin at the housekeeper.

"As I was about to say—" The older woman eyed him sternly before turning on her heel and striding toward the door.

"You love me, and you know it, Mrs. H." Gabe reached for the coffee carafe and filled his cup, his grin turning into a broad smile.

She harumphed and peeked at him over her shoulder before disappearing out of the dining room. "Sometimes...." Her voice diminished as she moved toward the kitchen.

"Do you always tease the hired help?" Kate placed bacon and pancakes on her plate and added butter and syrup.

"Only my favorite housekeeper."

His sparkling eyes stirred something inside Kate. Confused at the feeling she'd never felt before, she dropped her gaze to her plate.

"Doesn't she find you...annoying?" Annoying? Was

that too harsh?

"Annoying? Nah." Gabe chuckled as he filled his plate. "Our housekeeper can dish it out as good as she gets when she's in the mood. I suspect she's playing it cool this morning out of deference to you, our guest."

Kate remained silent as she took a bite. For some reason this man threw her off balance. Why had it been easier to talk to him at the airplane terminal? Because she'd thought she'd never see him again?

"Have you taken a tour of the ranch yet?" Gabe added cream to his coffee before taking a drink.

"No, I haven't. I've only been here a day, and yesterday I slept in due to coming in so late the night before."

"I see. Well, how about I show you around after breakfast?" He leaned his arms on the edge of the table and clasped his fingers above his plate. "I happen to know Matt's out working with one of the horses this morning, and Mark is in the ranch office working on the books. I have to stop in and talk business with him for a while, but I can show you around first. What do you say?"

Kate was torn between avoiding this man's company and wanting to see the ranch. Her desire to see the spread outweighed her discomfort in his presence. Besides, why *did* she want to avoid him? He seemed pleasant enough. Yes, but something about him drew her like a magnet, and right now, she didn't understand that. She didn't *want* that. Like she'd told her great-aunts at the airport. She wasn't interested in any man right now. Then why was her heartbeat telling her otherwise?

Chapter Four

Kate had only seen the front of the house from the outside the night she'd arrived. As gorgeous as it had been lit up, she was unprepared for what lay before her when she and Gabe stepped outside the rear of the house. A large year-around glass-enclosed sunroom with French doors led to a huge stone patio with a western firepit and outdoor furniture arranged around it. Wired clear bulbs were strung above the patio ensuring there would be beautiful lighting at night. How cozy would it be to sit around that firepit beneath those lights on a cool evening? Or any evening, for that matter.

Gabe led her across a wide expanse of yard to a huge barn where a corral stood next to it. Several men sat on the wooden fence watching what was happening inside the corral. Kate identified her brother in the middle with a horse.

"What's Matt doing?"

Gabe glanced in her direction. "What he loves doing most in the world. Working with horses. And in this instance, he's breaking one."

Kate's eyes flew to Gabe's. "Breaking one?"

"Yep."

"What does that mean?"

Gabe halted several feet from the corral and turned toward Kate. He pointed at Matt and the horse. "That horse is a new one that's either never had a saddle on it or has some issues with trust. Matt has to 'break,'—" Gabe made air quotes with his fingers, "—the horse of old habits. Whether that's not being used to a saddle and learning to have one on him so a rider can ride him, or if he has trust issues, Matt has to teach him to trust his rider. The horse has to learn that his rider won't harm him."

"I see. Can we watch?"

"Sure, but we have to be quiet. Notice none of the ranch hands are saying anything. There can be no distractions for the trainer and horse. Silence is crucial."

"All right." Kate followed Gabe to the corral fence where they stood with arms folded along the fence rail.

Kate watched as her brother spoke in gentle tones to the horse. She knew nothing about horses, but whatever kind it was, it was a beautiful black male. Matt walked it over to a stand where a saddle awaited. A blanket rested on the horse's back. Was Matt putting his life in danger? *Lord, You know. Please keep Matt safe.*

Matt crooned in gentle tones as he moved to the horse's head and stroked his muzzle. The horse tossed his head and snorted. Stamping a foot, he remained in place. Matt ran a hand from his cheek down his neck across his shoulder and patted him softly. He reached for the saddle and lifted it onto the horse's back, leaving it there as he moved back to the horse's head. As he stroked the horse's face and cheeks, Matt's gentle tones never stopped. Once again, he rubbed the shoulders and neck, taking his time. The horse remained still, eyes wide, watching his trainer. Matt slid his hand to the horse's belly and scratched, eliciting a nod from the horse.

A few ranch hands turned their heads and smiled. Kate noticed they never laughed out loud. Matt buckled the belly cinch on the saddle but didn't tighten it. He resumed scratching the horse's belly as little by little he began to tighten the cinch until it was snug. He patted the horse on the shoulder, took the reins and began walking the horse around. Little by little, he reached down and pulled the cinch tighter. His crooning grew louder as they walked. As they picked up speed, Matt continued to tug the cinch tighter. Kate was amazed the horse never seemed to notice.

Finally, Matt stopped the horse, grab the reins tight, sank his boot into the stirrup and flung his leg across the saddle. The horse bucked at first, trying to send Matt flying, but he hung on. Matt spoke in soft words to the animal. The bucking only lasted for a few moments, and seemed half-hearted before the horse settled down. Matt leaned forward and rubbed it's neck, crooning words close to its ear.

Gabe leaned toward Kate and whispered, "They've done this several times, and Matt has slowly gained his trust. A few more times and the horse will know he can completely trust him. Matt's been gone for several days on the roundup, they've had to go back a few steps, but it's not bad. He's good at this."

The whispered words sent a thrill tip-toeing down Kate's spine, and it took all she could muster to turn and meet Gabe's eyes. She swallowed. Hard. What was it about this man that…that what? Made her react in a way she never had before? She couldn't…no, she wouldn't allow that to continue. *I must get a grip.*

Dark, serious eyes met hers, due to the topic of his conversation. I must p*ay attention. That's my brother out there. I need to learn what's going on.*

"Yeah, I can see that. I wish I'd seen the two of them before they reached this point." Kate returned her eyes to the pair trotting in unison around the perimeter of the corral.

Gabe released a low mirthless chuckle. "I did. That stallion was wild. No saddle training or trust. They've come a long way."

Matt rode the horse in their direction, and the ranch

hands began to disperse.

"Is the show over?" Kate's eyes swiveled around.

"Afraid so. Besides, everyone needs to get back to work." Gabe lifted a hand toward Matt as he halted the horse beside the fence and slid from the saddle. "Hey, bro, good job. You've come a long way with Major. A few more sessions, and you'll have him in hand." Gabe reached over with slow movements and scratched the stallion on the forehead. The horse remained still, not shying away.

Matt stepped up beside the horse's head and rubbed his cheeks and chin. "You're right. Major's doing great. That little bit of bucking was for show. His heart wasn't in it; nor did it last long."

Gabe rubbed down Major's face. "Agreed. You're making your last stand, aren't you, boy? But you'll give in soon. Matt's your guy."

"What did you think, sis?" Matt shoved his cowboy hat back on his head and grinned.

Kate tipped her head to the side and observed her twin. "I don't know where you learned such skills, but I'm as impressed as I can be."

"From his father, where else?" A feminine voice Kate had never heard before spoke from behind them. She whirled around to see a dirty-blonde in a suede fringed jacket, blue jeans tucked into cowboy boots and a white blouse beneath the jacket with a burgundy print scarf tied loosely around her neck.

"Gina!" Matt tossed the horse's reins over the fence rail, vaulted the fence and hurried to the approaching young woman's side. "It's great to see you."

"And you, cowboy." The woman's words held a "come hither" tone as she stopped in her tracks and flung her arms around Matt's neck, tugging his head down to place a kiss on his lips.

Kate gaped at the two. She knew nothing about her brother's life. This must be his...girlfriend? Fiancée?

Whoever she was, Kate wasn't privy to their story, and it wasn't her business.

After a minute, Gabe cleared his throat. When they didn't come up for air, he cleared his throat again. Louder this time. It did the trick as Matt stepped back, an arm around the woman, color high in his cheeks. He brought her closer.

"Gina, I'd like you to meet my sister, Kate." He smiled at Kate, the color returning to normal in his cheeks.

The woman's mouth flew open. "Your...sister? But you already have a sister. Megan. How did you get another sister?"

"Kate's my twin. She's been living in Ohio all these years with our mother, and we didn't know it. Nor did Kate know she had a brother." Matt looked from Gina to Kate and back again. "It's pretty amazing, don't you think?"

Gina lifted her chin along with a skeptical eyebrow. A slight sneer painted her lips. "Yes, I do. Are you certain? Have you checked her credentials?"

A frown lowered Gabe's brows. "Are you kidding? Take a look at them, Gina. They look exactly alike. Can't you see it?"

Chin still in the air, her eyes darted between Matt and Kate and back again. "Not really. It could be coincidental."

Matt stared at the woman at his side even as ire rose inside Kate. Who did this woman think she was coming here and questioning her veracity?

"You need to get your eyes checked, hon." Matt stepped back from Gina. "Besides, have a talk with Dad. He can tell you the whole story. I have some work to get to."

"Oh, come now, Matty. Don't go away mad." Gina hooked a hand in the crook of his arm. Her chatter faded into the distance as they strolled away.

Kate turned to the horse standing by the fence. "Something tells me Matt wouldn't normally leave Major standing by the fence like this. Gina must have distracted him."

Gabe propped an elbow on the fence. "In a big way. I'm not sure what her deal was with finding out Matt had another sister. It shouldn't be any skin off her back."

"Me neither, but she doesn't like me for some reason. It was just like that." Kate snapped her fingers. "Ever have someone take an instant dislike to you? And I didn't do anything to her."

Gabe scrunched up an eye in thought. "No, I can't say I ever have, and no, you didn't."

"Does Gina live around here?" Kate circled a finger in the air.

Gabe shrugged. "Her dad owns the Circle H Ranch. He's Hank Harris, and his spread is about the size of this one. It's a couple ranches over. Gina's had her sights on Matt since they were four years old."

Kate smiled. "Looks to me like she's got him, hook, line and sinker, as they say."

Gabe crossed his arms over his chest and shrugged. "Yep. Looks that way. From where I'm standing, he doesn't seem to mind."

Kate shifted her gaze around the dinner table and took a bite of the tender pork chop Mrs. Holcomb had prepared. She attempted to concentrate on the delicious meal rather than the dirty-blonde sitting across the table sending a cold gaze in her direction. How could Gina go from a warm, sweet friend to Matt to ice-cold toward her in a split second? It was a good thing Kate lived in Ohio. Whatever Gina thought about Kate, she had nothing to fear from her.

Matt laid his fork on his plate and wiped his mouth with his napkin before leaning his arms against the edge of the table and clasping his fingers. "Dad, Gina doesn't believe Kate is my sister. She thinks Kate has come here under false pretenses. How about you tell her the story."

Warmth rolled through Kate. She'd much prefer this discussion take place when she wasn't present. She lowered her eyes to her plate.

Mr. Scott sipped his iced tea and returned his glass to the table. "Is that so? Why would you think that, Gina? All you have to do is look at the two of them and see they're twins."

Kate couldn't resist a glance at the other woman. Her eyes were on her host, her chin in the air.

Gina gave a careless shrug. "Sorry, Mark. I don't see it." Leaning back in her chair, her eyes moved to Kate. "So, what's the story about her?" As if she wasn't even in the room.

Matt turned toward her. "Stop being rude. She's a guest in our house and my sister whether you believe it or not. I won't put up with rudeness."

Gina blinked and shifted her eyes to Matt. "Sorry, Matt. I didn't mean to be…rude. It's simply that I find it hard to believe you've had a sister all this time, and suddenly she shows up out of nowhere."

"Don't apologize to me. You were rude to Kate, not me." Matt sat up straight and leaned slightly away from Gina.

Gina frowned, her eyes moving to Kate. "Fine. I'm sorry, Kate. I…I didn't intend to be rude."

Kate realized how utterly painful it was for Gina to utter those words. She waved them away and smiled at the other woman. "No problem. I'm sure it's difficult for you to understand the situation, but Mr. Scott can explain it clearly." She turned toward the older man. "Please, if you would do that for her, I would appreciate it."

"Mr. Scott?" Gina laughed derisively. "Why don't you call him Mark like Gabe and I do?"

Kate gave her the sweetest smile she could muster.

"Because I only met him two days ago, and I don't know him well enough to call him by his first name. Out of respect I'll continue to call him Mr. Scott until *he* decides I can call him whatever he chooses."

"Here, here." Gabe chuckled from his place next to Mr. Scott. Matt smiled from his right.

"Thank you, Miss Cigler." Mr. Scott tilted an appreciative nod in Kate's direction before turning his eyes toward Gina. "As for her 'story,' I can indeed tell you. They are in fact twins. I personally knew their mother."

He proceeded to tell the account he'd shared with the others. Gina sat back and listened, but Kate wasn't entirely sure she believed what she heard. Lips clamped tight and chin still in the air, the young woman crossed her arms over her chest.

Mrs. Holcomb served coffee and dessert, a chocolate torte with vanilla ice cream and caramel drizzled on top. When Mr. Scott finished his tale, Matt turned to Gina. "Well, what do you say now?"

She shrugged a dainty shoulder and prepared a bite of dessert on her fork. "What can I say?" She turned to Kate. "Welcome to the family," Gina said, her tone laced with cloying syrup.

As Kate brushed her teeth that night before bed, she stared at her reflection in the mirror. What was it about her that Gina disliked? She seemed to love Matt, but even though they looked so much alike, Gina didn't see it. Despite her welcoming words, Gina had taken a dislike to Kate. Her words didn't ring true either. Kate rinsed her toothbrush and laid it on the counter by the sink. An idea popped into her head. Did Gina think Kate would steal Matt from her or his money? What a ridiculous notion. Kate had no intention of remaining at the ranch when her search for mother's secrets was over. She fully intended to return to Ohio and carry on her legacy at the bakery. No, she would stay in touch with her brother, but she wouldn't stay here. Her life was in Ohio.

Kate climbed into the huge, soft bed and drew the covers up under her chin, sinking into their warmth and comfort. Could she find a bed like this back home? She discarded that idea. A bed like this would never fit in her room. She'd enjoy it while she could, and when she returned home, she'd hold its memory close along with the memories of this amazing place.

Perhaps there would be an opportunity in the future to visit Matt and Mr. Scott again someday. Of course, Matt would probably marry Gina. At the thought, Kate's idyllic bubble burst. She wouldn't want to come if Gina was head of this household. But somehow, she didn't think Mr. Scott would give up control to the likes of Gina. Her smile returned, joined by a little chuckle.

Dark gray eyes slipped before her mind's eye. Kate's heartbeat ticked up a bit. Ridiculous. There was no reason for that. Where was her mind going? Oh yes. Gabe lived here too. At least when he wasn't traveling. She had no idea how often that was, but the thought of Gina living here might affect that. Kate had the feeling Gabe wasn't enamored with Gina. It seemed Matt was the only one who was, although Mr. Scott seemed okay with her.

Gabe. He did things to Kate's heartbeat. Not to mention her ability to think straight. *Oh Lord. This shouldn't be happening. I didn't plan on this. My home is in Ohio, and I own a bakery, for goodness sake. I can't afford to fall for a guy in Wyoming who lives on a ranch and travels. Please, Lord, take this funny feeling away.*

Kate rolled to her side and punched her pillow. That pair of dark gray eyes remained before her mind's eye along with his amazing smile, both of which wouldn't leave her heart alone. *Lord?*

"Are things going as well as we expected with the purchase of that lot of cattle from Abilene, Texas? How many head did you say?" Mark relaxed in the leather armchair by the fire.

Gabe sat across from him in an identical chair. "One-hundred twenty-eight head. I inspected all of them myself. That took all day, believe me. We started at 6:00 am and ended at 10:45 pm. Talk about a long day. There were thirty-five more, but there were problems with them, so I rejected those."

"When can we expect delivery?" Mark ran a hand down his face.

"In a couple of weeks."

Mark hauled in a deep breath and released it slowly.

"Why? You don't look happy about that." Gabe leaned forward.

Mark shook his head. "Normally I wouldn't mind. That's the average delivery time from Texas for that number of cattle, but right now? I don't know. I—"

Gabe waited for him to finish, but when he didn't, he asked, "What's going on, Mark? What's wrong?"

Mark shifted in his seat. "I've had an idea rolling around in my skull since Kate arrived that I just can't shake. I'm contemplating a trip to Germany."

Gabe's face crumpled. "Germany? Now? Why? What's in Germany?"

Mark leaned forward and clasped his hands together, his elbows remaining on the arms of the chair. "I've been thinking it might be a good idea to take Matt and Kate to where their mother worked in Germany. To the place she sang. To where she lived. To where she escaped. It's only fair they know more about her. About her past." But not *everything*.

Gabe leaned back. "Okay. Maybe you're right. But what about this shipment of cattle? Do you want me to—"

Mark vehemently shook his head. "You must come with us. I'm not a hundred percent sure what we're going to find on this journey, but I want my lawyer along. While I know you can't practice in Germany, you know the legal jargon and can deal with lawyers. I'm not saying we'll need one, but just in case, mind you." He released a long breath. "We'll leave Clayton in charge. He's the most level-headed, and he's been in charge before. Clayton has headed up roundups when Matt couldn't go, so I have no doubt he can take on a shipment of cattle."

"I agree. Clayton's a good man. I trust him. It's a simple enough thing for him to call us if we leave him a number, and we can call him often enough to check in."

"Right. Don't say anything to the kids yet. I want to work through some details first." Mark started to rise but stopped. "Oh, and Gina is *not* going. Hear me?"

Gabe chuckled at the severity in his partner's voice. "I hear you, and you've got my support. Now if you can convince Matt."

"Don't you worry about my son. I'll take care of him." Mark climbed from his chair and left the room.

Chapter Five

Kate stepped outside the back sliding glass door onto the patio to find someone had turned on the tiny twinkling lights above the sitting area around the firepit. A fire danced delightfully, beckoning her to come sit a while. A chill in the air encouraged her to grab the fleece blanket tossed over the back of the outdoor cushioned-couch. Wrapping it around herself, she sat and stared into the star-bejeweled sky. Not even the twinkling string of lights above her head could dull the glorious milky way or the amazing brightness of the surrounding stars. So far out from any city or town, there was nothing to compete with them. Kate didn't think she'd ever seen such a bright night as this.

Silence filled her ears except for the occasional whinny of a horse in the barn or the lowing of distant cattle. Her heart was full. *You're up there, aren't You, Lord? It's so comforting to know You see me. You know I'm here. You know my problems. You knew Mother even before I did.* Kate inhaled and released a long vapor-ridden breath. *Who was my mother? What was she like before I knew her? Mother was so much more than I know. She did important things I suppose I'll never fully understand. Soon I'll go home. Then what? I need Your direction, Abba Father.*

Kate had wandered around the ranch earlier during the day exploring for the wonders this vast land held. Amazing scenery met the eye in every direction. Although the land stretched endlessly, distant snow-covered mountains rose to meet the sky. Kate guessed if she were to mount a horse, which she had never done in her life, she could ride for at least a day and a half and never reach them. She might be off on that estimation, but what did she know? The land was simply too far-reaching for her understanding. She'd watched Matt as he finished training Major. What a magnificent horse! He'd passed his final test, and would be used by Matt as a rider. Impressed by Matt's skills, Kate was proud of what her brother accomplished.

The sliding glass door opened drawing Kate's attention from the star-flecked inky sky. Gabe stepped out, closing the door behind him. He'd donned a suede jacket with a sheepskin collar.

"Well, what are you doing out here all by your lonesome?" A lopsided grin lifted a corner of his attractive mouth. Kate yanked her gaze back to the sky. This man was far too good-looking for his own good. And hers too.

"Some thoughtful person left a lovely fire burning, so I thought I'd take advantage of it." She tugged the fleece a little higher under her chin. "It may be a tad chilly, but it's such a beautiful night. I've never before seen a sky this bright with stars. It's...it's hard to put into words. Even when you live in a small town, there are too many lights that dull the stars. This is simply stunning."

Gabe dropped onto the other end of the short couch. "It is, isn't it? I lived in Casper most of my life so moving out here opened my eyes to the beauty of the night sky. It's something I'll never take for granted."

Kate turned her eyes toward him. "Who do you think turned on the twinkling lights and started the fire? There was no one out here when I came out."

He chuckled. "I did. Mark asked me to. He'll be out along with Matt shortly."

Kate's eyes widened. "Oh, how nice. A bit of

conversation around the fire. That'll be pleasant."

"I think so." His gaze moved to her, and his eyes roamed her features.

The sliding glass door opened again, and Mr. Scott stepped out. Two women followed him, one who looked to be in her early thirties, the other about Kate's age. "Good. You're both here. Where's Matt?"

"I'm here, Dad." Kate turned to see Matt approaching from the direction of the barn. "I was checking on Major. He's doing great."

"That's good to hear, son. I heard he passed his final test today." Mr. Scott ushered the women toward the sitting area, and as they sat, he also took a seat.

Matt dropped onto a second couch beside the older woman and wrapped an arm around her shoulders. "He sure did. With flying colors. I'll use him as my riding horse for a while, alternating between him and Plucky, my usual rider."

He turned toward the woman beside him. "Hey, Megan. How's it going?"

With blond, chin-length hair and dark-rimmed glasses, she turned and planted a kiss on his stubble-lined cheek. "Going great, darlin'. Can't complain. You?"

Matt shook his head and squeezed her shoulder. "Wouldn't do any good to complain. So why bother?" He chuckled and laid a kiss onto her temple.

"You two finished?" Mr. Scott chucked. "It's chilly out here, and my old bones feel it."

"You're not that old, Dad. Get real." The woman named Megan laughed.

This was Matt's older sister? Kate looked closer. The light from the over-head twinkling lights and the fire indicated a pretty face, if slightly plump as was her figure. She sported a ready smile and her laugh sparkled. Kate's eyes moved to the younger woman. Who was she? Not Matt's girlfriend. She'd already met that difficult.... *I mustn't be uncharitable.* If Matt loved Gina, so would she. Or she'd attempt to. *Would you help me with that, Lord?*

"Well, I still feel the cold, so let's get started." Mr. Scott stared down his daughter. "First, I'll make introductions. Kate, you haven't yet met my oldest child, Megan Howard. She lives in Gillette part-time and part-time in Casper. She's a journalist." He indicated the young woman sitting in a cushioned-armchair. "This is Skylar Simpson. Megan's assistant. Ladies, this is Kate Cigler, Matt's twin sister."

"It's a pleasure to meet you." Kate tossed them a smile. She expected a shocked reaction from both women, but when they responded with nods and smiles, she realized they'd already heard the story.

"You look a bit surprised, Kate." Mr. Scott smirked. "Yes, I've already prepared Megan and Skylar. It would've taken too long to tell them once they arrived. I had a long conversation with them by phone this morning when I invited them out."

Puzzled, Kate tilted her head. "Pardon me, but I don't understand. What's this all about? All of a sudden, I feel like I'm playing catch-up."

Matt withdrew his arm from his sister's shoulders and leaned forward, his hands clasped between his knees. "That makes two of us. What's going on, Dad?"

Mr. Scott crossed a knee over the other and folded his hands in his lap. Drawing in a deep breath, he released it slowly as if fortifying himself for the conversation. "I want to take you and Kate to Germany to visit some of the places where your mother lived and worked as a spy. I believe if you go there, you'll understand a little more about who she was. You'll be able to uncover some of those secrets you're looking for, Kate."

Kate's heart stuttered, her breath catching in her throat. *Germany.* How could she go to Germany now? No. She couldn't leave now. Her aunties and uncle were depending on her to come home and run the bakery.

Gabe touched her arm. "Kate, what's wrong?"

She shook her head. "I can't go to Germany. Not...not now. I simply can't." She lowered her gaze to her lap. "It's not possible."

"What's holding you back? You said your relatives work at the bakery. Can't they do without you for a time?" Mr. Scott leaned forward.

"No, I...I can't leave them right now. It'll have to wait, or you'll have to go without me." Kate squeezed her hands tightly together beneath the fleece blanket. As much as she wanted to know more about her mother, she had to save her and her loved ones' livelihood.

Kate lifted her eyes and met her brother's. Something there drew her. Did he somehow understand her dilemma? But how could he? He had no idea what was happening in her life.

His lips formed a gentle smile while his eyes never left hers. "Kate, something's going on in your life that's causing you difficulty, isn't it? Are you facing something you need to deal with? What's going on?"

Kate's gaze shifted around the group. All eyes were on her. How could she tell this group about her problem? It was her problem to deal with, not theirs.

"Kate." Matt's gentle tone drew her eyes back to his. Nothing had changed. Care and understanding remained in the depth of his eyes and stamped on his features. "You have a family back in Ohio, one you care deeply about, but whether you know it or not, we're your family now too." His smile widened. "We care about what you care about. If you have a problem, we have a problem. We want to help if we can. Look around. Yes, you only met us recently." He pointed at Megan and Skylar. "Two just this evening. But there are five of us with varied experiences and educations that may be able to help with what you're dealing with. Please, give us a chance. If we can't help, we may know someone who can."

Kate swallowed hard and scanned the group again. There was no judgment or censure on anyone's face. Only smiles and nods all around. Tears threatened, forcing her to blink them away.

She brought her hands from beneath the blanket and clasped them in her lap. "It's not in my nature to spill my problems to anyone I've only known a short time, but Matt's words make so much sense." She shifted her gaze around to include them all. "Something tells me he's right about this group being my extended family."

Matt's lips quirked as he sat straight up and propped his hands on his hips. "Of course, I'm right. Now how should I take that?"

Kate shrugged and gave him an impish grin. "As a compliment?"

He huffed and rolled his eyes. "Okay, sis." His face transformed into a smile.

Megan elbowed him. "Hey, behave yourself, or I'll give you a wallop like I used to." She gave Kate a wink. "You have my permission to wallop him anytime you want to."

Kate laughed. "Thanks."

"So now that we've got the family thing straightened out and you understand we're willing to help in any way we can, what's holding you back, Kate?" Mr. Scott shifted in his seat. "We want to help. Understand?"

Kate tugged the fleece around her again. "Yes, I believe I do." She paused to gather her thoughts. "The bakery is housed in a leased building, and although we are current with our payments, there's a property developer who's buying up buildings in our town. We've heard rumors that's he's interested in purchasing our building. It's situated at a prime location on Main Street. We do a huge business and sell out nearly every day, but if we have to move, or worse yet, shutdown completely, we'll be devastated."

"Who was the reliable source that said the developer was interested in purchasing your building?" Gabe asked.

Kate turned to meet his eyes. "The lawyer on the day he read my grandmother's will. That was about two weeks ago."

"Who owns the building?" Furrows creased between his brows.

"A local gentleman, but we make our payments through the bank in town. My grandmother left me some money that I can put toward the purchase, but it's not enough. However, it'll almost pay it off."

"No problem. It's quite simple." Mr. Scott waved a hand in the air. "I'll pay the rest and the building will be yours."

Kate stared at him wide-eyed before shaking her head. "Thank you, but I can't be beholden to you like that. If nothing else, I'll take out a loan when I return and pay off the rest."

Mr. Scott leaned forward, a frown darkening his features. "You'd pay out the nose in interest fees on a loan. I'd never charge you interest. Please, let me help you."

Kate stared into his pleading eyes. Sincerity stood out plain and simple. He truly wanted to help. "Let me think about it."

"Don't think too long, Kate." Gabe leaned forward, elbows on his knees. "Property developers don't wait. When he decides to move, you may not have a chance to do anything."

Kate turned to stare at his stern features before returning her eyes to Mr. Scott who nodded his agreement. She'd have to give her loved ones a call and do some praying. Borrowing money from an individual she'd barely met didn't sound like a good idea, yet she hated the thought of borrowing from the bank.

"Can you give me an answer by tomorrow evening?"

Mr. Scott grinned at her. "I'd like to get going on this Germany trip. The reason Megan is here is she'd like to do an article on our...adventure, if you will. And with yours and Matt's permission, she'd like to do a write up about your mother's service to our country. Elena was an extraordinary woman, and her service deserves to be recognized." He paused and turned to Skylar. "That's where this young lady comes in. She'll be traveling with us and recording our journey of discovery concerning your mother."

Kate turned to Matt and found the same dumbstruck expression she was certain must match hers. Mother had been a spy for the United States. Kate still had a hard time coming to grips with that knowledge. Perhaps seeing the places Mother had lived and worked would make it real for Kate. She had a decision to make, and before she could make that decision, she had a phone call to make.

"Yes, I'll give you a decision by tomorrow evening."

"Thank you. I look forward to hearing it."

Megan stood and walked around to Kate's side. Leaning over, she wrapped an arm around Kate's shoulder. "Welcome to the family, sis. Matt's sister is my sister." She stood and stuffed her hands into her coat pockets. "When I was about five, I remember a second baby when Matt was brought home to us. A little girl. And I have a faint memory of her mother, but she and the baby both disappeared. Shortly after, I was told they both died. That's what Matt and I grew up believing. I suppose there were reasons beyond what we all needed to know. Especially if your mom was a spy. Who can question those things?"

"You must be the little girl in the picture with the two babies." Kate pulled the photos from her coat pocket and sifted through them. "I've been carrying them with me because I never knew when I might run into someone I could ask about them." She handed the photo to Megan. "Do you recognize it?"

Megan accepted it and stepped closer to the fire light. "Wow, that was taken a long time ago, but yes, I do recognize it. That's me with the two babies that came to our house. I must have been about five or six years old. Matt stayed and you left with your mother." She straightened and handed the picture back to Kate. "I'm so sorry you lost your mom, but I'm glad you grew up happy and had a good life with her.

"I did. Thank you for welcoming me into your family, sis." Kate smiled.

Megan released a happy laugh. "You'll fit in just fine, darlin'. I know after the German trip you'll return to Ohio, but I hope you'll come back often to visit. And, yes, I have faith you'll be going to Germany."

Kate eyed the older woman. "Do you have real faith? I mean faith in Christ? Or just believing something will happen."

Megan winked. "I know exactly what you mean. I put my faith in Christ years ago." She turned to glance over her shoulder at the group chatting quietly behind them, then she returned her gaze to Kate. "I've been working on my father and brother for a long time, but they've been resistant. Are you a believer?"

Kate nodded. "Since I was a child."

"Great. Perhaps you'll help pray for them. Gabe's a believer, and he's been working on them and praying for them too."

"I'll be happy to, and I'll ask my family back home to pray as well. My Auntie Genevieve, when she gets a bone between her teeth, she won't let go. She'll pray hard for them."

Megan clasped Kate's shoulder. "Thank you. That would mean the world to me."

Kate prayed about her decision whether to accept Mr. Scott's offer that night and the next day before calling her aunties and uncle the following afternoon. The bakery closed at five eastern time, and she was two hours behind. Her loved ones would close the shop and begin cleanup, but they could stop long enough for her to tell them about Mr. Scott's offer and her alternate plan. *Lord, help them give me the sound advice You want me to follow. They have wisdom I simply don't have. If You want me to accept Mr. Scott's generous offer, please give them and me Your peace. And if not, give me the peace to take out a loan. Show us Your will.*

Except for mealtimes, Kate stayed in her room praying and packing some of her things. If she went to Germany, she'd need to pack, but if she didn't go to Germany, she'd need to fly home. Either way, she wanted to be ready.

At three o'clock, she sat in the chair by the little table in her room and picked up the receiver on the phone sitting there. She'd already obtained permission to use it. When she'd promised to pay for the call, Mr. Scott had waved her offer away, telling her not to worry. He could afford a long-distant call. In fact, he made them all the time. One more wouldn't make a difference on his bill.

Finger in the rotary dial, Kate placed the call to the bakery. After several rings, Uncle Rudy's voice finally answered.

"Hello. Cigler Bakery. We're closed. Can you call back tomorrow, please?"

"Uncle Rudy? It's Kate." How his familiar accent filled her with a homesickness she hadn't realized until that moment. Oh, but she couldn't let on about that.

A gasp rasped. "Is that you, my holčička? How are you? Are you okay? Nothing bad has happened, has it?"

Kate laughed. "No, Uncle. Everything is fine with me. How about all of you? Are you all well? How's the bakery?"

His guffaw filled her ear. "It's such a relief to hear your voice. We are all well. The bakery is flourishing. Not one pastry or pie left in the case—not a single crumb, mind you. Anna and Genny are washing up now before we go home to collapse. Aye, yiy, yiy. How busy we are."

In her mind's eye, Kate could see her uncle waving his hand in the air as he described his day. "Oh, Uncle, I'm so happy the bakery is still doing well, but you three are so busy when you should be enjoying your retirement. I feel so bad for you. Perhaps I should hire some folks to take your places so you can settle down and take it easier."

"Shush. Don't even mention that to your aunties." His near whisper was almost as loud as his regular voice. "They'll never go for that."

Kate snickered. "I'm sure you're right. Grandmother didn't retire until she was on her deathbed."

"You're right, God rest her soul." He sighed. "So, did you simply call to check up on us?"

"Well, no." Kate inhaled deeply, blowing out the breath all at once. "I called to ask for some advice. You may want to gather the aunties near, so the three of you can give it."

"Are you kidding me, holčička? They would only confuse matters. Let me give the advice. I have the business sense, what's left of it, in this family. Now spill the beans."

Kate stuffed down a giggle at his cliché, although she knew this fact of his business sense to be true. Auntie Anna and particularly Auntie Genevieve would argue about things. "All right. Remember that Mr. Calhoun told us the property developer, Mr. Hawthorn, is interested in our building? He's buying properties all around town." Kate reminded her uncle that she had enough money from the safe-deposit box to pay for part of the building but not all of it. She told him about meeting her twin brother and his family, about her mother's secret job as a spy, about the proposed trip to Germany, and Mr. Scott's amazing offer.

"Uncle, so much has happened in the week I've been here, it's been like a whirlwind. Mr. Scott's offer is generous, but I simply don't know if I should accept it." Kate paused. "As an alternate plan, I thought about taking out a loan to pay for the remainder of the cost of the building. I need your sage advice in which I should do."

Kate waited for a response from Uncle Rudy, but it wasn't forthcoming. Was he processing all she'd told him? "Uncle Rudy? Are you still there?" Had the connection dropped?

"That was a lot of information to process. I had forgotten your mother was a spy for the United States during the war." His voice held a note of awe. "That was so long ago."

Kate released a small chortle. "Is that as far as you got or did you hear everything I told you?"

"Oh, I heard it all, but I still can't see your mother as a spy. I never could. A singer, yes. A spy? Not at all. She was far too gentle of a creature to be a spy."

"That's what I thought as well." Kate cleared her throat. "Uncle, I need you to focus on Mr. Scott's offer of the loan. I've been praying about what to do concerning the bakery. These people are...amazing and generous. I hope you can meet them sometime. They believe Mr. Hawthorne won't hesitate to grab up the prime property of the bakery at any time. Even with me out of town. Please, let's just focus on the bakery's needs at this moment. We can talk about the rest later."

"Yes, I will. Your Mr. Scott has made a most generous offer. Will he charge you interest? A bank will charge you a lot of interest for a loan. You understand this, yes?"

"I do."

"How much is left to pay off the building after you pay what you can from what Margareta left you?"

Kate told him the approximate amount and waited for his reply.

"You will pay at least half that much in interest, if not more, if you take out a loan from the bank. My recommendation is to accept the loan from Mr. Scott, but get it in writing. Is there a lawyer nearby you can have write up a contract for you?"

Kate thought of Gabe and smiled to herself. "Yes, I believe that can be arranged."

"There, you have my advice, and you'll save yourself a lot of money. Just make sure the contract states there will be no interest."

"I will. Thank you. You've taken a huge burden from my shoulders and helped answer my prayer. I must go, but please, give my love and hugs to the aunties and know how much I love you."

"We love and miss you too. Please be safe when you travel in Germany. Your sweet mother's secrets will reveal themselves if they want to be revealed. We'll be praying for you."

"Thank you. I appreciate every prayer. Which reminds me—Megan, Matt's sister, asked prayer for Matt and Mr. Scott. She's a believer, but they aren't."

"Enough said. We'll all be praying for them. And you know your Auntie Genny. When she gets a bone—"

"Exactly." Kate laughed. "Take care of them. Bye for now."

Chapter Six

Kate drew in a deep breath and released it slowly as she settled into her seat on the plane. Gabe sat on one side of her and Mr. Scott on the other. Across the aisle to their left and by the window sat Matt and Skylar Simpson. Kate inwardly chuckled as she noticed the two deep in conversation, a grin on Matt's face at something the young woman had said.

In the three days since she'd met Skylar, she'd discovered the lovely brunette was a fellow believer. Kate liked her, and they'd had some great conversations. Perhaps she could work some magic on Kate's brother, and he would turn his life over to Christ. Maybe he would even turn his attentions away from Gina and toward Skylar. Gina wasn't good for Matt. Her attitude certainly wasn't. *There I go again, Lord. Help me with my own attitude toward Gina. She needs You. That would make a world of difference.*

Mr. Scott pushed a button on the side of his seat, and the bottom came up allowing his legs to stretch out in front of him at the same time the back reclined. Wow. And she thought sitting in business class on this huge 747 plane simply provided more leg room. She turned to find Gabe's eyes on her and a grin on his face.

"Quite the upgrade from our last flight, huh?"

"I'll say." She returned his smile. "I wasn't expecting

to travel in such luxury."

"Any time you want to take a nap, help yourself. There are buttons on the side of your armrest to make whatever adjustments you need."

Kate lowered her eyes to the area he indicated. "Knowing we'll be on the plane for a while, I might. Too bad I don't have more pastries to pass around."

His brows lifted. "Now that would be nice. One of these days I'll have to visit that bakery of yours."

"When I spoke to my uncle the other night, he told me they were selling out of everything."

"They must get up early to bake."

"They do." Kate leaned her head against the headrest. "We begin baking at four am and continue throughout the day. My aunts and uncle are in their seventies. They should be retired, yet they continue working six days a week. We close on Sundays. My grandmother was eighty-three when she died. She continued working in the bakery until she became so ill, she couldn't get out of bed. Her body simply gave out. They'll all do the same unless I can do something about it."

Gabe reached over and squeezed her hand laying in her lap. "You started by securing the building. It's all paid off and belongs to you now."

Kate turned to meet his eyes, her voice little more than a whisper. She didn't want Mr. Scott to overhear. "Not fully. I still have a payment to make, but I'm grateful to pay it. It's far less than the one I would've made with another loan."

Gabe smiled and squeezed her hand again before releasing it. "I'm sure that'll help out."

"Hugely. When I return home, I should be able to hire help to give my loved ones a break. At least part-time. I doubt they'll give up completely at first. If I can get them to work part-time, that'll be an accomplishment."

Two stewardesses moved carts down the aisle to begin

serving the meal. Kate turned toward Gabe again. "You know, I never properly thanked you for drawing up the loan contract for me. You ensured it had everything in it that I wanted. I appreciate your time and effort. But you wouldn't accept payment. What kind of lawyer doesn't take payment?" She laughed.

His shoulders lifted in a shrug, and he winked at her. "A lawyer who I hope is a friend?"

The grin he tossed in her direction faded as his eyes remained locked with hers. Kate couldn't tug hers away, and her breath caught.

One of the stewardesses stopped by with the food cart. "Can we interest you in lunch?" She listed the lunch choices.

Kate yanked her eyes toward the stewardess awaiting an answer. "Can you repeat that, please?" Goodness. Her words sounded a bit breathless. She cleared her throat.

Gabe scrubbed a hand over his mouth as if hiding a grin but turned his attention to the stewardess. Once she repeated the menu, Kate decided on one of the meals and Gabe on another.

"Would you like for me to wake him?" Kate pointed at Mr. Scott.

The stewardess shook her head. "That won't be necessary. We'll make a trip down that aisle shortly." She handed Kate and Gabe their meals. "The next stewardess will serve your beverages." With that, she smiled and passed on.

Kate enjoyed her meal and once again determined her aunts didn't have a clue what they were talking about when it came to airplane food. Afterward, she settled back for a nap and didn't awaken until the plane was preparing to land in Frankfurt, Germany. As she folded the blanket the stewardess had provided for her nap, she recalled what Gabe had told her when they'd first boarded. This particular plane, the 747, had only rolled into service this year. Pan Am, the carrier they were on, was the first to purchase and send flights out. Kate, for one, was impressed with the service the airline had offered on this trip.

As the plane touched down smoothly, a thrill ran up Kate's back as she thought about the fact they were now on foreign soil. Soon she would step onto that soil. Germany. The land her mother had lived and worked in. The country where she had hidden her identity in order to discover information from the Nazis. Mother's sacrificial goal had helped the United States win the war. *Oh, Mother, you truly were a heroine, weren't you? And I thought you were simply my mommy.*

Kate's heart thrummed as the plane came to a stop at the jet bridge and the plane crew prepared for deboarding.

"Kate? Are you all right?" Gabe's deep voice caught her attention. He was in the aisle removing their carry-ons from the overhead luggage compartments.

She nodded.

A soft smile lifted the corners of his lips. "A little nervous?"

She shrugged. "I'd never left Ohio before I went to Wyoming. Germany is a huge step for me."

Gabe held out a hand. "Come on. Let's get this adventure underway. You have things to discover about your mother. There's no telling what you'll find out."

Kate returned her gaze to his face. "Maybe that's what I'm nervous about."

He wiggled his fingers urging her to take it and tilted his head in the direction of the exit. "Come on. You're surrounded by people who care. Matt's as nervous as you are."

Kate reached for his hand, then he pulled her up. "I'm grateful I'm not in this alone." Once on her feet, she reached for her carry-on. "Lead on."

After going through customs, they found a black stretch limousine waiting outside baggage claim. Kate still couldn't understand how Mr. Scott had been able to procure her a passport in two days. He'd simply stated it was important to know the right people to get anything done these days. Matt had winked at her and explained the right people worked at the State Department. Kate decided she probably didn't want to know, but it likely had something to do with his days in the US Army.

The limousine driver piled their luggage into the huge trunk while they piled into the limousine. Kate was certain her chin must be dragging on the floor. How had she connected with people who rode in limousines? She thought about her Ford Mavrick rental car. Mr. Scott had sent a couple of his ranch hands to return it to the Gillette airport since she wouldn't be around to drive it. Kate had thought she had been in high-cotton driving that. At home she drove a non-descript beater car. This limo? Was she dreaming? When no one was looking, she pinched herself. Nope. She wasn't dreaming.

"So where are we headed, Dad?" Matt settled onto a white leather bench seat and fiddled with some buttons that turned on a small TV. "Oops. Sorry." He turned it back off.

Mr. Scott chuckled. "We're heading to a hotel here in Frankfurt. It'll be dark before long. Although Munich is our destination, that's almost a three-hour drive. I'm not up to that tonight after a transatlantic flight. Don't know about the rest of you, but I'm ready for something to eat then go to bed."

"Food? That sounds good." Matt opened a cabinet along one wall of the car. "Hey. I found some food." He reached in and pulled out some bagged snacks. "Anybody want some snacks?"

Mr. Scott breathed out a sigh. "I was thinking more along the lines of a meal near the hotel, son."

"That sounds better than these, I guess." When Matt's face fell, Skylar giggled. He grinned at her as he stuffed the snacks back into the cabinet.

Kate reached over and patted his arm. "It was a good idea."

He shrugged. "Thanks."

The limo passed through Frankfurt into the heart of the city to the Steigenberger Icon Frankfurter Hof, a huge hotel established in 1876—at least that was what Mr. Scott had said. Once again Kate clamped her lips together to keep from gaping at the amazing architecture. Darkness had fallen during their travel from the airport, and the vast number of windows were lit between tiered levels. Columns and arches were everywhere. The name of the hotel was lit above a balconied terrace where a columned-and-arched entrance welcomed visitors to come in.

The limo came to a smooth stop before the entrance, and a doorman opened the limo door and helped them out. A bellhop hurried with a luggage trolley to the trunk of the limo. Kate stood on the sidewalk, her eyes on the façade of the building. With the elegance on the outside, she couldn't begin to imagine what the interior must be like. Skylar slipped over beside her and placed her arm through Kate's.

"Is this as fantastic to you as it is to me?" Skylar's tone remained low, indicating it was meant for Kate's ears only.

Kate eyed the other woman, but Skylar's eyes stared upward. "Probably more so. I'm struggling to take it all in. First class on the airplane. The limousine. Now this." She waved a hand toward the building in front of them. "And this is just for overnight?"

Skylar lowered her eyes to meet Kate's, one brow lifted, a smile on her lips. "You're learning Mr. Scott doesn't do anything halfway."

"Yes, I am."

Skylar tugged Kate's arm gently. "Come on. Everyone's heading inside."

Mr. Scott led the way with Matt and Gabe right behind. Two bellhops waited for Kate and Skylar to follow. They apparently wouldn't go in until the women did. One even held out his hand directing the women to precede them.

"Oh, sorry." Kate tossed a wave, and they moved inside. Once in the lobby, she nearly dropped her chin again. Creams, golds and oak everywhere. It was magnificent.

Mr. Scott headed toward the reception desk. He had them checked in and on their way to their rooms in no time.

Before they entered the elevators, he paused. "Anyone wanting something to eat, meet back here, and we'll grab something local. I happen to know of a good place near here. At least I hope it's still open." Mr. Scoff eyed Kate and Matt. "If it is, I think you two in particular might be interested in it."

Kate's ears perked up. "I'll be here."

Matt shoved his hands into his jeans pockets. "I'll be here for two reasons. I want to know about this place, and I'm hungry."

Mr. Scott stepped into the elevator. "We'll meet in twenty minutes."

Gabe wasn't about to miss the restaurant where Mark was taking them to eat. One, he wanted to spend as much time with Kate as possible. Two, he wanted to find out what this place had to do with her mother. Mark hadn't specifically said it had anything to do with her, but he'd sort of implied it by saying Kate and Matt might be interested in the place. Whatever was of interest to Kate was of interest to Gabe. He was quickly losing his heart to this beautiful, meek woman. *Lord, I don't know why I should. She's given me no encouragement, but I can't help it. There's something compelling about her. I want to know more. Is that crazy or what?*

He waited by the elevators when Mark and Matt came

down, and within minutes, Kate and Skylar followed them. Gabe's heart quickened as Kate stepped off the elevator. She'd freshened up by changing into a casual dress and pulled her long hair up into a twist. *Wow, Lord. She's...gorgeous.*

Kate turned from saying something to Skylar, then met his eyes. A smile lifted her sweet lips and her eyes sparkled. That smile was directed at him, causing his breath to catch. How did he rate? He didn't likely. She shared smiles with everyone.

"Where's this restaurant, Dad?" Matt fell into step beside his father. "Do we need to call a taxi?"

"Nope. It's just around the corner. After our plane ride, a walk won't hurt any of us." Mark headed for the front exit, the others following.

"I'm certainly game to stretch my legs." Excitement filled Skylar's voice. "I'm keen to find out about this place, aren't you, Kate?"

Gabe eyed Kate for her reaction.

"Definitely. Does it have something to do with Mother, Mr. Scott?" Kate grasped the handle of her shoulder bag.

Mark paused and turned to face Kate. "First off, it's time you called me Mark. You're the only one in the group, except my son, who doesn't. Is that okay with you?"

Kate hesitated. "I was always taught to call my elders Mr. or Mrs. It doesn't feel right calling you by your first name. But...if you prefer that, I suppose I can, Mark."

He grinned at her. "I do, and that wasn't so hard, now, was it?"

"No, but I may slip up on occasion."

"We'll work on it. To answer your question, yes, this place does have something to do with your mother." He turned and headed out the hotel door.

Gabe chuckled inwardly at Kate's expression. Shock wasn't quite the right word, but surprise was too lame. He reached over and took Kate's hand, tugging her forward.

She met his eyes. "It's an adventure, right? We're here to discover your mother's story. You found out she was a spy. This is the beginning of that discovery. Remember, Mark knew your mother back in the day. He knew the ins and outs of what happened. Trust him. He's a good man. And if she was a spy and worked with him, most likely he was a spy too."

A question appeared in Kate's eyes.

Gabe shrugged. "Mark doesn't talk much about his time in the military, but if he's here to show you and Matt your mother's past, he may open up a little about his own."

Kate turned her eyes to the street as they walked down Kaiserplatz. to Kirchnerstrass. What was going on in that beautiful head? Kate had a lot to think about. She'd recently discovered she had a brother, and her mother was a spy. Now she would begin to learn more about that life her mother had lived. What would she discover? *Lord, help her as she soaks in all this earth-shaking information, and help me to be there for her. If she'll let me.*

The doorbell rang and Mrs. Holcomb made her way from the rear of the house to the front door. Whoever was there, certainly leaned on the bell incessantly.

"Good gracious. I'm coming," she murmured. "This is a huge house, and I don't live right by the front door. Have patience."

Nearly out of breath, she unlocked the door and swung it wide. A tall man about Mr. Scott's age stood with hands encased in black driving gloves folded in front of him. He wore a black leather jacket, a black turtleneck underneath, and black slacks. Wispy white hair peeked from beneath a black fedora, and dark sunglasses covered his eyes. Whoever he was, he appeared to love black.

"Yes, may I help you?" This was not the usual type of

visitor to the ranch, but it wasn't in her nature to be rude, so she plastered on her most genuine smile. After all, this man had driven miles to get here. The least she could do was be pleasant.

His chin lifted another inch as he removed his sunglasses and stared at her through narrowed eyes. "I'm looking for Major Mark Scott. Is he at home?"

Alarm bells echoed through Mrs. Holcomb's head at the man's accent. What could it be? She didn't particularly want to tell this man her boss wasn't at home, but what was she to do? Why had she ever opened the door? "He's not available right this minute, but if you'll leave your name and a way for him to reach you, he'll get back to you soon, I'm sure." She flashed her pleasant smile again.

The man drew in a deep breath and exhaled it all at once. "That will *not* do. I want to speak with him immediately." His chin lifted further, his tone haughty and impatient.

Mrs. Holcomb took a step back. "I'm terribly sorry, sir, but that's not possible. If you give me a few minutes, I'll go get the man in charge, and—" Before Mrs. Holcomb knew what was happening, the man reached out and backhanded her with his fist.

She flew backwards across the wide foyer to land several feet away, her glasses flying across the room. Just before she blacked out, a black shadow leaned over and said, "Tell *that* to Mr. Scott."

Chapter Seven

The group entered the tavern Das Schwarze Wildschwein around the block from the hotel on Kirchnerstrass. After the excitement of the day, Kate was glad they didn't have to walk too far. Her tummy had been talking to her for a while and telling her the meal on the plane had disappeared long ago. As they stepped inside the warm and rustic interior, she noticed several customers filled tables and sat at the bar, but a quiet atmosphere rested over the establishment.

A waitress in a traditional German *dirndl* approached with a tray beneath her arm and included them all in her welcoming smile. "*Guten abend*, everyone. Welcome to The Black Boar." She reached behind a tall desk against the wall and retrieved menus. "If you'll follow me, I'll take you to your table."

"Thank you." Mark led the group as they filed behind the waitress into the depths of the tavern. Kate's eyes soaked in her surroundings. If her mother had visited this place, Kate wanted to see every inch of it. Was it the same as it had been when she was here, or had it changed over the years? She could almost picture Nazi officers sitting at the tables around the room. Had her mother dealt with them often? What did her spying on Hitler's regime entail? Did Kate truly want to know? A shudder went through her as she stopped at the table and took the seat Gabe held for her.

"Are you cold?" He leaned close and asked for her ears only.

Kate shook her head. "I was thinking of my mother and wondered what she had to do to spy on the regime. It sent a chill down my spine."

Gabe gave her shoulder a quick squeeze and took the chair beside her.

Quiet chatter flowed around Kate as the group perused their menus. She decided on veal— *wiener schnitzel* with lemon, *spaetzle* and *rotkohl*, a red German sauerkraut. Kate's mouth watered in anticipation. She couldn't remember the last time she'd eaten German food.

As the waitress headed toward the kitchen with their orders, all eyes turned to Mr. Scott...er, Mark.

"Well, Dad, what's the scoop?" Matt's eyes roamed over the tavern before edging back to Mark. "Why is this place of interest to Kate and me?"

Mark leaned forward, his hands clasped in front of him on the table. "I've never told anyone any of this information, not even your mom, Matt. I still can't tell you everything I did, but I can divulge some of it. I was stationed in London with Eisenhower's Supreme Headquarters Allied Expeditionary Force, or SHAEF, as it's better known to some. This was the group that headed up and prepared for D-Day. A lot of—how shall I say it —"

"Spying?" Matt chuckled.

Mark lowered a brow at him. "For want of a better word, yes. In order to prepare, the allied forces had to find out what the Nazi's were up to, so we had to use every means at our disposal."

"—Including my mother." Kate piped in.

Mark's eyes met hers. "We didn't *use* your mother. She willingly accepted the mission. We made sure she knew exactly what she was doing before she ever left Washington, D.C. Elena trained for it and did a flawless job."

The waitress brought refills of their drinks and promised their meals would be out shortly.

"Thank you." Mark returned his attention to the group as she hurried away. "Elena took the train to Frankfurt occasionally under the guise of shopping, and I met her here at The Black Boar Tavern. She passed on information, and I in turn took it back to London. However, if there was information with a time restraint, she'd send me a telegram in code to a contact here in Frankfurt. The man worked for our side and sent the message on to London."

"How in the world did he not get caught?" Gabe shifted in his seat. "The Nazi's monitored things like that."

"They did indeed." Mark took a drink of his iced tea, a half-grin on his face. "Franz set up a special telegraph relay system to the resistance in Paris." Mark raised his hands, palms outward. "Don't ask me how it worked, but desperate times and all that. The Nazi's never caught on." His eyes returned to Kate. "Your mother's work was invaluable. She ascertained information that helped launch D-Day and helped the allies win the war. So, when you wonder about your mother's spying days, keep that in mind."

"Something you said a moment ago—" Kate folded her hands in her lap. "You said Mother took a train here to Frankfurt occasionally. That indicates she didn't live here. Where did she live?" All eyes pivoted toward Mark.

"I should've known you wouldn't miss that. Elena lived in Munich. That's where we're heading tomorrow." He lifted his eyes and smiled. "Ah, here comes our food."

The waitress brought out a tray and began serving their plates. As Kate began to cut her veal and took a bite, she attempted to correlate the mother she knew with the woman Mark described. In her mind, the woman who met him in this room so long ago and informed him of Nazi movements didn't mesh with the baker Kate knew. *It's hard to grasp, Lord. Help me see Mother in all this. If it's true, she was a national hero and deserves the recognition. But most of all, I simply want to see her for who she was.*

As they stepped from the tavern and strolled along the sidewalk to the hotel, conversation revolved around the delicious meal they'd enjoyed and how bedtime was next on the agenda.

"It's been a long day." Gabe matched his stride with Kate's, walking on the outside closest to the curb.

She stifled a yawn and clasped the strap of her shoulder bag. "It has—"

From out of nowhere, someone slammed into Kate, yanking her bag. She fell to the ground and landed hard on her shoulder and hip but managed to hold onto her bag with both hands. "No, let go," she yelled at the person, whom she could now tell was a man.

Gabe whipped around and dove for the man. "Hey, let go, buddy." With a balled fist, Gabe prepared to make contact with the side of his face, but before he could, the man released his hold and took off down a side alley.

Mark, Matt, and Skylar spun around and froze.

"What happened?" Mark demanded. "Kate, are you okay?"

Matt bent over his sister as Gabe helped Kate to her feet. "Are you all right, sis? What happened?"

Skylar wrapped an arm around Kate's waist. "I saw the guy run down that alley, but I didn't get a good look at him. Did he hurt you?"

All Kate knew was she still had her shoulder bag. Winding her arms through the strap, she grasped it to her chest and realized she was shaking. "I'm okay. I think."

Gabe reached for her hand and held it out. It shook. "Let's get you back to the hotel and bring you something warm to drink. A hot shower would do you some good.

You hit the pavement hard with your shoulder and hip. You'll likely have bruises tomorrow."

"Maybe a call to the hotel doctor is in order." Mark eyed her closely.

"No. I don't need a doctor. Let's just go back to the hotel. A hot shower, some aspirin and a good night's sleep will do me fine." She started to walk but winced at the pain in her hip.

"Uh huh." Wrapping an arm around her waist, Gabe lifted Kate into his arms. "I'll take the weight off that hip for now. At least until we get you back to your room."

"But...but...but—" Kate sputtered, holding her shoulder bag close.

"I've found it's useless to argue with a lawyer." Mark followed Gabe down the sidewalk, his chuckle mingling with Matt's. "You won't win."

Kate avoided Gabe's eyes. Heat radiated over her as she attempted not to notice how strong his arms were or how secure she felt nestled against his chest. Nope. She wouldn't think about those things. Drawing in a deep breath, she released it slowly.

Gabe's chest moved up and down as if he were laughing. A soft chuckle escaped him. Was he laughing at her? Before she could stop herself, she turned to meet his eyes. A grin rested on those handsome lips, and he winked. Kate sent him a glare before yanking her gaze toward the front. He was still laughing.

Skylar opened their hotel-room door, and Gabe stepped inside where he gently deposited Kate onto the end of the bed.

"I'll have some hot cocoa sent up. You—" he pointed at Kate, "take a long, hot shower and some of that aspirin you promised. I'm sure Skylar will help with whatever you need."

Skylar, standing close with arms crossed over her chest, nodded. "You bet I will. I'll start the shower, and she'll be finished by the time room service delivers that cocoa."

"Great. Have a good night, ladies. See you in the morning." He winked at Kate again. "Sleep well." With that he slipped out the door.

"I'll start the shower for you while you gather your things." Skylar headed for the beautiful spa-like bathroom.

Kate stood and found her muscles already beginning to stiffen. Pain arched through her shoulder and hip as she limped over to gather her nightclothes. She'd be uncomfortable for a day or two, thanks to the would-be purse-snatcher. Yes, she'd gone down, but she'd gone down fighting. Gabe had been about to punch the guy in the face. At least the stranger had thought better of sticking around.

"It's nice and hot for you. Check it before you get in to make sure it's not too hot." Skylar stepped out of the bathroom. "You might be in a sauna by the time you're finished."

Kate took her pajamas and toiletries and limped into the bathroom. "That wouldn't be so bad either." Undressing, she checked the shower temperature. Perfect. After climbing in, she stood beneath the rain-shower head, allowing the warm water to flow over her abused muscles. Oh, it felt so good.

Her mind returned to the incident. She supposed because she was the last person in the group, other than Gabe, that made her a prime target. It happened so quickly there wasn't much she could describe about the man. When they'd come out of the tavern, it'd already grown dark, and her assailant had been dressed in dark clothes with a dark hat pulled low over dark longish hair that stuck out from beneath the hat. The whole incident couldn't have taken more than thirty seconds, if that.

Kate soaped up and washed her hair. It felt good to clean up after traveling all day and falling onto the dirty pavement of the city street. She hadn't even looked at her dress to see if it had been damaged. Thanks to the purse-snatcher *not* stealing her purse, she still had some money if she needed to replace the dress.

Kate turned off the water and, grabbing a long, thick terry towel, gingerly dried off. Yep. She'd be sore tomorrow. Once dressed, she towel-dried her hair, took her comb and limped back into the bedroom where Skylar had already changed into her pajamas. Skylar was perched in a chair at the table where two mugs of steaming cocoa sat with whipped cream and cinnamon sprinkled on top.

"I thought I'd wait for you." Skylar indicated the mugs. "If you were going to be much longer, I was going to start without you."

Kate carefully lowered into the opposite armchair. "I don't blame you. It smells amazing."

Skylar pushed a bottle of aspirin toward her roomie. "You haven't taken any yet, have you?"

Kate shook her head. "Not yet, but I sure could use some. Thank you. You're a good roommate."

Skylar quirked a smile. "You're welcome. I have three sisters. All younger than I am. I know how to look after others."

"Yes, you do." Kate popped the lid on the aspirin bottle and poured two into her hand. She dropped them into her mouth and took a sip of her cocoa. "Hopefully that will do the trick. Mmm. This is delicious."

"Hopefully you won't run into anymore purse-snatchers." Skylar sipped her own hot beverage and, leaning back in the chair, gave Kate a sly grin. "So, what's with you and Gabe?"

Warmth rushed over Kate, and she sipped more of her cocoa, avoiding Skylar's eyes. "What do you mean, what's with us?" She shrugged her uninjured shoulder. "There's nothing with us."

Skylar lifted a brow and narrowed her eyes at her

friend. "I think you're doing that protesting-too-much thing because he stares at you, and you avoid his eyes. That's always a tell-tell sign. I nearly dropped my teeth when he grabbed you up and carried you back to the hotel after the guy tried to snatch your bag."

Kate waved a dismissive hand. "Big deal. I was hurt, and he was simply being helpful. Nothing more."

"Uh huh. So why was he chuckling and you were avoiding his eyes? Again." Skylar leaned forward, her fingernail tapping the table surface. "Seems to me something's going on, and you're trying to pretend it's not."

Kate shook her head. "I only met him a few days ago. How could anything be going on that fast?"

Skylar stroked her chin. "Well, I'm sure I don't know, but I've known Gabe for a few years now, and I've never seen him look at anyone like he looks at you." She crossed her arms over her chest, the expression on her face indicating she'd just won a debate.

Kate held her breath. Gabe looked at her in a special way? She sipped her cocoa. Skylar had to be mistaken. Except for the occasional wink, Gabe didn't look at her any differently than he had since they'd met the first day in the airport. And the winks? Well, they were mere teasing.

Skylar finished her cocoa and set the mug on the table. "Well, you might want to start noticing, my friend." She stood, and with a stop by her toiletry bag to grab her toothbrush and toothpaste, she headed to the bathroom. All of a sudden, she leaned her head back out the door. "Gabe, is a good Christian man worth the notice, Kate. I'll be praying for you." With that she withdrew into the bathroom.

The next day after their plane arrived in Munich, once

again a limo met them at baggage claim. Kate doubted she'd ever adjust to this luxury. She didn't want to because she'd have to face facts when she returned home to Ohio. Things would go back to normal when she drove her little beater around town. Grateful she had a beater to drive, Kate gingerly stepped into the limo and took a seat. Sore didn't begin to describe how her body felt when she'd rolled out of bed that morning, and it hadn't improved much throughout the trip. Skylar sat beside her on the plane and offered her another dose of aspirin which Kate gladly accepted.

Their destination in Munich was the Hotel Bayerischer Hof on Promenadeplatz. As the limo rolled smoothly to a stop in front of the entrance, Kate gazed up at the more modern façade than their last hotel's. Built on a side street away from the heavy thoroughfare a street over, with a small green park between, this hotel was still tall and wide with an enormous number of windows. Cobalt-blue awnings topped the arched walkway in front of the building with a much larger matching awning over the entrance. As the doorman held open the limo doors, they exited the car and entered their temporary home. Kate doubted this hotel would be any less luxurious than the last. If she'd learned anything about Mark Scott in the short time since she'd known him, it was that he enjoyed nice things.

Not yet lunchtime, Mark wanted everyone to settle into their rooms before they met for lunch in one of the hotel's five gourmet restaurants. He would let them know where to meet. That was fine with Kate. She wouldn't have any idea how to choose.

When Kate and Skylar entered their room, Kate picked a bed and cautiously lowered her sore body onto the duvet. "Oh, my goodness. This is so soft." She spread her arms beside her. "I've never felt anything so soft before. Wonder what it's made of?"

Skylar sat on her bed and spread her hands along the

duvet. "I've heard of eiderdown comforters before. Think that's what it is?"

Kate dropped off her shoes and edged further up onto the bed. "Eiderdown? Hmm, my mother told me about that. They used down from eider ducks to make pillows and duvets when she lived in Czechoslovakia with my grandparents when she was growing up. I had no idea it was so soft."

"I have a feeling we'll sleep well tonight." Skylar dropped back onto her duvet. "This must be what clouds are made of."

"Yeah. It's going to be hard to get back up again." Kate laughed. "Think we can order room service?"

"It would still be hard to sit up to eat." Skylar joined her in laughing.

The room phone rang, and they met each other's eyes. Skylar sat up. "I'll answer it. You're still sore." She reached for the phone receiver on the table between the beds.

"Hello?" Silence for a few moments. "Right. We'll be there shortly. If I can pry Kate from the eiderdown duvet on her bed." Skylar laughed and hung up the phone. "Matt said eat or sleep. Your choice."

Kate didn't move. "Don't tempt me." After a moment, she slowly rolled to her side and sat up. "Never mind. I'm hungry."

As they stepped out of the elevator, a man in dark clothes bumped into Kate nearly knocking her down. She gasped as pain shot through her hip and shoulder. The man didn't even turn to apologize, but kept walking. How rude!

Skylar steadied her friend and eyed the man with wide eyes as he turned a corner and disappeared. "What is wrong with the men around here? Don't they have manners?"

"Obviously not." Gabe hurried over and gently grasped Kate's elbow on her uninjured side. "Are you all right?"

Kate gave him what she hoped passed for a genuine

smile. She rubbed her shoulder. "I'm fine. It jolted me as well as surprised me. The man seemed to be in a big hurry. He likely didn't realize he'd run into me."

Skylar blew an unladylike raspberry. "Baloney. How could he have missed seeing you? He just kept going with no apologies."

A chuckle from beside them had Skylar turning her head. "So, where did you learn to blow raspberries?"

She lifted her chin at Kate's brother. "Don't know, but it's my way of calling foul on what someone says. This time it was something your sister said."

"Oh yeah? What'd she say?" Matt lowered his brows, his eyes on Kate.

Skylar explained what happened to Kate. Matt's expression grew concerned. "Are you okay? It's beginning to look like the male German population has it out for you."

Kate scowled at him. "Two men, Matt? Really? You're exaggerating. He likely didn't realize he'd bumped into me."

"That's why I raspberried her." Skylar rolled her eyes.

"Yeah, I'm with Skylar on this one. Rudeness to the max, if you ask me." Matt nodded.

"I'm in agreement—" Gabe, who'd kept his hand on Kate's elbow, led her in the direction of the restaurant Mark had suggested, "but, I'm not standing here having this conversation when Kate needs to sit down. Let's eat and find out what Mark wants to do for the rest of the day."

Kate thought that was a fantastic idea. The more she was around this man, the more she liked him. Yes, she thought the word *liked* was appropriate because she wouldn't allow herself to think anything stronger. She was headed home to Ohio when this trip was over, and Gabe Flanagan had a life in Wyoming. Those two lives couldn't mesh. *How could they, Lord? He's a lawyer, and I'm a baker with the responsibility of elderly loved ones. I can't afford to allow my feelings to grow beyond like for this man. No matter that he's a good, godly man. A strong, man of integrity. A handsome, strong man. A...a.... Enough. Help me stop it, Lord. There's too much going on right now with trying to discover Mother's past. I don't need to complicate the present.*

Chapter Eight

That evening after Kate, Skylar and Matt headed to their rooms, Gabe sat by the indoor pool staring out the bank of windows at the city lights. That afternoon Mark had the limousine driver take them on a ride around the city of Munich. They'd driven past the Oktoberfest grounds that wouldn't see the famous festivities until fall. Afterward they'd ridden out to Dachau Concentration Camp, a twenty-four-minute drive. They'd toured the awful remains of the death camp where thirty-two-thousand documented deaths took place, but thousands more were undocumented. Kate walked through the cold, horrible buildings with tears streaming down her cheeks, not even attempting to wipe them away. Gabe's own heart broke at the remnants of the horrendous history and the smell of death that still clung to walls in the gas chambers and the crematorium. The return ride into Munich was a solemn one as their group attempted to come to grips with what they'd seen and learned.

When Matt asked why his dad had taken them there, Mark had simply stated that Elena had been well aware of what was happening at Dachau. She had a larger picture of freedom as her goal for seeking information from the Nazis. Not only to keep America free from fascist ideology, but also to free those who were already under its hob-nailed boot.

"You're deep in thought."

Gabe turned from the cityscape to find Mark striding toward the table where he sat. A grimace marred the older man's features. "I suppose I am. Pull up a chair and take a load off. You look like you've received bad news. What's up?"

Mark dropped heavily into the chair opposite Gabe and leaned back, his hands on his thighs. He gave a slow nod. "That's because I have. I called the ranch to check in and see how things are going. I talked with Clayton. Apparently, a stranger came to the door yesterday and attacked Martha."

"What?" Gabe sat forward, his arms resting on the table between them. "What do you mean attacked? Is she okay? Who was it? What happened?"

Mark held up a hand and released a mirthless chuckle. "I can only answer one question at a time."

Gabe swiped a hand down his face. "Sorry. Your statement surprised me, I guess."

"No more than Clayton's did when he told me." Mark crossed an ankle over a knee and shook his head. "Martha's in the hospital, but she's stable. She said a man dressed in black clothes came to the door and wanted to talk to me. He had an accent. Martha didn't want to tell him I wasn't home so she said I wasn't available at the time. She offered to get someone else, and he plugged her. Right in the face. Sent her flying across the foyer. Just before she blacked out, he leaned over and said, 'Tell Mr. Scott that.'" Mark punched a fist into his palm. "I'd like to tell him a thing or two."

Gabe stared out the windows but failed to see the scene before him. "Do you have any idea who this man could be?"

Mark's lips tightened into a flat line. "I have an idea, but I thought he was either long dead or in prison."

Gabe yanked his eyes back to Mark, but the older man's gaze was on the city lights. "Who is he?"

Mark returned his eyes to Gabe's, dread in their

depths. "Someone I wish was long dead."

The next morning after a delicious breakfast in one of the hotel restaurants, the group set off in a limo for places unknown. At least to everyone except Mark.

"You enjoy these limos, don't you, Dad?" Matt chuckled as he settled onto one of the white leather seats. "I'm not complaining, mind you."

Mark released a chuckle of his own. "I didn't think you were. With the five of us, we'd be hard-pressed to fit comfortably in a taxi, and Mr. Gustafson is always available when we need him." He pointed in the direction of the driver. "So far, he's always been right on time."

"It's a great way to see the sights, and as you say, it's comfortable." Gabe tossed a thumbs-up. He sent a grin and a wink in Kate's direction. She'd been quiet this morning. Was she still sore from her fall two evenings ago? Or could she still be contemplating their visit to Dachau? His heartstrings tugged at the half-hearted smile she sent his way. It wasn't her usual cheery one. He'd have to see if he could discover what ailed her this morning. *Lord, help her through this difficult time.*

The limo wove its way through morning traffic until they came to a large open square where booths formed rows around the pavement and large numbers of people wandered from one to the next.

"This is Viktualienmarkt." Mark pointed toward the booths. "It's a daily food market that's been here for over two hundred years. During the war, food supplies weren't readily available, but farmers brought what they had to sell, and people still came to buy what they could afford—your mother included." He cast an eye toward Kate and Matt. "The people of Germany don't have the large refrigerators that Americans do, so they shop daily for their meals. Like most Europeans do."

He tapped on the window for the limo driver to continue on.

Kate shook her head. "I can't imagine Mother shopping here daily. And in wartime. It's so hard to comprehend all this."

Mark reached over and patted her hand. "I know, sweetheart. I hope things will become clearer in the end for you, but please, keep an open mind."

Kate met his eyes and locked on them. "This isn't going to get easier, is it? It may get clearer in the end, but not easier."

Mark continued to hold her gaze as the limo slipped through crowded streets. "Probably not."

Kate drew in a deep breath and closed her eyes, lowering her head to the head rest. *Oh, Mother. What life did you lead before I knew you? What kind of danger were you in?*

Next the limo rolled down a narrow street and stopped before a five-story building built of golden stone. Gray slate tiles lined the steep-pitched roof, and a row of gabled windows ran across the lower edge. A narrow, peaked edifice centered on the façade and rose to the center of the roof where a window sat in a line with the other gabled windows. Every window on the building sported window boxes with red geraniums.

"This is a lovely building." Skylar leaned over and peeked upward. "I love those flower boxes. They add a nice touch of color." She straightened and turned to Mark. "What is it?"

"This is where Elena lived while she was in Munich. In a third-floor apartment."

"It seems she lived comfortably." This from Matt.

"I would assume so. I never went inside." He cleared his throat."

"I suppose we can't go in." Kate leaned over to look up at the tall building. "I'm sure that apartment is occupied. Could we at least go into the lobby?"

Mark stared at the building before turning his eyes toward Kate, then shrugged. "I don't see why not. I'll have the driver move the limo so it's out of the way since it's a narrow street."

They stepped out and headed toward the square-arched entrance. Gabe held the door while the others entered. A mix of pine cleaner and something else less pleasant assailed Kate's nose as she stepped into the lobby. What was that musty smell? The building must be quite old, so the owner possibly dealt with moisture. The pine cleaner didn't quite do its job.

The inlaid marble floor, although lovely and still shiny, showed wear as expected from an old building, but the oak woodwork around the lobby was in great shape and quite lovely. A brass chandelier hung in the center of the room giving off a warm, gentle light. Tyrolian blue drapes hung at the front windows with white sheers, allowing in light from the street. Matching Tyrolian blue couches and armchairs clustered around a small gas fireplace to one side. The room emitted a welcoming warmth. A reception desk stood to the other side.

"*Willkommen.*" A soft, older feminine voice spoke from behind the reception desk, "May I help you?"

Mark stepped to the desk and explained their presence at the apartment building. "We won't stay but a few minutes."

"Ach, I see. What number was the apartment where their mother lived? Perhaps it is available. I have several openings at the moment." The lady turned to nod at the group. "Your mother. She lived here a long time ago, ja? Perhaps it is open."

Kate sucked in a breath. Could they be that fortunate? Mark tapped his chin. "I know it was on the third floor and faced the street."

The woman chuckled softly. "Sir, there are many apartments facing the street. Can you be more specific?"

"Of course, there are." Mark offered her a grin. "Would you give me a minute? I'll take a look from the outside. I'm sure I can tell which one it was from there."

The woman lifted a palm. "But of course. Take your time."

"Be right back." He sauntered out the door.

It was more like five minutes, but he returned, confidence in his step. "Yep. It's the three windows in the middle on the third floor."

A broad smile lifted the woman's lips. "Very good, sir. That is apartment 305." She ran her finger across a page. "Ah, and you are in luck. It is available." Turning, she opened a small box hanging on the wall and retrieved a key. "If you will follow me?"

Kate couldn't believe her ears. The apartment Mother had lived in was open and available for them to visit. Her heart began to hammer with excitement. She would get to see where Mother had lived.

On the third floor, the building manager slipped the key into the apartment door-lock and turned it. Kate's excitement built. This was yet another piece of the puzzle to Mother's past.

The apartment consisted of a living-room, a bedroom, a small kitchen, an eating area off the kitchen and a bathroom. It was big enough for Mother to be comfortable. Happiness filled Kate at that knowledge. She strode to the living-room window. A small park sat across the street from the building. Kate imagined Mother spending time there in the park reading one of her beloved books on one of the benches.

"This, of course, is not the original décor and furniture.

The building has passed through several owners since the war." The manager clasped her hands at her waist and turned to speak to them. "I do not own the building; I simply manage it."

"Kate, have you seen enough?" Mark called to her at the window.

She turned to Mark and the manager. "Yes, thank you. I appreciate you allowing us to come and see it. It gives me a better idea where my mother lived during the war."

"But of course, my dear. I understand you did not know your mother lived here?"

Kate shook her head and reached for Matt's arm. "Nor did my brother."

"Thank you for helping us, ma'am." Matt winked at the woman before tossing a smile at her.

"It is my pleasure." Pink suffused her cheeks before she ushered them toward the door. "If I may be of any further help to you, please do not hesitate to ask."

Once they were on the street again, Mark hurried to the curb to look for the limo. "It's down this way. Come on."

The limousine had found a parking spot at the end of the park. They had to walk a short distance to reach it. After glancing in both directions, Kate stepped out into the narrow street and began to cross it. Out of nowhere, a car bore down on her as she reached the middle. She gasped as it sped toward her. Kate almost felt the hot breath from its racing engine. Surely the driver had noticed her and would slow down, but he didn't. Instead of slowing, the car gained speed. Kate attempted to dash across the street but fear seemed to weight down her legs in place.

Just before the car reached her, strong arms lifted and carried her to the opposite side of the street where vehicles were parked close together along the curb.

"Hold on." Gabe's voice breathed in Kate's ear. "This is going to hurt."

They slammed into the hood of one of the cars before

sliding across onto the sidewalk on the other side. Kate landed on top of Gabe but still banged the side of her head. Residual, jarring pain shot through her shoulder and hip. Unsure if it was from landing on the car or the sidewalk, she didn't care. As the reckless driver sped away, Kate was relieved to get banged up instead of run over.

Cautiously she rolled to the side of Gabe. "Ouch. Oh, my goodness. Are you all right?" Kate eyed her knight in a button-down shirt and jeans, the shirt torn at the shoulder. She struggled to a sitting position on the pavement beside him, attempting to avoid her sore hip.

Gabe lay on his back, mouth twisted sideways, eyes fixed on the sky. "Why don't the rest of you go about your day and come back for me later. By then maybe I'll have the kinks worked out."

Kate took his hand as it lay on the sidewalk. "I'm so sorry, Gabe. You're injured. Can I help you up?" She rubbed the side of her head.

Gabe lifted a brow and met her eyes. "Are you kidding? In the shape you're in? I'm sure this didn't help you any. Did you get hurt worse?"

Kate felt the rising knot beneath her hair. "I'm going to have a goose egg soon." She grimaced. "It's already started to rise. I hit my head on the either the car or the pavement."

Gabe reached up and ran his fingers beneath her hair. His brow furrowed. "That's not good. We should somehow get you some ice."

She patted his hand. "We need to worry more about you right now. You haven't even sat up yet."

Matt ran over and knelt beside them. "Are you all right, buddy?" He placed a hand on Gabe's shoulder. "Gabe? You with us, man?"

"Sort of." Gabe closed his eyes and swallowed. "Maybe you can help me up."

"Sure thing." Matt held out an arm as Gabe opened his eyes once again and held up his arm. Matt gently lifted him to a sitting position.

Gabe groaned.

Matt held onto his arm and supported his back. "I saw the whole thing. Whoever that guy was, he aimed for you, Kate. There was no mistaking it. First, he wasn't there, the next second—boom, he was bearing down on you. Fast. He didn't even try to slow down."

Kate shrugged. "I seem to have become the target of these Germans. What did I do to deserve this animosity?"

Mark and Skylar hurried over, and Mark squatted down. "Is everyone all right? Gabe? You're moving too slowly. We need to take you to a hospital. You may have injured your back, buddy."

Kate met Gabe's eyes. "I'll feel horrible if you don't. You rescued me from what could've been death or at least severe injury. If you don't get checked out, I...I—"

"Won't ever speak to me again?" His smile didn't quite reach its normal brilliance, and his eyes held pain. "I couldn't live with that, now, could I?" He nodded slowly. "All right. I'll get checked out."

"Great." Mark stood. "I'll have the driver bring the limo around, so you don't have to walk far. He'll know where the nearest ER is."

Within minutes they arrived at the hospital, and ER staff rushed Gabe into the back.

"He's allowed one person to go with him," the nurse in a white uniform dress and cap said to their group. "You must decide who, and I'll take you back."

"Dad? You speak German." Matt eyed his father.

Mark shook his head. "Haven't you noticed most Germans speak English? It's not like it was when I was here years ago. Besides, my German is rusty." He waved a hand. "Gabe doesn't want me back there anyway. He'd rather have a pretty face to ease his discomfort. Kate why don't you head back there and see what you can do?"

Warmth invaded Kate's cheeks as all eyes turned on

her. "All right. I doubt I can do much except keep him company."

"I'm sure he'll appreciate it." Matt said before Kate followed the nurse.

She entered a small cubicle separated by patterned curtains. Kate's eyes instantly went to the man on the bed in the middle of the tiny room, his presence filling the space. She wanted to go to his side and take his hand, but the nurse directed her to a seat in the corner.

"Once I've taken his vitals, I'll leave you until the doctor is ready to come in." The nurse popped a glass thermometer into Gabe's mouth. "Close, *bitte*." She positioned her fingers on his wrist and eyed her wristwatch, her lips pursed and brows puckered. "Yes, yes." She lowered his wrist to the bed. "Your heartbeat is strong, Herr Flanagan. No matter what you did to your body, your heart is fine." She reached for a blood-pressure cuff and wrapped it around his bicep. "I usually make my patients remove their sleeves, but considering your pain and how you would have to remove your shirt, we will let it slide. Your shirt is fairly tight around it. I don't think it will affect the accuracy."

Kate eyed the bicep the nurse worked with, then forced her glance to the other side of the room. She'd noticed the size of Gabe's biceps and other muscles. How could she not? The man was in perfect shape. He'd lifted her from in front of that oncoming car and dove with her onto the hood of the parked car. Kate felt horrible that Gabe had landed so badly and injured himself. All while rescuing her.

"*Ja. Das is gut.* Yes, that is good. You have a wonderful blood pressure too. Now—" the nurse released the blood pressure valve, "let's check your temp." Out popped the thermometer. "No temperature. *Gut.* You are in great health. *Ja.* Injured only, I think." She removed the cuff and stowed it away. "The doctor will determine the rest." She turned a smile on both Gabe and Kate. "Wait here and try to relax. Dr. Müller will be in shortly." Sliding back the curtain, she stepped outside and left the cubicle.

Gabe turned his head and grinned at Kate, waggling his brows. "It's good to know I'm healthy."

No way could Kate hold back the laugh that bubbled out. She shook her head. "You're lying on an emergency-room bed, most likely in extreme pain, and you're making jokes?"

He scrunched up his face before pulling a crooked grin. "Yeah, well, you got the pain part right. My military training tells me I probably tore some muscles. If I don't try and make fun of it, it hurts more."

This was news to Kate. The Vietnam War was in full swing. Had he served there? She hoped not. How horrible. "I didn't know you served in the military."

Closing his eyes, Gabe turned his face back toward the ceiling. "It's not something I talk about much. I was in Vietnam. That's where I met Matt. We were sent over in '65 in a group of one-hundred-thousand troops to undertake offensive missions against the Viet Cong and North Vietnamese anywhere we found them in South Vietnam. Another one-hundred-thousand were sent over the following year. It was an uphill battle, but we fought with everything we had in us. President Johnson announced his decision in a news conference the year I went to Nam, but he didn't actually declare war or prepare the US economically for it." Gabe turned back to Kate. "Can you believe that? A president who doesn't prepare his country for war?"

"And we're still reeling from it." Kate lowered her gaze. After a few moments she returned her eyes to his. "But you, Matt and every soldier who went over did their job. You did what you were sent there to do."

A faint smile touched his lips. "We tried to. It's an ongoing battle that my military brothers are still fighting."

"How long were you there?"

"Thirteen months the first time I went. I came home at the end of that tour but returned for another seven months. I was injured during my second tour. Not severely, but enough to bring me home."

Before Kate could reply, the curtain to the cubicle slid back and a tall blond man who looked to be in his fifties stepped in and tugged the curtain closed behind him.

"*Guten tag.*" He nodded to them. "Good day to you both. I am Dr. Müller." He turned to Gabe and retrieved the clipboard from the foot of the bed. Perusing it, he nodded as he stepped closer. "I see you have possibly injured your back. *Ja?*" The doctor slanted a glance at Gabe over the rims of his glasses.

"Maybe. That's where the pain is."

"Let us see." The doctor replaced the clipboard. "I will help you sit up if you cannot do it on your own, but I need to see where your pain is."

With difficulty Gabe sat up holding onto the doctor's hand.

"Swing your legs to the side, and remove your shirt. We must see if there are any contusions or lacerations of course."

With the doctor's help, Gabe swung his legs over the side of the bed and unbuttoned his shirt. The doctor gently helped him slide his arms from the sleeves and helped him slip his undershirt over his head. Kate nearly gasped at the perfection of his muscular body and almost averted her gaze until she caught a view of the massive bruise on his back and side. She caught her breath.

"*Ja.* It is as I expected. The nurse informed me that you hit the pavement hard when you saved this young lady from being hit by a car. Is that the reason for your injury?"

Gabe winced. "Yes, that's right."

"The contusions of your back and side are massive, and the area is quite swollen. I dare say the muscles beneath are likely bruised and possibly torn. I would like to send you for an x-ray to see if you have broken or cracked ribs. Is this all right with you?"

"I suppose...."

The doctor waved a dismissive hand. "Herr Scott who awaits you in the sitting room, has informed me he's arranged all the finances for your care. He wanted me to assure you of this."

Gabe blew out a heavy breath. "Okay, let's do it."

Dr. Müller chuckled. "Whoever he is to you, Herr Flanagan, he is a good man to have on your side."

"He's my partner and dear friend."

"Indeed, he is." He turned and headed for the exit. "I'll return when I've studied the x-rays. The nurse will be in to help you dress."

True to his word, the same nurse came in a moment later and helped Gabe put on his clothes. "That is a lovely contusion you have, Herr Flanagan. One of the best I've seen recently. Quite a lot of swelling too. If I had a mirror, I'd show it to you. You'll have to take a look when you return home. It's a badge of honor as far as I'm concerned. I believe you saved this young lady's life."

"Yes, he did," Kate piped in. "Because of his efforts, all I got was a little bump on the head."

"Indeed?" The nurse eyed Kate as she helped Gabe lie back down and moved the head of the bed up, so he'd be in more of a sitting position. Once he was comfortable, she stepped in front of Kate. "Where's your bump?"

Kate waved a dismissive hand. "There's no need to look at it."

The nurse crossed her arms over her chest and stared down her nose at Kate. "Where is it?"

"You'd best tell her." Gabe chuckled.

Kate released a heavy breath and pointed at the side of her head. "It truly is nothing."

"I'll decide that." The nurse leaned over and felt beneath Kate's hair. "Any injury to the head must be taken seriously." After a couple of moments, she backed up a step. "Mm hmm. That's not a small bump; that's a goose egg, my dear." She straightened and headed for the curtain. "I'll be right back with an ice pack. You should have said something sooner."

"Something tells me she's used to getting her way." Gabe tossed a lopsided grin at Kate.

"Most likely." She rubbed the spot and winced. "It is rather sore."

"You hit the pavement with as much force as I did."

Kate stood and stepped to the side of the bed. "Maybe. But you took all the force when you saved me from that car. I can't thank you enough for that." She slipped her hand within his. "You're in pain because of me."

Gabe shook his head, his expression the most serious she'd ever seen. "I'm in pain because of the bozo who tried to mow you down with a car. I hate to put it into words, but something is going on. I don't want to frighten you, Kate, but think about it. Someone's targeting you. He tried to snatch your purse last night, and today he tried to run you down."

Kate's fingers squeezed Gabe's. "Do you really think they're related?"

He puffed out a heavy breath. "I don't know." A frown lowered his brow. "There was something else. What was it?" He thought for a moment then snapped his fingers. "Oh yeah. The man by the elevator at the hotel. The one who nearly bowled you over."

Kate's eyes widened. "Surely that was a coincidence."

"Three coincidences?" Gabe lifted her hand to his lips. "I think not. We'll simply have to keep a closer eye on you, lady."

Warmth rolled past Kate's collar to her hairline. She dropped her eyes to their linked fingers. "I suppose, but it's simply a string of bad luck, if you ask me." She stepped back as a technician slid the curtain back and rolled in a wheelchair.

Why would anyone want to harm her? The only person that came to mind was Mr. Andrew Hawthorn. He was the only one who had a vested interest in anything she was doing, particularly when it came to the bakery. That had nothing to do with Germany and her travels here. Did he even know she was here? Probably. Word traveled fast in small towns. With Mr. Scott's help, she'd paid off the bank loan and actually purchased the building the bakery resided in. It was hers and her family's free and clear as far as Mr. Hawthorn was concerned. He should have no further need to pursue the purchase of the building.

So why was she having difficulties here? Was the purse-snatcher, the man who bumped into her, and the man in the car all the same person? Or were they all simple coincidences as she thought they were? *Lord, no matter which case it is, please protect me while I'm here in Germany. I seem to have experienced a run of unfortunate incidents. Gabe thinks otherwise. Can Mr. Hawthorn truly be behind what's going on? Is he hounding me here? Whatever is going on, Gabe got hurt because of me, and I don't want him or anyone else hurt. Please protect us all.*

Chapter Nine

"I thought she was dead, but she's still alive. The photo you sent—she looks the same as she always did. I don't understand how. She hasn't aged a day since, but—" His accented voice cracked. "I will return to Germany soon. Do not lose her." The vehemence in his voice sent a chill through him.

"Do you want me to kill her?"

"No, of course I do not." His boss's voice rose in anger. "I will deal with her myself."

Oops. And here he had nearly run her over with a car yesterday. He'd have to be more careful. Thank goodness her traveling companion had taken the hit for her. "She's traveling with a group of people. There's an older man in the group. Do you know him?"

There was no response right away from the boss. He tapped the phone to make sure it was still connected. The boss's voice was low as he answered. "No, I've never met him, but I know of him. He was a major in the US Army."

"What should I do?"

"What you've been doing." Belligerence filled his boss's voice. "Continue to follow her and ensure she knows she's being followed. Make her life miserable, but make her wonder why. In the end she will understand that her past has caught up with her." His laugh held a mirthless ring. "She will regret what she did to me."

After Gabe's release from the hospital, he insisted he was famished. It mattered not that the x-rays indicated two cracked ribs and an ultrasound diagnosed torn muscles across his back. Since he'd spent several hours in the ER, food was far more important at the moment.

"I'm not going to stand in the way of a hungry man and his food." Mark stood back as the nurse wheeled her patient to the side of the limo and helped him inside. As she straightened and turned to leave, Mark stopped her. "Thanks for taking such good care of my partner. He means a lot to our family."

She smiled and patted Mark's arm. "I'm sure he does. He was a good patient." She leaned closer and lowered her voice. "Now if you can persuade the young lady to admit she's interested in him, that would be a good thing. His eyes say it all."

Mark snickered. "We're working on it."

"Good." She gave him an approving nod before turning the wheelchair toward the entrance to the hospital.

Mark chuckled and ushered his group into the limo. He knocked on the front window and instructed the driver to head back to the hotel. If Gabe was hungry, they'd eat in one of the hotel restaurants before urging him to get some rest. They wouldn't take in any more sights today. If Gabe was up to it tomorrow, they'd continue their sightseeing.

Since they'd missed lunch and eaten an early supper, they agreed room service later for snacks might be a good option. Mark escorted Gabe to his room.

"Mind if I come in for a few minutes?" He paused by the door as Gabe unlocked it.

Gabe tossed him a glance. "Of course not. Come on in, and I'll show you my 'lovely contusion,' as the nurse called it. I need to get out of this torn shirt anyway and put on something a little less constricting."

He closed the door behind them and strode to his suitcase, tugging out a loose, soft t-shirt. Removing the torn button-down, he tossed it next to the suitcase before removing his undershirt. "What do you think of that bruise?"

"Sakes alive, Gabriel. You did a number on yourself." Mark eyed the bruise from his chair in the sitting area of the room. "No wonder you have torn muscles and cracked ribs."

Gabe slid the clean t-shirt gingerly over his head and down. "Well, at least Kate's okay. She only suffered a goose egg on the side of her head and jolted her sore muscles. That was bad enough. I couldn't prevent that. The nurse gave her ice for the bump on her head." He eased himself into the chair near Mark's.

"Son, she's a lucky lady to have you looking after her. I don't want to think what would've happened if that car had hit her."

Gabe ran a hand down his face. "Neither do I. I can live with this knowing she's only suffered a bump on her head."

Mark grinned. "You're in love with her, aren't you?"

Gabe stared at the older man. "Love? That's a huge assumption, isn't it? Why would I be in love with Kate? We've only known one anoth—"

"Oh, cut the nonsense, son. This is me you're talking to. You forget I know you well." Mark crossed an ankle over a knee. "I can see it every time you look at her. It's as plain as the nose on your face. Right out there for all the world to see."

Gabe shifted in his seat eliciting a grunt and a wince. "Do you think she sees it?" He didn't even try to deny it this time.

Mark shrugged. "Probably not. The gals are usually the last to figure it out. You have to spell it out plain for them."

Gabe scrubbed a hand around the back of his neck. "Now's not a good time. She has so much on her mind—first with finding out she has a brother, and now with everything you're springing on her. What else are you going to surprise her with? Is there more?" A sheepish expression carved Mark's features. "Yeah. There's more."

After a nice hot shower that helped ease the soreness in her shoulder and hip, Kate slipped into her pajama's and took out the book she'd brought on the trip but had simply been too busy to read. Unless Skylar chose to chat after her shower, it might be a good time to crack the cover and enjoy a chapter or two. Kate piled the pillows up behind her and leaned back, opening the book. She read a few pages until Skylar strolled out of the bathroom.

"That was amazing." Skylar dove onto her soft bed and, crossing her legs, began combing her damp hair. "After spending the day in the ER waiting room, it's nice to relax in a hot shower."

Kate placed a bookmark in the page of her book. "I felt bad for the rest of you as you waited not knowing what was happening."

Skylar smiled. "I didn't mind. I spent some time praying for Gabe and read several magazines. Matt and I strolled down the street and grabbed some soft drinks and snacks for Mark and us. That was fun. Your brother is a funny guy, but he wasn't joking the whole time. He's interesting too."

"Really? What do you mean?" Kate rolled to her side, propping her head on her hand.

"Did you know he served in Vietnam? I knew it, but he opened up a little more about it today."

Kate nodded. "Just found out today that he and Gabe

served together. I'm thankful they both came home. With all the atrocities occurring over there, I can only imagine what they went through."

Skylar pulled her knees up, hugging them close to her chest, her chin resting on them. "Yeah. Me too. It's a terrible war. Some men from my church are over there serving now. Another one was killed recently, and a friend's brother is missing in action. We've been praying they find him. Soon."

"I'm so sorry." Kate had heard how soldiers were taken by the Viet Cong and held as prisoners of war. "I'll pray they find him."

"Thank you." Skylar shifted on the bed, a sly smile pursing her lips. "Gabe definitely is attracted to you."

Kate shook her head and rolled her eyes. "We've had this conversation, my friend. Gabe likes everyone. He's simply a nice guy."

"Yes, he is, but he has eyes on you, girl. He doesn't look at me the way he looks at you."

"You're mistaken. There's no reason a big ranch owner/lawyer would take an interest in a small-town baker. None whatsoever." Kate climbed off the bed and went to the desk to retrieve the room-service menu.

"Why not? What's wrong with a small-town baker?" Skylar slid to the end of the bed. "You're a pretty young woman, and he's bound to be attracted. Besides, you're the sister of his best friend. That's convenient, don't you think?"

Kate smirked. "Thanks for the compliment, but me living in Ohio and him in Wyoming is hardly convenient." She waved the menu. "Want to order room service? It's been a while since we ate."

"You're just trying to change the subject." Skylar crossed her arms over her chest.

Kate smiled. "Is it working?"

"No."

"Well, let's order anyway. Aren't you hungry?"

Skylar grinned. "Okay. Bring the menu over here, and let's take a look."

"Oh, my darling Katarina, it is so wonderful to hear your voice." Auntie Anna's distant words held tears as she spoke into the phone. "We miss you terribly. Ah, but the bakery is doing fantastic. We sell out of pastries every day."

Kate smiled at her precious aunt's excitement. "That's what Uncle Rudy told me the last time I spoke to him. That's incredible. The three of you are doing an excellent job of holding down the bakery while I'm gone, but I had no doubt you would."

"Ay, but we have a problem, Katarina. We don't know what to do. Even Mr. Calhoun, our lawyer, isn't sure. He's not a property lawyer, as you know."

Dread raced through Kate at the note of worry in her aunt's voice. "What's wrong?"

Auntie Anna mumbled something to someone away from the phone before speaking clearly in Kate's ear again. "Andrew Hawthorn is stirring up trouble again. His lawyer came to visit us. He told us he had found a loophole in…in something or other, and that Mr. Hawthorn could still take our building. Ay, Katarina. It sounds so bad. What are we to do?" Her voice rose with each word.

"Auntie, please calm down. How can he take what is clear and legally ours? We paid the owner the amount he quoted as payment for the building. You paid them my part of the payment, and Mr. Scott took care of the rest. Mr. Kendrick at the bank faxed the paperwork to Wyoming for me to sign, and we faxed it back. It was all done legally. Mr. Calhoun oversaw the whole process. He faxed those documents here for Mr. Scott's lawyer to ensure everything was completed correctly. I don't understand how Mr. Hawthorn's lawyer could find a loophole anywhere. He's simply attempting to stir up trouble and intimidate you."

"Well, it's working."

Kate's heart melted for the elderly loved ones who were holding down the fort while she galivanted around Germany. But they were the ones who sent her on this journey. Torn between wanting to hurry home to be with them and wanting to continue to find out about Mother's early life, Kate was unsure what to do.

"Auntie, take that deed to the bank and put it into a safe-deposit box. Bring the key home and hide it in a secure place where no one but the three of you know where it is." Kate drew in a deep breath and sent up a quick prayer of peace for her loved ones. "Neither of them should fall into anyone else's hands. Do you understand?"

"Yes, darling, I understand. I will send Rudy this afternoon to take care of it." Auntie Anna huffed out a sigh of relief. "I feel better after talking to you."

"Good. I'll talk to Mr. Scott's lawyer who, fortunately, is on this trip with us. Perhaps he can think of any loopholes they may be talking about. I still think they're trying to intimidate you in my absence, but we won't give them an inch on this. There's no telling what the scoundrels are up to."

"I agree about that."

"I have to let you go, Auntie. This call isn't cheap. I love you. Give my love and a hug to Auntie Genny and Uncle Rudy."

"You know I will, my sweets. Take care of yourself and be careful."

Kate hung up the receiver and went down to the lobby to meet the rest of the group who was gathering in one of the restaurants for breakfast. She wasn't sure if Gabe's injuries would allow him to sightsee today, but she'd soon find out. As she stepped into the elevator, she touched the knot on the side of her head. The swelling had gone down some, and it was still sore, but not as much. Apparently, the ice pack the nurse had given her at the hospital yesterday had helped.

The group sat at a table in a corner perusing menus. Gabe spotted Kate's approach and winked over the top edge of his. Her breath caught as she gave him a smile and slid into the empty chair beside him. She couldn't help but notice they'd saved that particular seat for her. If she didn't know better, she'd think the others were playing matchmaker.

A round of "good mornings" greeted her as she sat down and picked up her own menu. As Kate decided what she wanted for breakfast, Gabe laid his menu down and turned to her.

"Skylar mentioned you called your family in Ohio. Is everyone all right? How's the bakery?"

She lowered her menu. "They're doing fine, but the property developer who threatened to buy the bakery before we purchased it has reared his ugly head again."

"Now what?" Mark asked, leaning forward.

"It seems his lawyer paid my family a visit and threatened them with a loophole of some kind. They're still threatening to take the property. It has my aunties and uncle frantic."

"A loophole? What kind of loophole?" A groove formed between Gabe's brows as he clasped his hands on the table in front of him.

"My Auntie Anna had no idea, and she said our lawyer didn't either. He's not a property lawyer and had never heard of such a thing." Kate released a drawn-out exhale. "I advised her to take the deed and put it into a safe-deposit box, bring the key home and hide it someplace no one but the three of them would know."

"Good advice." Gabe nodded. "I'm not a full-fledged property lawyer, but I've dealt with a lot of property issues for Mark. However, I have a friend who's a property lawyer. Let me give him a call and ask him some questions. Since I've read over your purchase, I'm familiar enough with it I can talk with him about it."

Kate placed a hand on his arm. "Would you? That would be great. I could reassure my loved ones that there's truly nothing to worry about." When Gabe's eyes dropped to her hand on his sleeve, she yanked it back to her lap. "To be honest, I've been concerned that some of these things that have been happening to me might be connected to Mr. Hawthorn, the property developer."

Matt's brow rose. "You think he'd go so far as to follow you here and harass you?"

"Not him specifically, but I wouldn't put it past him to send someone. He's harassing my family."

"That building your bakery is in must be quite valuable." Mark propped his chin on his hands.

"Oh, it is. It's in the center of town." Kate smiled. "Why do you think they sell out of pastries every single day? Besides the fact they're delicious, of course."

"Of course." Gabe smiled. "We all know that."

The waitress arrived to take their orders before hurrying away.

Kate slid a side-eyed grin at Gabe. "And how are you feeling today? Well enough to see some sights or do you need another day of rest?"

"Nope, I'm well rested, and I've already told Mark I'm ready to go." He moved his cup over as the waitress returned to fill cups with coffee. "Besides, I'm not one for sitting around long. I'd pull my hair out if I had to do that."

"We'll take it a step at a time." Mark leaned back in his seat as the waitress refilled his cup. "I have a plan of where to visit, but I'm keeping my eye on him." He pointed from his eyes to Gabe. "We don't have to push or rush the sightseeing. If he starts getting tired, we'll head back to the hotel."

Gabe stirred cream into his cup. "Did you ever tell them about your call home?"

Mark's brows lowered. "No. There hasn't been a good time, what with your injury and everything that's been going on." He stared into his coffee cup and remained silent for several moments.

Matt, sitting beside him, rubbed his dad's back. "What's up? Has something happened back home?"

Mark turned his cup around and around between his fingers. After a few moments, he lifted it to his lips. Setting it back onto the saucer, he eyed the group. "I called home to see how things are going. I had a chat with Clayton." He told them about Martha's encounter with the strange man and her subsequent hospital stay. "I called again last night, and she's still in the hospital. She's doing better, but she's having some vision problems. Everything's kind of blurry. The doctor's said she has a detached retina in one eye. The other is having trouble compensating. She's going to need surgery."

Kate's hand flew to her mouth. Who was this evil man? Someone related to Mr. Hawthorn? What was going on?

"The words the man said to her— 'Tell Mr. Scott that,'—what could they mean? Do you know who this man is?" Matt asked.

"I have an idea." Mark clasped his hands around his cup

After several seconds when he offered no more explanation, Matt leaned toward his dad. "Well?"

"It's someone I'd thought was long dead or in prison. Someone…someone I'd rather not discuss right now."

"All right." Matt leaned back. "So what about Mrs. Holcomb?"

"Clayton has everything well in hand. I asked if he wanted me to come home. He said he'd take care of her. I trust Clayton."

"You bet. He's more than capable."

The waitress brought their food and the subject changed.

Chapter Ten

The limo dropped the group in front of the National Theater on Max-Joseph-Platz. As they exited the vehicle, Kate stood soaking in her surroundings. The theater in front of them appeared to be neo-classical in architecture with eight Corinthian columns along the front. Many stone steps led up to the portico behind the columns where seven entry doors awaited with the same number of tall arched windows above them. Carved neo-classical statues filled the peaked area above the columns. To Kate, the building looked similar to the ancient ones she'd seen in pictures of the Parthenon in Athens.

She turned to stare across the square and identified the back of a seated statue in the middle of a cordoned-off, cobblestoned circle. It must be a memorial to someone famous.

Beside her, Skylar snapped pictures and jotted notes in her notebook. "Impressive, isn't it?"

"Yes, it is. To think Mother sang here." Kate breathed softly. "It's still hard to grasp."

Skylar wrapped an arm around her in a quick squeeze. "I can't imagine what you're dealing with. When you try to envision this place under the control of Nazis, it's even harder."

In her mind's eye, Kate attempted to swap the vehicles driving past with the jeeps and vehicles of World War Two.

She imagined officers and soldiers dressed in Nazi military uniforms and other people dressed in the clothing of the era. It boggled the mind. How hard could it be for Mark to return here after so many years? Surely, he must remember those things.

"Kate? Skylar? Are you coming?" Matt's voice broke into her reflection of the past.

Turning, they followed him inside the entrance. In the massive lobby, Kate turned around and around taking in the luxurious Greek, neo-classical décor. Her feet sank into the carpet as she noticed the beautiful white velvet drapes hanging at the windows and the gray marble walls. Red velvet and gold benches lined the walls while crystal chandelier sconces lit the outer edges of the lobby. Marble Corinthian columns stood at both ends of the room, and a gold Greek-design border broke up the marble wall two-thirds of the way up. A huge crystal chandelier hung from the two-story ceiling surrounded by gold plasterwork and painted friezes.

Kate elbowed Skylar who stood beside her craning her neck to stare at the ceiling. "I hope you're writing all this detail down. It's...magnificent."

"Oh yeah." Skylar lifted her notebook and jotted some notes. "Sorry. I got caught up in the beauty of this place."

Kate released a long whoosh of air. "Yeah. Me too."

"*Guten tag. Willkommen.*" An unfamiliar deep male voice drew Kate's attention from the ceiling. A man wearing a woolen Werdenfelser jacket with forest-green trim and forest-green trousers strode toward them. When he reached their group, he bowed and clicked the heels of his shiny black shoes.

"Herr Scott, I presume." He turned his attention to Mark before turning his gaze to peer at the group. "Welcome to the National Theater. We are happy to have you here."

He held out a hand to Mark who shook it. "It's our

pleasure. I take it you're Herr Becker."

"Indeed. I am the theater manager."

Mark introduced the group. When he came to Kate and Matt he added, "These are the young folks whose mother sang here during the war."

Herr Becker's brows rose and a smile lifted the corners of his lips. "Ah, yes. It is a pleasure to meet you. If you all will follow me, I will show you around. At the end of our tour, I have something special to show you that I believe you will find of great interest. Come with me please." The man turned and led the group across the soft carpet past the box offices to a set of double doors in the middle of the lobby. He swung one wide and held it open for them. "Please step inside and wait for me."

Following his instructions, they waited just inside the door which he closed behind him. "Now, please wait here. I shall return for you momentarily."

They waited in the near darkness for what seemed an interminable amount of time. Kate grew antsy. What could be taking him so long? This had to be the auditorium. She could barely make out the seats next to her. The red exit lights around the edges of the room were the only bright spots in the space.

All of a sudden, the stage lights came on, nearly catching Kate's breath. Even though the house lights remained dark, everything lit up. The stage curtains were deep red velvet with gold scrolling along the bottom and middle edges. The upper curtains were also deep red velvet with gold tasseled, lower edges. The upholstery on the audience seats matched the deep red velvet of the stage curtains as did the tiered theater box seats along the sides of the room. Red figured wallpaper decorated the walls while gold scrollwork decorated the fronts of the tiered theater boxes.

The group stood beneath what Kate assumed must be a balcony. She walked down the aisle until she could clearly see the ceiling. A crystal chandelier hung from the center of a domed ceiling matching the one in the lobby, and the artist who had mastered the plasterwork and painted friezes in the lobby had accomplished the same work here. Candle sconces lined the front of the various balcony and theater boxes. The large room exhibited meticulous and magnificent décor.

She turned to Mark. "Have you been here before?"

A faraway look settled across his features as he stared at the stage. "Once. I dressed as a Nazi and slipped in to hear your mother perform. Actually, it was her final performance." A slight smile lifted a corner of his mouth. "She sang...well, she sang as she always sang. Perfectly."

Kate laid a gentle hand on his arm, drawing his eyes to hers. "As I look at that stage, I can't imagine my mother standing up there and performing."

His eyes locked with hers. "I know. I'm sorry about that, but it's important that you and Matt take this journey. More for you, I suppose, than him. He never knew her. You did."

Herr Becker approached them from up the aisle. "Well, what do you think? Is not our theater quite something?"

"It's...it's more than beautiful, Herr Becker." Kate waved a hand encompassing the huge room. "Though something tells me this isn't what it looked like back in World War Two."

He wagged a finger in her direction before clasping his hands behind his back. "You are an astute young woman, Fräulein Cigler, and you are correct." He half-turned toward the room. "As you are likely aware, bright red was Hitler's color, and the swastika was everywhere. This room was no exception. During the occupation of the Third Reich, the Nazi banner hung from every theater box and all along the walls. You may or may not be aware, the swastika is now banned in Germany as well as in a few other European countries. That emblem may not be displayed anywhere in this country." He paused for his words to sink in. "This theater was nearly destroyed during the war. It took many, many years for it to be rebuilt, although it was almost decided to tear it down completely. They did a wonderful job in rebuilding our theater. It is much more pleasing to the eye without the swastikas, do you not think so?" He turned to see their reaction.

"You bet it is." Gabe swept his gaze around the interior of the room. "Sadly, I can almost picture what it must have looked like during the war. I've seen too many pictures of Hitler's Germany. My father fought in the war and helped liberate your country. He told me about his experience."

Herr Becker clapped him on the shoulder, eliciting a bit of a wince. "I thank him for his part in what he did for Germany. Not everyone in our country approved of the political atmosphere of the time, but people's hands were tied. Thousands and thousands of Germans were sent to concentration camps for their disagreement of the Nazi government, and many of those were killed for it."

"We know, sir. You don't have to explain." A soft smile settled on Matt's features. "That's why people like his dad, my dad—" he patted Mark on the back, "—and my mom did what they did in the war. To help people like yours."

Herr Becker gave him a watery smile. He tugged a handkerchief from his trousers pocket, blew his nose, and returned it to his pocket. "Indeed."

Kate wondered at the possible story behind this man's emotions. Everyone seemed to have one, especially in this part of the world.

"Please, if you'll come with me." Herr Becker motioned for them to follow him across the rear of the theater and down to the stage where they climbed steps beside the orchestra pit. Walking across the stage, he led them behind the curtain backstage to the dressing rooms.

"I did research to find which dressing room your

mother used when she sang here during the war. It took some time, but I went back into the theater records and found out Elena Jäger dressed in this room." He swung wide a door and turned on the light.

"You must be mistaken, Herr Becker." Mark tugged at the gentleman's arm pulling him back while the others stepped inside. "Her name was Elena *Cigler*."

Kate turned to see what Mark and Herr Becker were talking about. Confusion crossed Herr Becker's face as he stared at Mark. "Cigler? But—"

Matt stepped in Kate's way, preventing her from seeing the two men just outside the door. Were they whispering?

"Yes. Cigler." Mark said.

Where had Herr Becker come up with the name Elena Jäger?

"Ah, yes. I am mistaken." Herr Becker released a nervous laugh. "You are correct, Herr Scott. It was Elena Cigler who used this dressing room. My apologies. I must have confused her with an actress named Jäger."

After the two men entered the small room, Gabe stepped out. "It's a little crowded in here. I'll look on from the doorway."

"This room has changed through the years, as I'm sure you must understand." Mr. Becker spread his hands. "However, Elena *Cigler* used this room for a couple of years. She was widely popular, and shows sold out three times a week as audiences came to hear her sing." He stepped to the doorway. "Come with me. I have a special treat to show you."

They followed him to a long, carpeted hallway along one side of the theater where small chandeliers hung and a plethora of pictures lined both sides of the walls. About halfway down the hallway, he paused beside a picture of a young woman in a long, dark silky evening gown.

Kate gasped as she edged closer for a better look.

"That's...that's Mother." All of a sudden, it was real. Mother *had* sung in Germany. She stared at the picture attempting to memorize it.

"Wow. She was beautiful." Matt breathed the words softly as he slipped an arm around Kate's shoulder. "I've never seen a picture of her. You look like her, sis."

Kate leaned her head against his shoulder and laughed. "So do you. In a masculine sort of way."

He chuckled. "I suppose. You know, she seems real to me now. Before, she was just someone you told me about."

Kate turned to him, her brow furrowed. "Did I not show you the picture of her and your dad?"

Matt shook his head. "I don't recall it."

"I brought it with me from Ohio. How did I not show it to you?"

"Excuse me, sir." Skylar cleared her throat. "Herr Becker? That photo. Is there a negative available somewhere? Is it possible to obtain a copy of it?"

The gentleman turned a questioning eye on her. "Well, I'm sure I don't know. I'll have to check in the business office and see if they know anything."

"If not, we can have a copy made from this one, with their permission of course." Mark piped in. "I know the kids would love to have a copy of their mother's picture."

"Oh, yes. Please." Kate straightened and turned to the theater manager. "As Mr. Scott told you, we're just learning about this side of Mother. We never knew she lived and worked in Germany during the war, and we never knew she sang here at the theater."

Herr Becker nodded. "I understand. The war was hard on families all over. I will see what I can find out. Will you remain in Munich for a few days?" He turned to Mark.

"As long as it takes. We still have more to see."

"*Gut.* Please leave me the name of your hotel, and I will be in touch soon." He shook hands with them and led them back to the lobby where he bade them a good day.

After lunch the group decided to take the rest of the day off. Gabe could rest and make a phone call to his lawyer friend in the US concerning the supposed loophole Mr. Hawthorn's lawyer had found.

Too restless to settle down in the room and wanting to give Skylar time to make some phone calls of her own, Kate grabbed her book and took the elevator down to the coffee shop in the hotel. A cup of coffee in a corner with her book would be a good way to while away some downtime.

Facing the room so she could keep an eye on any strangers who entered the shop, Kate placed her order, sat back and opened the book she'd barely started. Once her steaming cup arrived, she doctored it the way she liked and dove into the pages of her romantic suspense. She'd barely read a paragraph when a familiar voice spoke from beside her booth.

"What are you doing here by yourself?"

Kate raised her eyes to meet the questioning ones of Mark Scott. His lowered brow and frown indicated he wasn't overly happy she was alone.

"Reading and enjoying a cuppa as they say in England. Of coffee that is."

"We're not in England." He dropped onto the bench opposite her. "We're in Germany, and someone's been bothering you. It isn't wise to go anywhere alone."

She grinned at him and waved at the seat where he'd already sat down. "I'd love some company. Want some coffee? It's delicious."

"I'd love some. And quit changing the subject." Mark raised a hand to grab the attention of the barista. After placing his order and telling her to place Kate's order on his bill, he returned his attention to Kate. "So why not order room service and read in your room? I'm sure it's far more comfortable and quieter, not to mention safer."

"I'm giving Skylar some privacy. She's making long distance calls to Megan to talk over the article and then to her mom. It would be hard to read with that going on, and it's hard to talk with someone in the room." She shrugged. "Voilà. I'm here. Besides, I'm sitting in a corner with my back to the wall. I can see if a stranger comes in."

He looked at her as if she had a green face. "I doubt that. You're reading a book; you're not paying attention, girl. Until I spoke to you beside the table, you didn't see me."

Kate attempted not to look sheepish. "Well, I was trying."

"Okay. Whatever you say."

Kate slipped her bookmark into her book as the barista brought Mark's coffee. He didn't bother to doctor it and drank it black. "Since you're here, I have a question for you."

"Shoot."

"Is this hard for you? Returning to Munich after so many years, I mean. You were here when all the Nazi flags flew everywhere and Nazi soldiers marched along the streets."

He pursed his lips before nodding. "Yeah, I know what you mean. It's definitely different. There were checkpoints everywhere back then, and you couldn't throw a rock without hitting a Nazi soldier in this town. Did you know the street across from the National Theater, called Viscardigasse, became known as Shirkers Alley? There was a shrine just down the street from there to Hitler and his thugs and to a night back in 1923, when the Nazis attempted to overthrow the German government.

"Nazi guards stood forcing Germans to salute the shrine as they passed. People didn't want to salute it, so they began slipping down Viscardigasse to avoid it. It wasn't long before the Nazis caught on, and they started shooting and killing the German shirkers." Mark shook his head, sadness marring his features. "These weren't Jews. They were fellow Germans killed in cold blood because they didn't want to salute a stupid shrine." He took a sip of his hot brew.

Had he even tasted his coffee? Kate briefly closed her eyes. "I can't imagine what you and Mother went through in those days. However, I know what got her through."

Mark's eyes met hers, wariness in their depths. "You mean her religion?"

Kate sent him a gentle smile. "She didn't have religion. So many belief systems. So many people believing there's a lot of ways to heaven. They believe you can get there on your own by doing good works." Kate rolled her eyes and cupped her hands around the hot cup. "The Bible clearly states that Christ is the way, the truth and the life. Mother had faith in Christ. It's called relationship; not religion. That's what got her through every day, no matter what she faced." Kate shook her head. "I can't comprehend all that she dealt with as a spy, but her faith helped her face the Nazis. What got you through?"

Mark's eyes shifted over Kate's shoulder. "There were days I had no idea if I'd make it through or not. I trained for it, yet at times I was terrified, and Elena...well, she always seemed at peace. She seemed so strong. Much stronger than I, that was for sure." His finger circled the rim of his cup. "The night I helped her escape from Germany, she hadn't planned to leave. A Nazi officer was on her tail. He'd found out about her, and she was forced to leave. She had a strength in her...."

Kate waited but he didn't continue. "Were you in love with my mother?"

His eyes flicked to hers and he half-grinned. "Who wasn't? Maybe I was a little. I certainly admired her, but I had a wife and young daughter back in the US. There was never anything untoward between your mom and me. Everything was always aboveboard and professional."

"I thought as much." Kate patted his hand. "You did a great job of changing the subject, by the way, but I won't let you get away with it. The topic is too important."

"Topic?" His brow shifted upward.

"Megan told me before I left Wyoming that you've never put your faith in Christ. If you identified my mother's faith in action, why did you never turn to Christ?"

Mark blew out his cheeks and stared into his cup. "My wife was a Christian. She and Martha Holcomb always attended the little wooden church a few miles down the road from our ranch. Quite a few ranchers in the area attended there. Martha and even a few of my ranch hands still do. Carolyn, my wife, always tried to persuade me to go with her, and I did a few times, but I never thought much about Christians. My father raised me to believe they're nothing but a bunch of hypocrites."

"Do tell." Kate crossed her arms along the edge of the table.

"Well, I don't know. They tend to look down their noses at people. Know what I mean? They judge others and do wrong themselves."

"If you mean that Christians are human and sometimes make mistakes, then yes, I do know what you mean. But in my experience at our church, the people there generally head to the altar and ask forgiveness for their sins and attempt to do better, or they do that in their quiet time at home. They help one another, lift one another up when they fall, pray for one another and give mercy where it's needed. I often need mercy and try to give it as much as I receive it. We're all sinners, and none of us will be perfect until we get to heaven. Only one man who ever walked on this earth was perfect and lived sinless, and that was Jesus Christ. He died on the cross so the rest of us could one day live in heaven and have a sinless life. Until that time, we have to keep giving mercy and forgiveness and ask for it in return." A sheepish grin lifted a corner of Mark's lips. "You sound like your mom."

"Thank you. That's a compliment I'll always accept. She delivered the same message to you?" Kate chuckled. "Several times. So did my wife."

"You know what? It sounds to me like the Lord might be trying to get through to you. You've heard the message of Christ dying to save your soul before, haven't you? Also, you know how much He loves you and wants you to give your life to Him, right?"

He tilted his head to the side. "Yep. Megan still talks to me about it."

"So why not let go and let God have your life? Don't you think you'd be happier if you had true peace?"

"Probably."

Kate shrugged. "You have so much to lose if you don't, you know. But look what you have to gain if you do."

"I'll have to think about it."

"Haven't you been thinking about it for over twenty-five years?"

His grin grew. "Yeah. I have, but—"

"No buts, Mark. You're not promised tomorrow. No one is." Kate laid a hand on his. "Don't delay too long. You've already delayed a quarter of a century. Who do you think was looking after you through the war? It wasn't you."

Mark's grin disappeared as a thoughtful expression replaced it. Kate nodded. *Lord, please continue to convict him until he turns to You. Don't let him find rest until he makes You his Savior.*

Chapter Eleven

After dinner as everyone left the restaurant, Gabe touched Kate's elbow. "Feel up to a stroll?"

She halted just outside the entrance and turned with a tilt of her head to observe him, a brow raised in question. "I could ask you the same thing."

Gabe's heart picked up a beat at the smile in her eyes. He waved away her words. "I'm fine. I have to keep moving or I get stiff. A walk will do me good."

"Can you give me a few minutes to run up and grab my coat? I thought Wyoming was chilly, but it has nothing on Germany in early April."

Gabe tilted his head in the direction of the elevators. "You bet. Let's go. I need to get mine too."

Within a short time, they were heading out the front entrance of the hotel and into the evening. The city streets were already lit and vehicles rushed past to reach their destinations.

"I come from a small town so I don't think I could ever get used to living in a city this size even if everyone spoke English." Kate tugged her coat collar higher beneath her chin. "I'm simply a small-town girl. Guess I always will be. But you come from Casper. I only landed at the airport which wasn't large. What size town is it?"

Gabe chuckled and stepped beside Kate, taking her elbow. He'd stick close and keep a watchful eye around her. "I suppose it depends on your idea of big. Our population is around forty thousand. Certainly not big when you compare it to, say…Munich or even Cleveland."

Kate shrugged. "No, but it's bigger than Dogwood Station. Our population is less than ten thousand."

"Yeah, that's small." Gabe grinned. "I have an apartment in Casper but spend a lot of time out at the ranch. Occasionally I travel when the partnership has legal issues or a business deal that needs to be checked out."

"You think a lot of Mark, don't you?"

"I do. He's a man of integrity, and I could do worse for a business partner. He's raised his son to be the same. Meeting Matt in Vietnam was the second-best thing that ever happened to me."

"What was the first?" Kate stared up at him as they came to a street crossing, and Gabe took her elbow and guided her across.

He turned to meet her eyes and smiled. "Putting my faith in Christ." His breath caught at the beautiful expression that settled on her features. The desire to touch her soft skin nearly overwhelmed him. Instead, he jammed his hand into his jacket pocket.

"I'm glad. I talked with Mark earlier today in hopes of persuading him to put his faith in Christ, but all he said was he'd think about it." Their steps slowed as they strolled down the street. "He said my mom had told him the same things. I advised him that he'd had twenty-five years to think about it, and it was time to trust Christ now."

"I'm glad you told him that. I've been praying for Mark and Matt for a long time." Gabe edged Kate through a small crowd of people, keeping an eye on everyone as he led her to a small bistro. "Want some coffee? I don't know about you, but I could use some warmth."

Kate stared up just as tiny white snowflakes drifted down. Her mouth grew wide with a smile. "Oh, look. It's snowing." Lifting her hands, she caught tiny white flakes on her dark gloves. They vanished as the warmth from her hands seeped through the wool and melted them.

The happy tinkle of her laugh sent a thrill tiptoeing down Gabe's spine. This woman was pure delight. He chuckled. "Hey, the snow's getting a little heavier. Let's grab that coffee."

"Yes, please."

As they stepped inside, Kate removed her white knit toboggan and gloves. She attempted to smooth her flyaway hair. They laughed as they took a seat at a table as far from the door as they could.

After placing their order, Kate unbuttoned her coat and slipped out of it. Gabe spotted concern on her face as he removed his jacket.

"How are you feeling? Still sore?"

"A little." He shrugged and settled into his chair. Had he winced when he'd removed his jacket? She didn't appear to miss much. "I hope you know I'd do it all over again if I had to."

Kate's eyes locked with his and a lovely shade of pink rolled over her cheeks. As a beautiful woman, that hue looked amazing on her. He watched as she drew her lip between her teeth, uncertainty painted plainly across her face. *Captivating* didn't begin to describe her. The beat of Gabe's heart picked up and his breath caught. Did she understand what he'd just said? Of course he'd save her life again. In a literal heartbeat.

"I know that, and I appreciate it." Kate lowered he eyes and smiled as she steepled her hands on the table. She thanked the waiter as he set their coffee in front of them. When he departed, she met Gabe's eyes. Hers were contemplative. What was she thinking about now?

"You know, it's been hard for me to accept the information Mark's been giving us about Mother's past. That is until today when I saw her picture in the National Theater. I can't get that image out of my mind."

"I'm sure you can't. She was a courageous woman."
Gabe reached across and clasped Kate's hands in his. "You
look like her, you know."

"I'll take that as a compliment." Kate's eyes darted to
their joined hands, but she didn't pull hers away. "I'm used
to seeing her in slacks, a blouse and an apron, not an
evening gown. In fact, I can't ever recall seeing her in
anything more formal than a Sunday dress. In that evening
gown, she was gorgeous. With the combination of that and
her singing voice, no wonder the theater sold out."

"Do you sing?" Gabe squeezed her hands before
releasing them and picked up his cup.

"Only at church." Kate met his eyes and tossed him a
teasing smile. "I did not inherit my mother's voice."

"One out of two isn't bad."

Kate's brow puckered as she tilted her head in
question.

"You inherited her beauty, remember?"

Color flooded her cheeks again, delighting Gabe.
"Anyone ever tell you how lovely you look when you
blush?"

Kate hid behind her coffee cup as she lifted it to take
another drink. "I don't blush."

"Keep telling yourself that." He chuckled and finished
his brew. "By the way, I wanted to tell you I spoke with my
lawyer friend who knows property law. He couldn't think
of a single loophole that would allow your property
developer to take your building from you. My friend
recommended ensuring your deed is recorded at your
county clerk's office. That should've been done at the time
of the purchase, but have your relatives make sure. Once
that's done, put that deed in a safe-deposit box at the bank.
Also put any property sale paperwork there as well. The
lawyer said that should ensure your property is safe. Tell
your loved ones not to fall for anything the harassing
lawyer says. If he continues to harass them, we'll call your

local police and have them set up a restraining order. That behavior cannot continue. Period."

"Thank you. They don't deserve this, especially when I'm not there to help." Kate's distressed expression tugged at Gabe. "I appreciate you finding out this information for me. When we return, I'll call them."

"Good. Are you ready to head back to the hotel?" He cast an eye toward the window. "The snow's grown heavier. We want to return before the sidewalks become slippery."

Kate eased her chair back and stood. "I'm ready."

Gabe helped her on with her coat. He required Kate's help donning his, then he turned, giving her a helpless grin. "I don't generally allow a lady to help me on with my jacket, but under these circumstances...."

Kate patted his forearm. "I'm happy to help. May I remind you that you were a gentleman first?"

He held out his elbow for her. "My pleasure. Shall we, my lady?"

"Why thank you, sir." Kate slipped her hand within the crook of his elbow, and Gabe tightened it against his side. He would once again do all in his power to protect this precious woman.

When the bill was paid, they stepped outside to find the snow had indeed become heavier, and sidewalks were slushy. Keeping Kate close beside him, Gabe returned her to the hotel. Once inside where it was warm, he was grateful there hadn't been an incident of any kind. He'd nearly decided not to ask Kate to go for a stroll but instead trusted the Lord to look after them, and Gabe remained vigilant the whole time they were gone.

Back in his room, he sat on the edge of the bed and he closed his eyes. *Thanks for watching over us and for the pleasant time spent in this delightful woman's company. Father, You know I've fallen for Kate, don't You? I'm not sure what to do about it. How can we have a relationship when she lives in Ohio, and I live in Wyoming? How in the world can that work out? Only You can do a miracle or take these feelings from me. Thy will be done, Lord. Thy will be done.*

The next morning at the direction of Mark, the limo driver turned the long vehicle down a narrow street in what looked to be a forlorn section of Munich. It certainly didn't look like it had the last time he'd been here. During the war, the street had been lined with row houses but now warehouses replaced them. Only a few houses remained, and they were in sad shape. Was the one he was looking for still here? Mark's heart sank as his hopes began to fail. What if it wasn't? What if *she* wasn't here?

The limo drove slowly past large trucks parked in front of busy warehouses. Men with hand trucks loaded and unloaded them, eyeing the stretched limo as it passed. Mr. Gustafson finally stopped the limo behind a panel truck parked in front of an old row house on the right. Its shutters hung loose and the gray paint had long ago cracked and peeled. One downspout leaned away from the roof at a precarious angle. The house possessed a neglected appearance. She would never have left it in such disrepair. Mark sighed inwardly and shook his head. Where was she? Could she possibly still live here among the warehouses?

The front door stood wide open. Surely someone was here, considering the panel truck parked in front. Mark shoved the car door open and climbed out. "Hang out here. I'll be right back."

He stepped onto the cracked and uneven sidewalk just as a man carrying a box of supplies hurried out the front door and skipped down the steps. Mark approached him.

"*Guten Morgen.*"

The man dropped the box into the back of the open

panel truck and turned with a nod to Mark. *"Guten Morgen."*

"Do you speak English? My German is a bit rusty. I haven't used it in a while."

The man flashed a crooked smile. "I speak English. What can I do for you?" His curious eyes aimed at the limo then returned to Mark.

"I came here during the war when this was a bakery." Mark tossed a thumb toward the house. "I knew the lady who lived here. Do you know where she might be? Is she still living?"

The man shrugged. "I don't know anything about a lady who lived here, but I know there's a bakery on Marienplatz in Old Town Munich. This is the supply warehouse for it. I am the deliveryman." He stepped to the side of the panel truck and pointed to the sign. "See? Beraneks Bäckerei—bakery, in English." A huge grin lifted the corners of his mouth.

Mark followed him to the side of the truck, and he returned his grin. "I see. That's her last name. It doesn't tell me if she's still living, but it leads me in the right direction." He held out his hand and the other man shook it. "I know where Marienplatz is. Something tells me her business may have grown. Thank you. We'll pay a visit to the bakery. Maybe they can tell me more."

"Indeed. Good luck, friend." He tossed Mark a wave.

With a nod, Mark returned to the limo and instructed Mr. Gustafson of their next destination. Climbing in, questions peppered him before his rear hit the seat.

"Who was that?"

"What is this place?"

"What did you ask him?"

"Who were you looking for here?"

Mark held up his hands. "Just hold on a second. I'll tell you if you give me half a chance."

Silence settled inside the vehicle as all eyes trained on

Mark. He slanted his gaze at them and amusement settled on his face. "That's better. Now I'm not going to tell you everything, but I will give you some information. A lady used to live here from before the war, and she ran a bakery out of her home. She was a good friend to your mother. An exceptionally good friend." Mark turned to stare out the car window as memories flooded back, especially of that night so long ago when he came to help Elena escape to America.

"Dad? Is that all you're going to tell us?" Matt's voice broke into Mark's memories and snapped his attention back. He turned from the window and read the same question in everyone's eyes.

"Well, I will tell you that the woman who lived here helped your mother escape the night she left Germany for America. Elena hadn't planned to leave, but I came in, and we convinced her that she'd been discovered. If she didn't leave right then she'd be—it wouldn't go well for her, that was for sure. Thank goodness she listened to us." He cleared the emotion from his throat. Even after all these years the memories of that night still got to him. They'd come so close....

"Where are we going now?" Kate waved a hand toward the window.

"The nice German man told me of a bakery in Old Town Munich that has the same name as the one she ran in her home during the war. Hopefully we can find more information there." Mark folded his hands in his lap and stared out the window once again.

"She?" Gabe asked. "Who is 'she'?"

"Hopefully we'll find her if she's still living." Mark remained unclear as to the woman's identity. He missed the exchange of glances among the other occupants of the limo, but he wouldn't share any other information. They would simply have to wait until they found her. *If* they found her.

Chapter Twelve

The limo dropped the group at the entrance to the Marienplatz in Old Town. Kate thrilled to see the open area free of cars, where tented booths were set up for vendors. Unfortunately, they wouldn't be visiting them. They were on a mission to find a bakery somewhere amongst the Gothic, Baroque and Renaissance architectures of the buildings. On their left as they passed the tall tower of the Town Hall the glockenspiel started playing.

"Look!" Kate pointed at the figures as they began to move in time to the music. "Look at the knights on horses moving around. There are two levels of figures, but only the upper-level figures are moving."

They stopped and watched. "Are those knights jousting?" Gabe stared up at the tower.

A passing German man stopped beside them. "Pardon me for intruding, but it seems you are unfamiliar with our Rathaus-Glockenspiel. Is this true?"

"That's right." Gabe waved a hand in the direction of the tower. "It's fascinating."

"Indeed. It tells the history of the marriage of Duke Willhelm V. In honor of his marriage, a joust of life-sized horses and knights were made for the glockenspiel. The blue and white represents our region of Bavaria, and they win every time." The man chuckled. He pointed to the lower-level figures of dancers in Bavarian costumes.

"Those dancing figures are coopers—makers of barrels and casks. They dance to celebrate the end of a severe plague that happened in 1517. This dance will take place in an hour. *Auf Wiedersehen*." He tipped his hat and strolled away.

"How interesting." Skylar jotted notes in her ever-present notebook then snapped several pictures of the glockenspiel.

"It's fun if you ask me." Kate stared at the figures in the tower. "To think those figures are life-sized."

At the end of the show, they strolled around the square until they found Beraneks Bäckerei. Tantalizing aromas emanated from the business even before the door opened, and a customer hurried away.

"Wow, that smells good." Matt rubbed his stomach.

"Something tells me we'll be leaving here with more than information." Mark reached for the doorhandle and pulled it open. "*Eintreten, bitte.*"

"English, Dad." Matt lowered a brow at him.

"I said, enter, please." Mark chuckled. "Every once and a while some German returns to me."

Matt rolled his eyes and entered behind Kate and Skylar.

Kate breathed in the delectable smells that tempted the palate. Her stomach growled. A low laugh beside her drew her eyes to Gabe's.

"I can't help it," she whispered for his ears only. "It just smells so good in here."

"Tell me about it."

She glanced around the brightly lit bakery to find a glass case that ran the full length of the shop, it's lights displaying all kinds of delicious sweets. Glass-covered pedestal-platters held more pastries on top of the glass case. A table ran along one wall filled with wedding-cake samples while two more stood by the front windows with German breads, kuchen and rolls. The windows displayed all kinds of samples of what the shop offered.

A young woman behind the counter eyed their group with curiosity. "May I help you?"

Mark approached the counter. "In a bit perhaps, but may I ask if your manager is in? I'd like to chat with him or her, if I may?"

A shadow of concern crossed the woman's features. "Yes, of course. If you'll wait a moment, I'll get her for you."

"Thank you. Please don't look concerned. It's nothing bad."

Relief chased the concern away. "Thank you. I was worried."

"Nothing to worry about."

The young woman nearly smiled. "I'll be right back."

Within minutes, she returned with an older woman who looked to be in her sixties, a curious but pleasant smile on her face. Her graying brown hair was gathered at the back of her head in a bun. With hands folded in front of her, she rounded the end of the glass case and came toward the group. Her blue eyes held curiosity as well as a smile.

"*Guten tag*. My name is Freida Hofmann. My assistant tells me you wish to speak to the shop manager, but that it is nothing bad. I am pleased to hear this. What can I do for you?"

"Ms. Hofmann, my name is Mark Scott." He turned to the group and introduced each one. "I knew about this bakery when it was in the private home of Zofia Beranek during the war. This morning I went to her home but found she no longer lives there. A kind gentleman who serves as a deliveryman for your bakery told me I should come here to find out more. Do you possibly know Mrs. Beranek? I'm trying to locate her."

A gentle smile lifted the corners of Ms. Hofmann's lips as she tilted her head slightly. "I do indeed, Herr Scott. Mrs. Beranek is my mother. I used to work with her in her home bakery until the Nazis destroyed it. They came in and searched her home one night looking for someone, but obviously didn't find them. Another time they returned and searched more thoroughly. That time they destroyed her bakery and most of her home. They still found nothing, but they cared not. The Nazis took my mother away for questioning, but she told them nothing. She was beaten and released."

Kate gasped even as Mark flinched at the woman's words. Who was this woman, this Zofia Beranek that Mark searched for? She had helped Mother escape, but was there more? Was that why Mark looked for her, or was it simply to see her for old times' sake? Apparently, she'd been a friend to Mark as well as Mother.

"I'm so sorry, Ms. Hofmann. Your mother was a strong woman and a good friend."

Her smile grew. "She still is, and please, call me Freida. I am a widow now, and my mother lives with me. Might I suggest you all come round this evening after dinner? Say about six? Mother is a night owl so it's not like she'll be heading to bed early. Please say you'll come. She'll be delighted to see you."

"We'd love to." Mark agreed. "While you're writing down the address, we'll check out your array of pastries and purchase some. I haven't had true German Kuchen in...well, since the war. Since your mother's."

"Mother doesn't work in the bakery anymore. Her arthritis no longer allows it." Freida waved a hand toward the pastry case. "Now, peruse to your heart's content. I'll return shortly."

While they waited, they explored the bakery cases and chose several pastries to take back to the hotel. Freida returned with a slip of paper with her home address written on it. When they attempted to pay for the pastries, she waved a hand and said they were on the house.

"Just come this evening and make my mother happy."

Freida handed the bag of pastries to Mark, a broad smile on her face. "I remember *Mutter* mentioned you once, but afterward she warned me never to say your name. She'd let it slip and became angry with herself."

Kate couldn't comprehend the danger for Mother and Mark during those dark days, both spying on the enemy and attempting to keep from being discovered. How had Mother managed to survive under such circumstances?

"She was always careful." Mark aimed a mock salute at Freida and edged toward the door. "We'll see you this evening. And thank you." He held up the bag of pastries.

"You're welcome." Freida waved. "*Auf Wiedersehen.* Until this evening."

Gabe spotted the small green Volkswagen sitting at the curb across the street as they climbed into the limo. He'd seen the same car sitting down the street from the house they stopped at earlier when Mark had talked with the deliveryman. Was it really the same car, or one that looked similar to it? Could it be the same one that had nearly plowed over Kate? He hadn't caught a glimpse of it as he'd gathered her close and landed on the parked car and then the sidewalk. It had sped away.

Before climbing inside the limo, Gabe again paused to stare at the VW. The driver turned and stared in their direction before starting the compact car and driving away. The man's face had been shadowed, and there was no way Gabe could get a good look at his features. With a disgusted groan, he climbed into the limo and settled into his seat. Something told him the guy was following them. Was he also the same guy that nearly knocked Kate over by elevator and tried to steal her purse? Had the purse-snatching been real or a mere ruse to get close to Kate for some other reason? It all seemed like a pattern, yet disjointed at the same time.

"You okay, Gabe?" Matt asked.

"Yeah, I'm okay." Gabe gave Matt a brief smile before turning to stare out the window. He'd have to tell Mark of his suspicions and see what he thought.

They returned to the hotel to find Herr Becker from the National Theater had left a message at the front desk for Mark. He wanted him to call as soon as possible. Said he had good news for him. After reading the message, Mark approached the desk clerk.

"Excuse me. Is there a house phone I can use to make a call?"

"Why yes. Right over by those chairs." The clerk pointed to an arrangement of arm chairs situated by a table with a phone and a lamp on it. "Please, help yourself. Local calls can simply be dialed. If you must make international calls, a direction sheet is attached to the table for your convenience."

Mark tossed him a wave. "Thank you. It's local."

"Very good, sir." The clerk bowed slightly and returned to what he'd been doing.

Mark strode to the phone and placed a call to the number in the message and waited for Herr Becker to answer.

"Guten Tag."

"Herr Becker. This is Mark Scott. You left a message for me to call you. Your message indicated it's good news."

"Why yes, indeed it is. We do not have the original photo or the negative for the photograph of the singer you were querying about; however, we were able to locate the original photo through the newspaper office. Miraculously, it survived the war in the archives in their basement. They are willing to reprint it for you."

"For a price, I'm sure." Mark added for him, giving a chuckle.

"Ach, Herr Scott, there's always a price to do business as I'm sure you understand."

"Of course, I do. I'm a businessman, and I don't mind. Please have them print two for me. Preferably, smaller than the one in the theater."

"Most certainly. I will let you know when they are ready to be picked up. Will you be in Munich for a time?"

"For a time. If our plans change, I'll let you know."

"*Sehr gut*, Herr Scott. Auf Wiedersehen."

Mark replaced the receiver, but remained seated for a moment. He glanced up as Gabe approached him. "You look like a fellow with something on his mind."

Gabe halted before him and crossed his arms over his chest. "You could say that. Got a minute to talk?"

"Sure I do, but let's find someplace else in case somebody needs to use the phone." He stood, tilting his head in the direction of the table. "I just received good news from Mr. Becker at the National Theater. They located the picture of Kate and Matt's mother in the archives. One of the newspaper offices have it. He's going to have them make a couple of photos for Kate and Matt."

"That's great. They'll appreciate it." Gabe fell into step beside Mark as he headed across the lobby to another seating area.

"Will this be all right or do you want some place more private?" Mark indicated the empty seats.

"This is fine. I wanted to tell you something I observed today and get your take on it." Gabe lowered himself carefully into an armchair while Mark took another.

"Tell me what you saw that has your thoughts swirling." Mark crossed an ankle over a knee.

"I located a green VW down the street a little way from the house when you were talking to the deliveryman this morning. At first, I didn't think too much about it, until

I caught sight of it again at Marienplatz parked across from the limo. As we were getting into it after our visit to the bakery, I stopped and stared at the driver. His face was in shadow, and I couldn't see him well, but I sensed he stared back before he drove off."

A grimace settled on Mark features. "Yeah, I spotted it too. First at the house then at the square. If I don't miss my guess, I'd say it was the same car that nearly ran over Kate."

"Exactly. Aren't you concerned about us being followed?"

"Sure, I am." Mark scrubbed a hand down his face. "I don't know what I can do about it right now. Even if I walked up to the car and asked the guy why he's following us, he'd likely drive off before I could get close."

"Do you think it has anything to do with the man who hurt Martha?"

Mark suspected that would be Gabe's next question. He discharged a grunted breath. "I'd like to say no, but I'd be lying if I did. I can't figure out what the guy in the green car is up to, but even if he's not the man who hurt Martha, he's probably connected to the guy who did. It's a mystery." Mark dropped his foot to the floor and leaned forward, his elbows on his knees. He met Gabe's eyes and stared hard at him. "If the man who hurt Martha does show up, it will not be good. He's evil. Pure evil."

Skylar had just stepped from her room when she ran right into Matt. "Oh, my goodness. I'm terribly sorry."

Matt caught Skylar's shoulders and steadied her to prevent her falling from the impact of nearly running him down. He chuckled. "You should watch where you're going. You never know who's lurking in the hallway."

She hugged her notebook to her chest and stared at

him. "You're right, so my question is, why are *you* just lurking in the hallway?" Tilting her head to the side, she lowered a brow and narrowed her eyes at him.

He dropped his hands from her shoulders and took a half-step back. "Well, I heard you mention to Kate you might head down to the café for some coffee. Thought I might ask if I could join you, especially if you're going alone. It's not safe for young women to go around foreign countries alone."

"Really? But I'm not leaving the hotel. I'm sure I'll be fine."

"You mean you don't want me to come along?" Matt batted his eyes and affected the most forlorn expression.

Skylar spewed out a laugh. "You're laying it on a bit thick, don't you think?"

Lifting a brow, he gave her a side-eyed stare. "Is it working?"

"Well...I wouldn't want you to worry about me being in a foreign country all by myself, and I never said I *didn't* want you to come along—"

"Great. Let's go. I need coffee, and I'd like to spend some time with you." Matt grabbed Skylar's hand and tugged her toward the elevators.

"What?" Skylar tugged back, but Matt kept moving them toward the elevator.

He punched the down button and turned toward her. "Yes, I just said I'd like to spend some time with you. Is there something wrong with that?"

The elevator dinged, and a moment later the door opened.

"Well, no, but—"

Matt pulled her inside and pushed the lobby button. "No buts. No questions. Let's simply drink coffee and enjoy...talking."

"No strings?" Skylar tugged her hand from his and wrapped both hands around the notebook clasped to her chest. "You have a girlfriend, remember?"

Silence filled the tiny space as Matt stared straight ahead, a pucker forming between his eyes, and his mouth set into a flat line of...what? Displeasure? Unhappiness? Dissatisfaction? Skylar couldn't decide which, but her comment had given him food for thought, that was for sure.

"I remember." The solemn tone of Matt's voice and the look on his face ripped at Skylar's heart. For a long time, she'd attempted to shove this man from her thoughts, but it had been impossible. She'd prayed he'd come to know Christ, but so far, he hadn't. He'd chosen a woman who was self-centered. *Forgive me, Lord. It may be the truth, but I need to pray for Gina and not think badly of her. It's not my place to step between them, but coffee can't hurt anything, right? Matt's simply a friend and the brother of my boss, and he* did *invite me. I just have to keep in mind that he's in a relationship. Always.* Her heart ached at the thought.

Chapter Thirteen

It was already dusk when they arrived at the address Freida Hofmann had given them that afternoon. The limo stopped in front of a row house in a lovely neighborhood with flowerboxes in the windowsills and well-trimmed shrubbery along the sidewalk and beside the steps leading to the front doors. Kate wondered how these folks managed to keep flowers growing even in colder weather. Lights shone through the houses' windows up and down the street while street lights illuminated the sidewalks leaving a mellow glow along the cement path.

Mr. Gustafson let them out at the curb before driving away to return when Mark would call him back. They climbed the steps to the front door and rang the bell.

Within minutes Freida opened the door and ushered them inside to warmth and the delicious aroma of baking.

"Willkommen. Please let me take your coats and jackets." She hung their coats on a rack along the entrance wall then ushered them inside. "Mother awaits in the living room."

Overstuffed armchairs and a couch nestled around a gas fireplace. Everything was decorated in forest-green and cream. Kate thought the room was quite cozy and welcoming. An elderly lady sat in an armchair near the gas fire, crocheting an exquisite lace doily, her sensible black shoes barely reaching the floor.

"Mother, we have guests." Freida waved a hand toward them and folded her hands in front of her waist.

The elder woman set her project aside in a work basket by her chair as they entered. The woman's solid white braided hair wrapped around the back of her head. Her skin was thin and delicate, her narrow fingers bent with arthritis as they rested in her lap. Rheumy blue eyes gazed at them from behind rimless glasses. A smile lifted her fragile lips. "Guests, you say? And who are these guests? Since you speak in English, Freida, they must be from America, Canada or England. Where are you from, my friends?" She spoke with a frail and reedy voice.

Mark stepped forward and knelt beside the woman's chair. "Do you remember me, Zofia? A lot of years have passed since we last saw one another, and I've aged a lot since then."

The woman studied his features for several moments before she reached out a hand to cup his cheek. "So have I, Major Scott. So have I." Her smile widened. "I would recognize you anywhere, even with your salt-and-pepper hair."

Mark laid his hand over hers on his cheek. "I went by your old home this morning looking for you only to find you were no longer there. I feared the worse."

Her smile grew. "You cannot get rid of me so easily. The Nazis tried, my friend. They did not succeed," she cackled.

"I'm glad they didn't." Mark took her hand from his cheek and held it between his hands before laying a kiss on it. "Remember the package Elena and I smuggled out of Germany that night?"

She nodded slowly. "How could I ever forget the night my dear Elena left my life forever?"

Mark turned to Kate and her heart leaped. He waved her over along with Matt. "Kids, I'd like to introduce you to my dear friend, and your mother's dear friend, Zofia

Beranek. Zofia, this is Kate and Matt. These are Elena's twins."

Zofia's hand went to her mouth. "My goodness. Elena's twins? Her tiny *kinder*. Her children." Tears welled in her eyes and trickled down her cheeks. "I cannot believe they are here." She held out a hand to Kate, and Kate placed hers within it. "You, Katarina, holčička, look exactly as your mother did. She was so beautiful." Her gaze soaked in Kate's features before moving on to Matt's. "And you. Mathias. You look like your mother too. A handsome man. Neither of you will remember this—" She slipped her hand from Mark's to hold both of their hands. "When your mother was pregnant, she came to me so her pregnancy would not be discovered. I took care of you until such a time as Major Scott could arrange to have you smuggled from Germany. You were the package your mother sent away."

"What?" Kate exclaimed. "But...I don't understand. Why? Our father was an American soldier who died in the war. Why would they have to smuggle us out of Germany?" Kate did a double take. "Did you just call me little girl in Czech?"

The old woman smiled then turned her eyes to Mark. "You have not told them everything, have you?"

"No, I haven't." He avoided Kate's glance.

The old woman shook her head and tsked. "Then you must all have a seat, and I will tell you. But first, Freida has coffee and kuchen to share. Please, sit and make yourselves at home."

Kate's mind swirled with this news. She and Matt were the package that was smuggled out of Germany? What had happened? There was more to the story, just as she'd thought.

As delicious as the German pastry was, Kate barely tasted it as she anticipated Zofia's explanation of the past. Mother had been involved in far more than expected. Kate laid her plate on the table and sipped her coffee. Hot and delicious, it warmed the cold spot of uncertainly that had formed inside her.

Mark introduced Gabe and Skylar before asking Zofia to continue with Elena's story.

"Yes, yes. It was so long ago, but first I will tell you that I, too, am Czechoslovakian. I came to Germany as a young bride many years ago. My Heinrich passed when Freida was only fifteen. That seems a lifetime ago." Sadness cloaked the elderly woman, but she waved a dismissive hand. "You are not here to listen to that story. I will continue with the story of the night I will never forget. After Elena, your mother, came to me to have her babies—" she turned to Kate and Matt, "—you two, I kept you in my home and cared for you. It was only for about a month or so, but I cherished every moment." Zofia clasped her hands to her heart. "Elena came to see you as often as she could, but it was difficult for her to get away. The night she came to send you with Major Scott, we urged her to leave with him. You see, the SS was following her. If she had not gone as well, they would have imprisoned her. Or worse. You see, they had discovered she was a spy."

Kate glanced at Mark, who said, "That's not all, Kate."

"No, it is not." Zofia continued, "What did your mother tell you about your father, Katarina?"

"She said he was killed during the war." Kate frowned. "Now that I think about it, I'm not sure she actually told me he was an American soldier. Perhaps I always assumed he was since we were Americans." She lifted her shoulders. "I don't know what to think anymore."

"It's all right, child." Zofia's voice held a soothing tone. "No matter what you are told now, remember your mother did what she had to do for her country. She was an American through and through, and her principles were borne out of her love for America. She told me on more than one occasion that she would do anything to help

America win the war, and she did."

Kate gripped Matt's hand and felt him return her squeeze. "Who was our father?"

"Your father was Maj. Gunther Jäger, an SS officer with the Third Reich." Sadness filled the old woman's eyes as she gazed at the twins. "He…he was an officer in charge of executions at Dachau. As you may know that concentration camp sits just outside of Munich. Your mother's cover as a spy was singing at the National Theater here in Munich. Major Jäger had a penchant for opera and came often to the theater. Make no mistake. The major loved no one but himself and the Third Reich." Bitterness edged Zofia's words. "That did not stop him from insisting your mother remain at his side."

Nausea welled within Kate, but she could do nothing to stop the continuation of Mother's story. She leaned into Matt's shoulder, and he wrapped his arm around hers, drawing her close.

"What does that mean?" Kate's words were hoarse with dread.

"It means he wanted to marry your mother so he could flaunt her to the rest of the officers." Zofia shook her head and lifted her hands. "You must understand, child. With a renowned singer on his arm, he walked proudly among the SS, the Luftwaffe, the Gestapo and all German officials. Elena was well aware of this. As such she did not go into this relationship with blinders on."

"Did she marry him?" Matt's voice was strained.

"She did indeed. Elena would not live with a man under any other circumstances." Zofia lifted her chin. "She did not love Major Jäger, but she acquired valuable information through him. By your mother's sacrifice, some of the most crucial information reached the right US officials concerning the D-Day invasion as well as other US victories against the Third Reich. Because your mother, my dear Elena, married Major Jäger, she was able to attend many functions where high-ranking Nazi officials were present. Elena gleaned much information for the US. She passed that information on to her contact." Zofia tilted her head toward Mark, then turned her eyes once again toward the twins. "Lest you think your mother prostituted herself for no reason, think again. Elena sacrificed much for her country. She nearly sacrificed her life."

Kate swallowed hard as she attempted to come to grips with what Mother had done for the war effort. Yes, she'd married the enemy, but what she'd gained for the US had helped win the war. *Lord, she married someone she didn't love. I am the product of lies.*

All for the cause of freedom, a still, small voice said deep within.

She wasn't the only one to risk it all, was she, Lord? Others did similar acts of heroism, didn't they?

The still small voice repeated. *All for the cause of freedom.*

I get it, Lord. Thank you for a mother who was so brave. Help me accept these facts about her past and of my father. Kate lifted her purse from the floor where she'd placed it when they'd first sat down. She opened it and pulled out the photos Auntie Anna and Auntie Genevieve had given her from the little wooden box. "Zofia, I have a photograph I'd like to show you." She handed it to the elderly woman. "Is that our father standing next to Mother?"

Zofia adjusted her glasses to see the picture. Squinting, she stared at the images on the photo, then peered up. "Yes. Yes, that is Major Jäger standing beside Elena." She straightened, handing the photograph back to Kate. "She doesn't look happy to be with him, does she?"

Kate looked at the photo and handed it to Matt. "No, she doesn't. It's difficult to hear about Mother's past, but I see her bravery in your words. I'm beginning to understand why she did what she did." Kate paused as she sought the right words. "What I don't understand is why Matt and I were smuggled out of Germany. Why did she hide the fact she was pregnant? Wouldn't our father—" she blinked away the tears that threatened at the knowledge her father was such a horrible man, "wouldn't Major Jäger have been thrilled to have children?"

Sympathy and kindness filled Zofia's eyes. "I believe you will have difficulty in understanding what I'm going to tell you. Major Jäger would not have been thrilled to have twins. A single child, perhaps. Twins? Well, Elena was terrified he would turn you over to Dr. Joseph Mengele of Auschwitz Birkenau—also known as the Angel of Death. He did genetic research experiments on prisoners at the concentration camp, but his greatest interest focused on twins. Mengele cared not for the health or safety of his victims, and many died at his hands.

"When Elena found she was pregnant, and, before she began to show, she told Jäger she was going away to visit a family member in Czechoslovakia. She actually came to stay with me for a time until you were born, and you remained with me to keep you hidden. Because you were twins, Elena increased in size early on, so she suspected you were twins. I found a discreet doctor willing to help her and to deliver you. He did not turn her in, and he confirmed her suspicions that she was pregnant with twins."

Matt squeezed Kate's shoulder. "I can't comprehend the mindset of a man like Jäger. How evil he must have been."

"He was, Mathias. Major Jäger was pure evil, yet Elena maintained her marriage to him until we convinced her to escape." Zofia shifted in her armchair. "The night she and Major Scott took you and your sister to America, Jäger arrived at my front door looking for her only moments after you all escaped. The major, of course, found nothing. He returned a few days later and searched again, this time taking me to the SS headquarters in Munich. They tried to beat the information out of me." Zofia's voice broke on the last words. She swallowed hard but lifted her chin, a tight smile shaping her lips. "I told them nothing, and they never found the escape tunnel beneath my house."

Freida approached her mother and wrapped an arm around her frail shoulders. "Ah, Mutter. You have always been a strong woman. You are a wonderful example to us all. It is because of you, Elena Cigler, and Mark, as well as the allies who fought in the war, that the Nazis are no longer in power. We have so much to be grateful for."

Zofia cupped her daughter's cheek. "God is gut, my dear. It is because of Him we have strength to do what has to be done." She shifted her eyes to Mark. "Is this not so, Major Scott?"

A sheepish expression settled on his features. "I'm beginning to understand after more than twenty-five years. If you can't lick 'em, you might as well join 'em." He grinned.

"You mean you still have not given your life to Christ?" A look of horror crossed Zofia's face. "Has life not shown you that Christ is the only way to peace and contentment? He alone will give you the strength to face each day."

He nodded. "As you and everyone else has told me. Except Matt." He turned his eyes to meet his son's. "It's time to stop thinking about it and turn to Christ. How about it, son?"

Matt eyed Skylar. "Somebody's been talking to me about it too. She told me she's been praying for me. Maybe it's time."

"She's not the only one, my friend," Gabe piped in.

"I know." Matt grinned at his friend. "You've been praying for me since we met in Nam."

"There is no time like the present." Zofia lifted a hand to Freida who helped her up. Leaning against her daughter she closed her eyes and began to pray. "Our Abba Father in heaven, there are two souls here this night who need You more than anything. If they do not accept Christ, they will spend eternity apart from you in eternal damnation. Oh, Father, they have come to the realization that they need You. Help them to put pride aside and ask forgiveness from all their sins and turn their lives completely over to You. In Your precious Son Jesus' name, I pray, Amen."

Zofia opened her eyes and looked at Mark and Matt. "It is up to you now. It is as simple as asking forgiveness for your sins and asking Christ to live in you. He has done all the work for you, but you already know that, do you not?"

Mark chuckled. "I've been told several times."

"Me too." A sheepish expression appeared on Matt's face.

"So, what do you wait for? Everyone here will rejoice with you as will the angels in heaven when you come to know Christ as your Savior." Zofia lifted her arms as if directing a choir.

Mark knelt to a knee and prayed. "Father God, I'm a sinner, and I've done nothing but put this off far too long. You've been patient with me for decades, but time is up. I ask forgiveness for my sins, and I want Christ to take my life now. I haven't done the best with it up to this point. You can take it from here. Forgive me, Lord."

Silence followed for several moments before Matt dropped to his knees beside Kate, her hand in his. "Lord, God. Forgive me for all my sins. Please take me and be my Lord and Savior. Use my life however you want to. But if it's okay, I'd like to still work with horses. Amen."

A round of soft chuckles skittered around the room as Mark and Matt retook their seats. Zofia laughed. "I believe the Lord will allow you to continue working with the horses if that's your heart's desire, Mathias. There is nothing wrong with that."

Matt swiped a hand across his forehead. "Whew.

Thank goodness. I love working with horses."

As the room settled down after shoulder claps and hugs for the two men who had just made the most important spiritual decision they could ever make, Zofia cleared her throat as she retook her seat. "I have something else to tell you and something to show you."

All eyes trained on the elderly woman.

"There is something else you do not know about your mother. During the war if this information were to leak out, her life would have been worth nothing." Zofia stared at her fingers in her lap.

"What is it, Zofia?" Kate asked. "There's been so much about Mother I didn't know. This can't be anything worse."

"No, child. It isn't worse. But I suppose it can affect you if you let it. Elena chose not to let it affect her." Zofia paused for a moment. "Your mother was born in Russia to Jewish parents, and her village was destroyed during the Russian pogroms in 1917 when she was a mere baby. Cossacks killed her parents when they destroyed the village. Neighbors rescued your mother—a couple who'd escaped the pogrom. They traveled to Czechoslovakia where eventually Elena was adopted by your grandparents. When they immigrated to the US, she, of course, went with them."

Kate smiled softly, shaking her head. "The news you shared isn't bad news. There's so much about Mother I never knew. Chalk it up to one more thing. I'm not at all upset to find she was Jewish. My grandparents raised her to know Christ as her Savior."

Mark leaned forward and said, "You have to understand, Kate. Your mother had hidden so much during the war that she never stopped hiding it. When she returned to the US, she put all that behind her."

"I can't blame her," Matt shrugged. "If the Nazis ever caught wind of the truth, she would've been sent to a concentration camp and likely exterminated."

"With her light brown hair and brown eyes, I'm surprised she wasn't anyway," Kate suggested.

"Do not think that all Nazis had blond hair, my dear." Zofia smiled. "Hitler himself had brown hair even if his eyes were blue. It was your mother's voice and the fact Jäger was attracted to it and her beauty that prevented harm from coming to Elena. Jäger did exactly what the US allies intended him to do." She turned toward her daughter. "Freida? Will you bring the envelope please?"

Kate's eyes darted to the rest of the group as Freida left the room. Did they feel the sudden tension as much as she did? From their expressions she guessed so. Envelope? How many more secrets of Mother's past were there to absorb? Kate still reeled from what she'd already learned.

Freida returned several moments later and handed Zofia a worn yellow manila envelope. Zofia accepted it and carefully removed some documents. "Elena gave this to me a few days before she escaped. She had stolen it from her husband, your father. Elena wanted it for you two, Katarina and Mathias. She had faith that the Third Reich would fall at the hands of the allies and that Major Jäger would be imprisoned for his terrible deeds. As a result, she would have stayed and continued to gather information to pass on to the US if we had not intervened. She only had moments to make the snap decision to leave. She'd left this with me earlier in case something should happen to her."

"What is it?" Matt asked.

"It is a deed to Schloss Jäger near Salzburg, Austria. She wanted something as insurance for your future. Your father had no relatives. There were no siblings and his parents had passed. As such, there was no one to stake a claim of the property. Elena had researched all this before taking the deed." Zofia removed a key from the envelope. "This is a key to the schloss, but according to the paperwork in this envelope, Major Jäger had arranged to always have caretakers on the property. I am unsure if that is still the case, however. There is no guarantee as to the condition of the property twenty-five years after the war. It is possible there could be damage from the war itself, or perhaps squatters have taken it over. Who knows?" "What's a...what did you call it? A schloss?" Matt asked.

Zofia grinned. "A schloss is German for a chateau or a...castle."

Matt's eyes widened. "A castle? Mother left us a...castle?"

Zofia slipped the deed and the key back inside the envelope. "Indeed. It is yours, my dear ones. The schloss belongs to you. There is a map in the envelope to guide you to its location."

Amazed at the turn of events, Kate accepted the envelope and handed it to Matt. "Why don't you hang onto it until we follow the map to check it out." She turned to Mark. "I assume that'll be our next stop."

He nodded, a crooked grin lighting his face.

"Did you know about this?" She lifted a questioning brow.

He shrugged, a smirk settling on his face.

"Of course, you did. You knew about all of it." Kate released a heavy sigh, and rolled her eyes at him. Sobering, she turned back to Zofia. "What happened to Major Jäger after the war?" She couldn't bring herself to call him her father. Not with him being the kind of man he was. She'd have to pray about that long and hard.

Zofia stared into the distance, as if she were seeing into the past. "When the allies marched on Munich and freed the prisoners at Dachau, Major Jäger was caught and imprisoned, but he escaped along with other soldiers. I heard he'd made his way to Argentina where so many Nazi officers fled. You know the rumor mill. It's not always to be trusted. I also heard he was killed attempting to escape.

We do not know what happened to him. I struggle in my desire to see him get what he deserves. But do we not all deserve justice? We are all sinners. Christ died for Major Jäger the same as He died for us. He needs forgiveness the same as we all do. I hope somewhere along the way He found it."

Kate's heart tugged at Zofia's words. *Yes, Lord.*

"You know, what Mom did was wrong when she stole the deed." Matt held up the envelope. "Don't you think so?"

Zofia shrugged. "At the time, she was a desperate woman attempting to provide for her children's future. Much time has passed since the war. It was your father's property, and when he became a war criminal, it became hers legally. Now it is rightfully yours. There may be nothing there worth keeping, but you must go and find out for yourselves."

"Agreed." Mark stood. "We'll go check it out. Thank you for explaining everything, Zofia. You were the only one who could."

"Yes." She held her hands out to Kate and Matt who stood and placed their hands within hers. "Dear ones, whatever you do with the property, carry on your mother's legacy. She was a special woman. Live for the Lord and trust Him always."

Kate's heart lifted. No matter how terrible some of the news she'd learned had been, the Lord was with her, and her brother had accepted Christ as his savior. What an emotional visit it had been. *Lord, You reign supreme no matter what craziness comes into our lives. Thank You. I couldn't do this without You.*

Chapter Fourteen

"Did you notice the green VW sitting down the street from Zofia's house this evening?" Gabe asked Mark as they strolled into the hotel after their visit to the elderly woman.

"I did." Mark crammed his hands into his jean pockets. "You know, Gabe, I've never been able to turn off the surveillance part of me. I trained to keep my head on a swivel, and I still do. It's something that will never change."

Gabe clapped him on the shoulder. "That's not a bad thing, is it?"

Mark shrugged. "Not unless you count being on edge all the time."

"Well, there is that."

"I suppose that's why I love the wide-open spaces of Wyoming and living out in the middle of nowhere." Mark elbowed his partner as they followed the others toward the elevators.

"I get what you're saying. What are we going to do about the green VW?"

"Not a thing, except stay vigilant and wait. I'm praying that he'll leave Kate alone."

Out of the corner of his eye, Gabe saw a man in a black leather jacket approach the rest of their group as they stood by the elevators. He sidled up beside Kate, suddenly grabbed her purse, then turned to run away. Matt kicked out a foot just in time and tripped him.

The man went down and hit the marble floor hard. "Hmph." His chin hit the floor.

"I think you spoke too soon." Gabe called over his shoulder to Mark as he rushed over when the man bolted to his feet. "Oh, no you don't. Where do you think you're going?" Gabe shoved the guy back to the floor with his foot and yanked Kate's purse from his grasp. "That doesn't belong to you."

"That's mine." Kate accepted it from Gabe and slid it back onto her shoulder, holding it tightly between both hands. "We should call the police."

"*Nein, nein.*" The guy protested. "I made a simple mistake. Please allow me to stand."

As Gabe and Matt helped him up but held onto his arms, he begged, "Please do not call the Polizei. I mistook the lady's purse. Truly. I thought it was my girlfriend's. I'm terribly sorry. My mistake."

"Yeah, I don't believe that." Matt flashed him a skeptical eye. "Not for a minute."

The hotel manager hurried over, wringing his hands. "*Was ist das*? What is this? What has happened?"

Mark explained what had happened. "You should call the police and let them handle this."

"But of course. I will be happy to call them right away. However, can we all move into my office out of the view of other hotel guests? I'm sure you'll understand my request." The manager wrung his hands as he guided them toward his office. He made the call and within minutes the city Polizei responded to deal with the erstwhile purse-snatcher.

As the Polizei hauled him away, Gabe turned to Mark. "Do you think he drives a green VW?"

With a tilt of his head and a shrug, Mark watched as the man was shoved into the back of the Polizei vehicle. "Don't have a clue, but if we don't see it around for a while, I guess we'll know."

Gabe caught up with Kate as she headed toward her room. "Hey, are you okay?"

She turned and offered him a tired smile. "I suppose so. This evening was a bit overwhelming what with all the new information Zofia unloaded on us." Her fingers tightened on her purse shoulder strap. "Then, the purse-snatcher...." She shook her head. "I can't figure out if he's the same guy from that first night in Frankfurt, and if he is, why would he try again here in the hotel in Munich? What does he think I'm carrying?"

Gabe tugged her close and wrapped his arms around her, tucking her head beneath his chin. "All I know is it's been a rough time for you and Matt the last few days but maybe rougher for you because you knew your mother. Matt has never met her, so it's a little less personal for him. His mother was a rancher's wife. You're discovering a side of your mother you never knew about. It's been tough."

Kate nodded against Gabe's chest. "I'm trying to soak all this in. Mother did what she had to do in order to help win the war. I see it and understand it, but it's hard to accept who my father was. All this time I thought my father was an American soldier only to find he was an evil man who would've destroyed Matt and me without a second thought. I'm glad she escaped and became the mother I knew."

"Hold onto that, sweetheart, and remember her that way. You can be proud of the mother she was before you knew her." Gabe stroked Kate's shoulder without thinking then caught himself. Had she noticed his touch? Comforting her came so easily to him. Would there come a time when he would be free to share his feelings with her, or would the distance in their lives play against them.

The next morning at breakfast Mark announced they would be taking a road trip.

"A road trip?" Kate laid her napkin in her lap. "To Austria?"

"You got it." He grinned and held up the map Zofia had given Kate and Matt. "We're heading to Austria."

"To the location of the schloss, right?" Gabe loaded his fork with eggs and bacon.

"Yep. Near Salzburg just as Zofia told us. Matt and I pulled out the map last night and took a gander. It's only an hour and twenty-two minutes by car. I've already talked with Mr. Gustafson, and he's rarin' to go." Mark slapped the folded map across his palm.

"When do we start?" Skylar set down her fork and leaned back in her chair. "How long are we staying?"

"Good questions." Mark laid the map beside his plate and took a drink of his coffee. "We're leaving in the morning and will stay as long as necessary. Since we have no idea the condition of the place or anything about it, we're staying at the nearest B&B. Since there aren't any big hotels in that area, we'll stay at the next best place."

"A B&B sounds cozy." Kate nibbled her toast.

"I think you'll like it." Mark sipped his coffee and wiped his lips with his napkin. "Pack your things and be ready to go first thing in the morning. We'll head on down to Austria. Also, make sure you have your passports handy."

The B&B stood on the side of a rolling hill covered in a light layer of snow. The edifice was typical of Austrian alpine homes. Two balconies, painted white and rustic wood walls with green-shuttered windows gracing both balcony levels. Hardy flowers already bloomed in the flower boxes along the balconies.

The limo parked in the small lot in front, and the group climbed out. As Mr. Gustafson removed the luggage, Gabe, with the rest of the group, went inside to find an immaculate interior with spotless white walls and oak woodwork. Deep red velvet chairs and a red plaid couch clustered around a fireplace where a warm-and-inviting, crackling fire danced. A bell above the door jingled as they entered, and a lady in a green wool sweater and black skirt came in to greet them.

"Willkommen. My goodness, there are a lot of you. Do you have a reservation?" Her eyes widened.

"Yes, ma'am, we do." Mark stepped forward and checked them in.

Gabe wandered over to where Kate stood before the fireplace warming her hands. "This seems like a nice place."

Kate's eyes met his briefly before taking in the whole lobby. "It does. If our rooms are as cozy as this, I'm sure we'll feel almost at home." Although she avoided looking at him, he could see the rim of red around her eyes and a slight tremble of her chin.

"Are you all right?" He touched her elbow.

Gazing into the fire once again, she nodded. "Perhaps I'm feeling a little homesick. I miss my family. Learning all these things about my mother reminds me that my great-aunts and my great-uncle knew most of this about her, yet they weren't allowed to tell me. It took the death of my grandmother to set all of this in motion."

Gabe wanted nothing more than to pull Kate into his arms and comfort her. The sadness she exuded ripped at his heart. "This will all be over before long, and you'll head home. They'll be waiting for you, and you'll have lots to share with them."

Kate finally turned to meet his eyes. "You're right. Somehow this whole thing about the schloss seems more like a technicality than anything else, but we have to deal with it."

"Of course. If a schloss had been left to me, I'd sure want to check it out." Gabe tossed her a gentle grin. "It might be in better shape than Zofia or Mark are suggesting. You never know."

Kate shrugged. "I suppose."

Gabe elbowed her gently. "Just keep trusting. The Lord has a plan. Even about the schloss."

"You're sort of wise about things, aren't you?"

Her smile caused Gabe's breath to hitch. He swallowed. "I don't know about that, but I'll take that as a compliment."

"Come on, everybody. Here are the keys to your rooms," Mark's voice interrupted their conversation.

Gabe stepped back and laid a hand at the back of Kate's waist, allowing her to precede him. The smile she aimed in his direction turned his world upside down. What he wouldn't do to have this woman by his side from now on, but could he have what he wanted? Could it work out for them? Would she even be interested? Gabe's heart suddenly felt heavy.

After a hearty lunch at a nearby restaurant that Mrs. Schmitz, the B&B proprietress, recommended, the group enjoyed a car tour of the region until they arrived at a set of large iron gates. Mr. Gustafson pulled the limo up to them and parked the limo but left the engine running.

"What's this place?" Matt asked, peering around.

The gates were closed and only a short bit of pavement was visible before a curve in the paved driveway prevented any further view. Light snow covered the heavy, unkempt scrubs that lined the pavement, and large cracks marred the driveway. Trees shaded the snow-covered yard past the shrubs.

"This is the entrance to Schloss Jäger." Mark shifted in his seat to view out the window.

Kate stared down the driveway as far as she could. It didn't look inviting, and from the shape of it, it hadn't in years. Her heart sank even further than the homesickness that had struck her earlier. She wished to take care of this technicality and go home. But what would it take to get this over with? Had Mother's good intentions saddled her and Matt with a huge lemon? And in a foreign country no less.

"Wow, if that driveway is any indication of the house, we're in trouble," Matt spoke what Kate was thinking. "Are we heading in now?"

"No, I'd rather go in early in the day." Mark knocked on the plexiglass divider between them and Mr. Gustafson. The driver moved the vehicle away from the gates and down the road. "We need to start fresh and see what's going on with the property. Think positive, kids. Maybe the house is in better shape."

Please let be it so, Lord. Kate stared out the window hoping to catch a glimpse of the house, but it must be set way back from the road. She identified nothing but rolling snow-covered lawns, trees and vegetation with nary a building in sight.

Turning her eyes to the surrounding countryside, Kate had to admit, it was breathtakingly beautiful here, especially with the snow cover. Crystal-clear streams met rushing rivers as the limo passed. The lovely, rolling hills met the tall snow-capped mountains that reached in angular peaks to the blue sky. Little villages dotted the landscape, and Austrian alpine homes dotted the countryside in various configurations. Pedestrians dressed for cold waved as they drove by.

Despite her homesickness, Kate was falling in love with the charm of the region. *You made a beautiful country here, Lord. I love it. Now help me to trust You with the next leg of this journey. Whatever this technicality is, it's in*

Your hands.

Eventually they returned to the B&B and headed inside to the warmth and charm of another home away from home. Mrs. Schmitz had arranged a smorgasbord that Mark had ordered for their evening meal. Since there were no other guests at present, she and her husband joined them.

Once back in his room, Gabe slipped on his jacket and stepped onto the balcony outside his room. Leaning his elbows on the wooden rail, he stared across the snowy valley. The sun had already dropped below the high mountains. Lights in homes across the scene lit up like fallen stars. What a beautiful place Austria was—at least the countryside they'd spent the afternoon driving through. He'd enjoyed the expression of wonder that crossed Kate's features as she'd taken in the sights. When they'd first stopped at the gates of Schloss Jäger, she'd looked almost discouraged, but a smile had settled where a frown had been.

Gabe wanted so much to make things right for Kate. Although he wanted to help her through her legal difficulties, he wanted to do more than ask questions as a lawyer. As much as he might want to approach Kate with his feelings for her, he didn't want to throw one more thing at her that might overwhelm her. At least not until all this was over. *Am I doing the right thing, Lord? Is waiting the right thing? My head says wait, but my heart says, tell her. What do I do?*

A sliding door opened behind him, and he turned to find Mark stepping out onto the balcony.

Mark closed the door behind him and paused beside him at the railing. "Well, have you told her how you feel?"

Gabe gave him a withering glance.

"Why not?" Mark leaned his arms along the rail.

"You're gonna miss out if you don't tell her. And don't give me that stuff and nonsense about now's not a good time because of everything I'm springing on her. You already tried that one on me. Have you seen her lately? She needs the support of a strong shoulder, preferably from someone who loves her deeply. We all love her, but not like you do." He shoved Gabe's elbow.

Gabe stared across the valley again only this time he didn't see the scenery in front of him. Kate's features settled before his mind's eye—a place where she rested often these days. He drew in a deep breath and released it slowly.

"What if she doesn't have the same idea I have about things? What if—"

"She's not in love with you? You won't know if you don't ask, son. Why sit and wonder when you can find out? You just might find she's in love with you too."

"Maybe."

"Yeah, you're gonna 'maybe' yourself right out of a good thing." Mark huffed, "Anyway, that's not why I came out here. I wanted to know if you noticed that green VW around anywhere we went today. I was looking for it but never located it."

Gabe straightened and rubbed his back, stretching his muscles as he did. "No, and I was watching for it, believe me."

"Yeah. Maybe the guy at the hotel was the green VW guy after all, and he's sitting in jail." Mark made a fist and lightly pounded the railing. "Sure hope that's the case. I don't want him reporting back to his boss."

Gabe eyed Mark. "Think he's secured someone else to follow us?"

Mark tilted his head and shrugged. "That, my friend, is the $64,000 question."

The door slid open behind them, and they turned to find Kate stepping out. With coat, toboggan hat and gloves on she appeared to be dressed to stay out in the cold for a while.

"Where are you heading?" Mark chuckled.

"Nowhere. I thought I'd step out here for a bit to enjoy the evening."

Kate's smile appeared forced, and Gabe's heart grew heavy at the sight of it, wishing he could help lighten her load.

"I'm heading back in." Mark waved her over. "My old bones don't allow me to stay out long in cold weather these days, but come keep Gabe company."

Gabe chuckled to himself. Mark worked on a ranch in Wyoming and even in cold weather, nothing stopped that man. Did Kate see through his excuse like Gabe did?

"Goodnight, y'all." Mark headed toward his door.

"Goodnight" Kate said.

"Sleep well." Gabe turned to Kate as she rested her arms along the balcony railing, her eyes scanning the valley scene.

"It's lovely here no matter when or where you look at it, isn't it?" A half-smile lifted her delectable lips.

"Yeah, it's breathtaking."

Gabe heard the huskiness in his voice and realized she must have heard it too. She turned to meet his eyes, a question in them as her smile faded. She must have recognized he'd been staring at her and not the scene before them.

Of its own volition, Gabe's hand lifted and his fingers grazed her cheek then slid down to her chin. His touch elicited a tiny gasp as her lips parted, and her tongue darted out to lick them before disappearing again. Gabe's heart hammered in his chest. His forefinger tipped her chin up as his gaze delved into hers.

Huskiness tightened his throat and he coughed to clear it. "There's something I've been wanting to ask your permission for—something I've wanted to do for a while now. I've wanted to kiss you more than you'll ever know." He lifted her hand and removed her glove, shoving it into his pocket. Unzipping his jacket, he placed her hand over his heart. Kate's eyes widened. "Can you feel that? That's what you do to me, Kate Cigler. Now, if you don't want me to kiss you, you'd better tell me now."

Gabe lowered his head slowly, waiting for Kate to stop him, but she didn't. Her eyes closed, and she lifted her face to him. A thrill tip-toed down Gabe's spine. She wanted his kiss. He touched his lips to hers, lightly at first. Oh, so amazing. Kate tasted...sweet, delectable. Just as he'd imagined. He increased the pressure on her soft lips. Gabe wanted more, but he dared not scare her away. He could tell she'd never been kissed before. This amazing woman had allowed him, Gabe Flanagan, to be the one to kiss her.

He lifted his lips and rested his forehead against hers. Kate's eyes remained closed and her breathing rapid. Her hand still rested against his chest. Did she feel his heart racing? Somehow in the middle of the kiss he'd drawn her close, his hand pressed against her back.

"Kate, sweetheart, can you feel what you do to me?" Gabe heard the huskiness in his voice and didn't care.

Kate's eyes slid open, and she moved her head back to stare at him but didn't pull away from his arms. "Yes, I feel it. I...I don't understand it, but I feel it."

Gabe's chuckle was low. "What do you mean you don't understand it?"

"I feel the racing of your heart beneath my hand, but I don't understand how I can make you feel that way."

Gabe's heart nearly sank. "Did I not make you feel something when I kissed you?"

It was hard to tell if Kate blushed in the darkness and cold, but her gaze skittered away. "Well, of course you did. I could hardly breathe, and my heart's about to pound out of my chest."

Heartened at her words, Gabe forged on. "Good. So,

you do feel something for me?"

Her gaze remained lowered as she nodded.

A finger below her chin, he lifted her face. "Lift those gorgeous eyes so I can see, sweetheart. There's nothing to be ashamed of. If you don't understand, I'll explain what you've done to me. You've made me fall in love with you. Almost since I laid eyes on you at the airport in Cleveland, you've held my heart in your hands. I can't explain how someone can fall in love in such short a time, but I have. Of course, I can't answer for you, but there you have it plain and simple. I've laid my heart out for you to do with as you will." Gabe gathered Kate's hand from his chest and lifted it to place a kiss on her palm.

Another tiny gasp escaped, but she shook her head.

Gabe prepared himself for the worst as she stared into his eyes. Instead of joy as he'd hoped to see, sadness filled them. In the light from the moon that had risen above the high-peaked mountains, tears slipped down Kate's cheeks, and Gabe's heart sank.

"I don't see how we could ever make it work, Gabe." She sniffed. "I live in Ohio and run a bakery. My elderly loved ones depend on me for their livelihood. I can't turn my back on them or the business my grandmother left me. My loved ones won't be able to work much longer." Kate sniffed again as tears continued down her cheeks. "You live in Wyoming where you have responsibilities with the ranch. How can these two lives ever mesh?"

Before he could respond, Kate slipped from his arms and strode across the balcony to enter her door. As it closed behind her, Gabe stared across the darkened valley. How could one go from elevated joy to crashing misery within minutes? He hadn't even learned if Kate loved him or not. She simply stated it wouldn't work and left him. Maybe she was right. When one looked at the variables of the situation, it did appear quite hopeless. Variables or not, his heart felt as if it would break into pieces.

A sliding glass door opened, and Mark stepped out. He approached and leaned against the railing. "You gonna let that stop you?"

Gabe turned to stare at him. "Were you listening?"

"Nah. Thin walls."

"Somehow here in Austria, I doubt that." Gabe huffed.

"Well, you gonna let that stop you? I've never known you to let a little problem keep you from getting what you want. Just saying." Mark side-eyed him.

"Like how? It seems hopeless."

"Well, I'm sure I don't know, but if it were me, and I was in love with a young lady, I wouldn't let anything get in the way of having her in my life. Again, just saying." Mark headed back toward his room but stopped. "Think on it. And while you're at it, you might want to pray about it too." He winked at Gabe and headed inside.

Gabe returned his gaze to the night scenery he wasn't actually seeing and leaned against the railing, cupping his cold hands together. Blowing warm breath into them, he prayed. *Well, Lord, I've been told by Kate that things won't work out, but You're a mighty big God. You work on a different level than we do. Your plans are not our plans. You know how much I love Kate, and I suspect she loves me, although she didn't say so. The response of her kiss...well, it.... You know better than I. Lord, she's allowing circumstances to get in the way. I need You to move a mountain or two for me and work these things out so we can be together. How? I have no idea, but guide me, Lord. Show me the way.*

Chapter Fifteen

"We're back." Kate said as the limo stopped at
the iron gates of Schloss Jäger the next morning. She'd had
a rough night sleeping after Gabe's declaration of love and
his amazing kiss. Even now her heart quickened at the
thought. She'd felt like a heel as she walked away after
throwing cold water on his declaration, but she'd been
raised to be practical and face facts. Kate saw no way clear
of their circumstances. It broke her heart that she'd hurt
Gabe in the process. Her heart broke too. As she'd stepped
back into her room last night, the tears had flowed. How
much she loved that man. How was it even possible their
two hearts had entwined in such a short time? Kate didn't
understand it, but she knew it to be a fact; still, she didn't
see a way to make things work.

As the others discussed the best way to enter the
property, Kate's eyes were drawn to Gabe who had been
quiet all morning. As their eyes met, he winked and smiled
at her. She returned his smile then glanced away.

"All right, all right. Hang on a minute." Mark shoved
the car door open. "I'll check the gate to see if there's a
way in."

They all watched as he approached the entrance. Mark
searched for a way to open the gates. After a few minutes,
he fiddled around the center of the gates and turned with a
triumphant grin, flashing a thumbs-up. After swinging them

open, he waved the limo through before closing the gates behind it. Hurrying back to the vehicle, he climbed in. An expression of wonder crossed Matt's face. "How'd you do that?"

"Simple." Mark settled onto his seat. "A chain held the gate closed, but it was only fastened with a clip, not a lock. Interesting, if you ask me. The hinges moved smoothly, as if they were well-oiled."

As the limo drove slowly along the driveway, Gabe asked, "Don't you think it's interesting that there's no snow on the driveway? It's almost as if it's been plowed."

"Yeah, I thought about that by the entrance." Mark peered out the window. "I'm beginning to wonder if there's somebody taking care of this place after all."

"What about the disrepair of the driveway and the unkempt vegetation?" Skylar asked.

"Well, I'm sure upkeep isn't cheap even if someone is taking care of it. I'd bet some things aren't a priority."

"Can you imagine looking after this place all these years?" Kate eyed the landscape as it passed by the window.

"It's been a long time. We still don't know anything yet," Mark reminded her. "We have no clue what happened to your father."

Her father. Kate had no desire to be reminded of…that man. A flash of the photo of him and her mother came to mind. She closed her eyes for a moment and reminded herself that Christ died for the sins of the world, including Gunther Jäger. Sin was sin. Whether it was a lie or the murder of one or thousands. In God's eyes all sins were the same. Her sins equaled the sins of a Nazi officer, and she had no business looking down her nose at him. *Forgive me, Lord. I have no knowledge if he's dead or alive or if he ever came to know You or not. Only You know these things. All I know is he was my father. Forgive me for judging him. That's Your place, not mine.*

"There it is. Wow! It's fantastic."

Kate's eyes snapped open at Matt's words, and she searched out the window for a glimpse of the schloss. The limo drove around a curve in the driveway, and Kate caught her breath. Built of golden stone blocks, the schloss's two-story entrance had double arches on the lower level and a row of smaller arches on the second level, indicating a covered walkway between the two wings on either side of the entrance. Bits of red peeked from beneath the snow on the roof indicating its color. Smaller stones and a whole section of timber and plaster-work made up the front wall of the right wing while paned windows and peaked gables allowed light in. The snow-covered roof on the wing showed spots of red. To the far back corner of the wing and the entrance, a tall square tower stood above the rest of the schloss, its red roof covered with snow. The left wing incorporated golden stone blocks and the smaller stones throughout the front walls. More paned windows lined the wall, and an arched doorway stood on the lower level. The driveway ended at the entrance to the schloss, and beside it stood an ancient well covered by a tall, peaked roof held up by four sturdy square posts. Snow covered the lawn and vegetation.

"How breathtaking." Kate's voice held a note of awe. "The outside looks well-kept, but it's hard to tell anything about the roof with snow on it."

"Let's go see if anyone's home." Mark opened the door and stepped out. "Matt, make sure you have the key."

Matt followed him out. "It's in my pocket."

As the group approached the entrance, there were no outward signs that anyone was here. The place was so big, it was hard to tell. A side road off the main driveway they'd passed could have led to a back entrance. Perhaps there was a garage and other outbuildings back there. A solid oak door awaited behind the double-arched entryway. Worn paved stones beneath their feet would likely bespeak of centuries of guests who had entered here. Just how old was this schloss? It had certainly stood the test of time. It must have weathered the onslaught of the war and come through with little or no damage if Major Jäger hadn't returned to make repairs. Or had caretakers done that? Had the war even touched this part of Austria?

Mark lifted the door knocker and banged it on the iron plate beneath it. If there was someone here, surely, they'd hear that. Glancing around at the size of the building once again, Kate wasn't so sure. Would they hear if they were in a distant wing? Mark knocked a second and third time.

"It doesn't appear anyone's here." Mark tried the door handle before turning to the others. "Locked. Why don't you hand me that key, Matt."

As Matt dug the key from his jeans pocket, a sound from the other side of the door met Kate's ears. The door swung wide to reveal a man who looked to be in his mid to late sixties, dressed in his shirt sleeves and slacks, his hair salt and pepper.

"Guten Morgen. *Kann ich Ihnen helfen?*" His eyes roamed over the group, curiosity in their depths.

Mark stepped forward. "My German is a bit rusty. Do you speak English?"

"Ja." The man gave a single nod. "May I help you?"

"Indeed, you can." Mark waved a hand indicating Kate and Matt. "These are the children of Maj. Gunther and Elena Jäger. They have the deed to the schloss left to them by their mother, Elena."

Shock filled the man's eyes as he stared at the twins before they locked on Kate. A gentler expression replaced the shock as a smile lifted his lips. "Ach, *Fräulein*. You look like your mother. I remember *Frau* Jäger well. She was the kindest lady I ever met." Blinking rapidly, his features softened further. "Frau Jäger never failed to show kindness to all the household staff. We missed her after she…went away. It saddened us that we never knew what happened to her."

Kate smiled at him. "Thank you for your gracious words. Mother was kind to everyone she met."

The man stepped back opening the door further. "Please come in. My name is Friedrich Kraus. My wife and I have been the caretakers of Schloss Jäger since before the war." He closed the door behind the group and held his hand out toward the main house. "Please follow me."

Kate marveled at the beautiful solid-oak woodwork that graced the walls of the entryway and the arched doorway leading into the house. Paintings of what looked like ancestors hung on the walls. A suit of shiny armor stood beside an archway. Kate tried to imagine some ancestor wearing that into battle. Suddenly it struck her. It would've been *her* ancestor wearing that.

Passing through the archway, they followed Friedrich down a short dark corridor and into what appeared to be a large living room. Friedrich indicated they should make themselves comfortable while he fetched refreshments. Kate took a seat on a cushioned settee that lacked the cushion. Gabe lowered himself next to her.

"Not the most comfortable seat in the house, is it?" he whispered.

"I'm not sure. The rest of the seats could be just as bad, if not worse." Kate couldn't prevent the tiny giggle that escaped. She observed the huge marble fireplace. "You can tell they weren't expecting guests. It's rather chilly in here."

She huffed out a breath, and a wisp of condensation formed in front of her face. "You know it's cold when that happens."

Friedrich re-entered the room carrying two log carriers. "This room is where formal guests were welcomed. I shall start a fire and make it more comfortable for you. We live in the rear of the schloss and rarely light the fires in the rooms up here. However, we keep everything in running order." He knelt beside the fireplace and opened the flue. "My wife, Maria, is preparing a warm beverage for you. She will bring it out shortly."

"That will be nice, thank you." Kate leaned forward. "Is it just you and your wife that live here?"

Friedrich laid kindling on the andirons before adding small logs above that. He struck a long match and lit the kindling. "No, our son and his wife also live here. We all work to keep up the schloss. A trust was put in place before Major Jäger went to war. Perhaps you are aware his family was quite wealthy. It has kept the schloss running all these years." He spun on his knee and faced the group. "I must give credit to my wife who keeps the finances. As a penny pincher, my Maria has stretched the funds as far as she's been able. You may have noticed the driveway isn't in the best shape. We chose not to repair it as often as, say, the roof or other more important parts of the schloss."

"I can see how that would be a wise choice." Mark nodded. "Was the schloss damaged during the war?"

Friedrich added a few larger logs to the flames. "Nein. We were most fortunate."

A lady in her sixties dressed in a wool sweater and skirt strode into the salon carrying a tray with steaming mugs. Her hair was more salt than pepper, but a welcoming smile lit her face.

Friedrich climbed to his feet. "Ah, this is my wife, Maria. Here, *mein liebchen*, let me take that tray from you." He set it on the polished surface of the coffee table standing in front of the couch where Matt and Skylar sat. Maria passed out the steaming mugs of hot cocoa.

"You are Frau Jäger's son, are you not?" Maria held a mug out to Matt.

"Yes, ma'am." He took the mug from her.

Maria straightened and nodded. "Ach, you have her eyes, and the color of your hair is hers. You are a handsome young man." Her eyes moved between Skylar and Matt.

"And this your intended young lady? She's quite beautiful."

"Oh...oh, no," Skylar stammered.

Matt lifted a brow at Skylar, a question in his slanted glance. "Well, not yet." He laid an arm along the back of the couch behind her, and took a drink of his hot beverage.

Skylar's head whipped around to stare at him.

He merely grinned and shrugged.

Maria's brows lifted high, a smile tugging at her mouth between her rosy cheeks. She crossed over to hand cocoa to Kate. "And you. You look like your mother, Fräulein. My Friedrich told me he said the same to you, and it's true. How uncanny. Frau Jäger was so kind."

Kate accepted the cocoa. "Thank you. I've enjoyed meeting people who knew Mother during her time in Germany and Austria."

Maria handed Gabe and Mark cocoa before retreating to the back of the house.

Friedrich added more logs to the fire. The warmth spread to where Kate sat, and she began to relax. The delicious taste and warmth of the cocoa helped, and the solicitous care of Friedrich and Maria made her feel welcome in this huge place. Perhaps this visit would go better than she'd hoped.

"I'll return in a few minutes to answer any questions you have." Friedrich turned back to them. "Warm yourselves. We'll talk shortly." He left the room.

Silence reigned as the group soaked in the warmth from the fire and enjoyed their warm beverages. Kate took the time to observe the salon. The walls were painted deep green and a few ancestral paintings hung amongst beautiful landscapes. There were no windows in this room. Several glass-front bookcases held old books and porcelainware. Light sconces lit the edges of the room between the paintings, the lights most likely upgraded to electric. Rugs covered the hardwood floors, and a bear skin rug lay in front of the fireplace.

A large portrait of some military man hung over the fireplace, but he didn't appear to be from the twentieth century, nor did he wear a Nazi uniform. He didn't look like the man in the photo of her father.

"I wonder who he is?" Gabe's low voice so close to her ear nearly made her jump.

Kate turned to meet his eyes. Had he read her thoughts? "We can assume he's not dear ole' dad."

"He's not, I assure you," Mark said from across the seating group. "I'd know him anywhere."

"I thought you said you never met him," Kate pinned him with a stare.

Mark's brow lowered. "I didn't. Doesn't mean I didn't know who he was."

Friedrich returned and stood by the fire, stirring the logs and adding a couple more. With the fire blazing, he stepped toward the group. "Now, I'll be happy to answer any questions that I can. I have been here since before the war. As I didn't serve in the military, I remained to care for the property. Major Jäger assigned me to do so, so I was given a waiver. To be honest with you, I was relieved to receive it. I think you will understand why."

"You didn't want to fight for a cause you didn't believe in." Gabe set his mug on the table beside the settee.

Friedrich bowed his head slightly. "You do understand. Although Austria followed the cause of the Third Reich, there were those of us who did not agree."

"We understand that." Mark lifted a hand in acknowledgment. "Hitler steamrolled over Europe in an attempt to bend every country to his will. Many people did what they had to do to stay alive. Others stood up for what they believed and paid the price. You were fortunate you had that waiver."

"Friedrich, whatever happened to Major Jäger? Did you ever hear from him after the war?" Kate was unsure if she wanted to know the answer to her question, but curiosity won out.

"Yes, Friedrich, do tell them." An unfamiliar accented voice spoke from the doorway. "Tell them you haven't heard from me since after the war because I had to go into hiding. But you did not know that, did you, Friedrich?"

Kate caught sight of Friedrich's blanched face as he stared at the entrance to the room. He seemed to shrink into himself. Mark jumped to his feet as did Gabe, who whipped around to face the entrance. Kate twisted to see who stood in the doorway. A white-haired man in a black leather jacket and black slacks stood with a gun trained on them.

He strode into the room and over by the fireplace. With the gun he motioned for Friedrich to move. "Join them if you will, Friedrich. I see you've been a dutiful caretaker and taken good care of my schloss all these years."

His eyes roamed over the group before they settled on Kate. His voice softened as he spoke again. "Ach, my darling Elena. You've returned to me." A brow lifted as he shook his head. "I don't know how you've defeated time to continue to look so young and beautiful. It's quite amazing, mein liebchen. Time has stood still for you, even if you betrayed me."

"Elena's dead, Jäger." This came from Mark. "That's your daughter, Katarina. And this is your son, Mathias. Elena escaped to save not only her own life. She had twins and took them where you could never find them."

Jäger's nostrils flared and his lips curled as his eyes raked Kate's features before moving to Matt's. "She knew, did she not? Elena knew I would hand them over to Dr. Joseph Mengele at Auschwitz-Birkenau." A less than humorous chuckle escaped him. "He enjoyed working with twins, our Dr. Mengele. Unfortunate for them, many did not survive."

Kate gave him a pathetic stare. "You would've handed your own children over to him? Don't you think that's evil?"

"My dear daughter, I would have sacrificed everything for the Third Reich." The sneering smile he sent in her direction turned Kate's stomach. "So, Elena gave me children after all. Children to carry on the Jäger name."

"I will never take your name." Kate breathed the vow. "Why do you think Mother sent us away other than to save our lives? She didn't want us to have anything to do with you."

Jäger waved the handgun carelessly. "Perhaps. I wouldn't have cared for you then, and I care nothing for you now that I know of your existence. Since we've established our family connections, perhaps we can move on and straighten out our family home."

"Aren't you even curious as to why Mother isn't here?" Kate's brows pinched above her nose as a sickening suspicion swirled in her mid-section. "You *were* expecting her, weren't you? You thought I was she."

Jäger sniffed, his sneer firmly in place. "I care not. She betrayed me long ago. Other than the desire to see her beautiful face one more time, it does not matter."

"It matters to me." Kate's suspicions were confirmed. This man didn't care a flip what had happened to Mother. Anger filled Kate at the man's arrogance and lack of caring. "Elena Cigler was an amazing woman to so many people, and she left this earth far too soon. You may not care, but I do. I lost her to leukemia when I was eighteen. Although I didn't have a father to care for me or comfort me, I did have other loved ones who did. They filled that empty place that you left vacant because of Mother's fear that you would dispose of us." Kate shook her head. "I don't understand how someone can give themselves completely to such an evil ideology. And even though it's been removed, you have no remorse for your actions. How utterly sickening."

The veneer of Jäger's sneer weakened. "There was a

time when I cared for Elena in a small way. She was so beautiful and had the voice of an angel." His chin lowered as his face hardened. "Then her betrayal. So, Elena is dead. I still care not. She received what she deserved as far as I am concerned. Now, may we continue with my property concerns?"

An arm wrapped around Kate's shoulders as she was about to speak. "Let it go, sweetheart. He's too far gone to convince him otherwise." Gabe's whisper in her ear halted Kate from further words. He was right. This man had been too long entrenched in his evil ways for her to convince him otherwise. It would take the Lord changing his heart to do any good.

Jäger waved his handgun in a circle. "Now, where was I? Ah, yes. Before I left Germany for Argentina where I have lived for the last twenty-five years, I went to retrieve the deed of my schloss. To my surprise it no longer occupied the secure place where I'd left it." Jäger's brows lowered. "My darling Elena had stolen the deed. I did not know this until after she departed Germany. A few days before she escaped, I began to suspect her activities as a spy. That last night she sang at the National Theater, we were due at a party with other high-ranking Nazi officials. She wanted to return home to pick up a gift that she'd forgotten for one of their wives. However, she did not go home. Instead, I followed her to the home of a baker. I searched the place but found nothing. A few days later, I brought the baker in for questioning and had her beaten. She still told me nothing, so I released her. Elena had disappeared. I never found her."

"You didn't because I helped her escape." Mark crossed his arms over his chest. "Not only her but the twins. Elena only married you to spy on the Nazis. D-Day's success was due in part to Elena's 'efforts,', as well as other allied victories. Her spying provided them with valuable information they needed to win the war."

Jäger's chin rose. "Perhaps. Do not fool yourself into thinking I loved Elena. She was merely a tool—a beautiful woman who looked wonderful on my arm."

His icy eyes met Kate's, and bile rose in her throat. She swallowed and attempted to control the nausea that stirred in her midsection. "That may be so, Major, but Mother was the bravest woman I ever knew." Kate tipped her chin high. "You were merely a proud man boasting a beautiful woman on your arm, but she had a mission to accomplish for the allies that helped bring the Third Reich down. I've seen the picture of her standing by your side. No doubt she had no love for you either."

"You have a smart mouth, daughter." His eyes narrowed as he sneered.

"No. I'm simply stating the truth. And here's another bit of truth for your information. You were married to a Jew. Were you aware of that?"

His eyes flamed. "You lie. Elena could *not* have been a Jew. I could smell a Jew from a mile away."

"Then there was something wrong with your sniffer, Jäger. Elena was indeed a Jew," Mark piped in.

Jäger glared at him.

"That makes your children half-Jews." A tiny smile curled Kate's lips, her tone holding a note of triumph. "And while I'm on a roll, let me say this. I have no idea what all you did during the war, but I'm quite aware of your job at Dachau. I hope you feel remorse for the many people you had executed. One day you'll stand before God, just like the rest of us, and answer for the sins you've committed. It doesn't matter what we think of as the severity of our sins. It matters that we committed them. We must all face God one day. If you haven't put your faith in Christ Jesus who died on the cross for your sins, He'll say, 'I'm sorry, I never knew you.' You'll be cast into everlasting death, and *you*'ll pay for your sins."

His sneer grew. "As if I believed in God. I make my

own way in this world."

Kate shook her head. "I feel sorry for you. Simply because you don't believe doesn't make it less true."

"You needn't feel sorry for me. Now, I know one of you has the deed to my schloss. Hand it over."

"I don't think so, Jäger. You aren't going to need it where you're going."

Jäger lifted the gun higher. "Is that so? And just where do you think I'm going? I am the one holding the gun, Mein Herr."

A confident smile lifted the corners of Mark's mouth as he lifted his voice. "Come on in, Captain."

The sound of many footsteps preceded the appearance of a number of Austrian Armed Forces soldiers who filed into the room—all pointing rifles at Jäger. Where in the world had they come from? And how had Mark known they were there? What had he...? How had he...? When—?

An Army captain stepped forward, his own handgun pointed at the former Nazi officer. "Drop the gun, Major Jäger. There's no escaping this alive."

The color drained from Jäger's face. He bent slowly, lowered his gun to the floor, straightened back to standing, and held his hands in the air. His eyes darted wildly from one soldier to another. Two of them shouldered their rifles and approached to handcuff Jäger's hands behind his back.

The Army captain stepped in front of him as they handcuffed him. "You, Maj. Gunther Jäger, are under arrest for crimes against peace, crimes against humanity, war crimes and conspiracy to commit the criminal acts listed in the first three counts."

Mark took a few steps toward Jäger. "If you wonder what's happening, Major Jäger, you're going to be tried for what you did during the war. Way down there when you were hiding in Argentina, did you hear about the Nuremburg Trials that took place after the war ended?"

Jäger remained still, not replying.

"Well, let me explain if you didn't." Mark continued. "Your Nazi buddies were rounded up—at least as many as could be found, and they were tried in Nuremburg for the same crimes you were just arrested for. Ever since the Nuremburg Trials ended, every time a Nazi is unearthed, they must stand trial for their war crimes. So don't think that simply because it's 1970, the statute of limitations doesn't apply to yours." Mark chuckled. "Oh, yes, indeed. They certainly will."

Mark's eyes roamed the room at the surrounding Army troops with rifles still aimed at Jäger. "Justice will be served. Perhaps you should've stayed in Argentina, and forgotten about your little schloss here. As for the property deed, it's already passed on to your children. As I told you before, you won't be needing it, even if you manage to escape execution." Mark tossed him a mock salute. "Farewell, Major. Your just desserts are coming. You might want to think about what Kate told you before you meet your Maker."

Jäger's eyes swiveled to meet Kate's. She nodded. "I'll be praying for you."

"I have a couple questions for you, Jäger." Mark rubbed a hand over his chin. "How did you know to come looking for me at my ranch in Wyoming?"

"Ja, you would not know that, would you, Major Scott?" Jäger peered down his nose at Mark. "After you and Elena made your escape from Munich, I continued to search for her. The trail led me and my soldiers to a farm near the Swiss border where you and Elena stayed one night. We found the farmer—most helpful. We…persuaded…him to divulge your name." A mirthless smile lifted the corners of Jäger's lips. "I had to return to Munich, but my soldiers continued to follow your trail; however, they lost you." His smile turned to a bitter twist of his mouth. "After the Third Reich fell, and I escaped from prison and then Germany, I swore that someday I would find Elena and the man who helped her escape and make them pay."

Mark smiled. "Didn't quite work out for you, did it?" He paused. "Who was the guy you set on our trail since we landed in Germany? You know, the one driving the green VW. He was your lackey, wasn't he?"

Another scowl settled on Jäger's features. "Of course, he was. I wanted Elena to know she wasn't...welcome... She had betrayed me all those years ago, and until I could look into her eyes, I wanted her to know what betrayal felt like."

Kate started to speak, but before she could, Mark did. "Your lackey nearly killed our Kate. He almost ran her over with a car. If it hadn't been for that young man—" he pointed at Gabe, "—he would have. You and your accomplice are despicable. And if you don't know yet, he's sitting in the Munich jail." He turned away from the German.

Jäger frowned and stared at the ground.

"Oh, one more thing before you take him away, Captain." Mark turned back toward Jäger. "Did you strike my housekeeper when you visited my property in Wyoming?"

Jäger's chin rose. "I found her to be quite...uncooperative when I asked to see you."

Before anyone could anticipate his next move, Mark stepped toward him, reared back, and punched the man in the face.

Blood spurted from his nose. Jäger screamed before blurting German words Kate had never learned. Jäger touched his nose. "*Was ist das?* What is this? Why did you punch me?"

With a satisfied expression etching his features, Mark rubbed his knuckles. "Where I come from in Wyoming, men don't hit women. For *any* reason." He turned to Friedrich. "Sorry about the blood on the rugs."

A smile lifted the caretaker's lips as he bowed from the waist. "Do not worry, sir. It is with great pleasure that I will remove the stains."

Mark turned to the captain. "I think we're done here."

The captain nodded with a grin, then motioned with his head toward the major. "Remove him at once."

After the soldiers escorted Jäger from the room, the captain approached Mark. "Thank you for the tip. This criminal has been on the run for a long time. Any time we can bring down a Nazi official, it's a good day."

Mark shook his hand. "I still know a few folks in high places. Thanks for showing up right on time, Captain."

The officer grinned. "It's my pleasure, sir." He gave Mark a salute and headed out the door.

"So you had that all planned out." Matt turned to his dad. "How did you know Jäger would even show up?"

"Gabe and I have been tracking his accomplice."

All eyes turned to Gabe. "Seriously?" Kate propped a hand on her hip. "Why didn't you say something?"

"Now don't blame Gabe." Mark lifted a hand. "I suspected Jäger would show up eventually after Martha got hurt. The man that came to the door and attacked her fit his description, and no one else would do such a thing. I almost flew home, but decided he'd come here eventually.

"Gabe and I noticed a little green VW following us. It could have been the same vehicle that nearly ran Kate over before backing off. That's when the police hauled the guy away at the hotel. After that, the green VW no longer showed up. If another vehicle picked up where he left off, we couldn't tell. Something in my bones told me Jäger would show up sooner or later. Where best than at his schloss? I made some phone calls and arranged for the Austrian Armed Forces to march in. Actually, they were here before we were. Even Friedrich didn't know it." He turned and grinned at the caretaker.

Friedrich shook his head. "*Meine Güte.* Oh sorry. My

goodness. When I got up to milk the cows this morning, I had no idea this day would go as it has."

"Cows?" Kate blinked in surprise.

Friedrich smiled. "Ja. Cows. We have four Guernseys. Gentle souls, they are. Well, all except Gertrude. Not so gentle that one."

Kate laughed and elbowed Gabe. "Ever milked a cow?"

"Of course. We have cows on the ranch, remember?" He chuckled.

She snapped her fingers. "Oh, that's right."

Matt laughed. "Yeah, we'll have to work on your education, sis."

"So—" Friedrich clapped his hands together, "now that the excitement is over, may I see the deed? I know it is a technicality, and you both look like your mother, however—"

Kate strode over to Friedrich and slipped her arm through his. "Friedrich, I'm not in the least offended that you ask to see the deed. Matt, please do the honors. Afterward, I'd like a tour of our schloss. What do you say?"

Epilogue

Mid-May
Dogwood Station, Ohio

"May I help you?" Kate approached the young man perusing the bakery case. She wiped her hands on her apron and tugged on a pair of latex gloves from a box behind the counter. "I'm sure there's plenty here to tempt your palate."

His eyes flashed to Kate's before returning to view the huge selection of pastries. "That's the problem. There's so much to choose from. Maybe you can help me out."

"I'd be happy to. One of our best sellers is our *Koblihy*. It's a fried donut filled with custard. This one." Kate opened the back of the case and pointed at the puffy donut. "Another favorite is our cinnamon roll." She pointed at the huge pastry roll dripping with icing. "I could go on and on because there are so many good things to choose from, but these are my favorites."

He smiled broadly. "I'm sold. Give me one of each and a large black coffee to go."

"Great." Kate gathered the pastries into a bag and dispensed the coffee from a large, old-fashioned urn on the counter behind her. The customer paid and hurried away with a smile.

Uncle Rudy stepped up beside her and slipped an arm

around her shoulders. "My holčička, it's good to have you home. You've returned to work like you never left. The only difference I see is a sadness that wasn't there before. Even with the uncertainties before you left and having lost your dear grandma, God rest her soul, you weren't this down. Did learning your mother's secrets hurt you so much?"

Kate peered around the shop and didn't see any customers at the moment. She leaned her head against Uncle Rudy's shoulder and wrapped her arm around his ample waist. "No, I accept Mother's secrets. Some were hard to hear, but she did what she had to do for the sake of her country. It's hard to understand how she could've married the enemy to fulfill her mission, and it makes my skin crawl at the thought. My...Major Jäger was evil to the core, but I'm trying to accept it all because I love Mother."

"Then what has you looking so sad?" He tipped her chin up and stared into her eyes. "Ah, I see. It's a man." Uncle Rudy's arms tightened into a hug, and he dropped a kiss onto her temple. "You gave your heart to someone but could not give him your life. Is that so?"

Kate blinked at the tears that threatened. "If I deny it, you'll simply tell me you've been around too long to believe me, so why deny it, right?"

"Right." He chuckled. "Who is this man? Must I go and bust a knuckle on him?"

Kate lifted her head. "Uncle. Of course not, he's a great guy. He wanted to pursue a relationship with me, but I was the one who walked away."

Uncle Rudy lowered a brow at her. "Is he a Godly man?"

Kate nodded.

"Holčička, why would you do this?"

"I live in Ohio and have a business to run and loved ones to care for. He lives in Wyoming and is a partner in a ranch. I simply couldn't see a way for our lives to...to work together."

Uncle Rudy chuckled. "Ah, the foolishness of youth. You know a great God, but you underestimate what He's capable of. You see a huge obstacle in your path, but you only see a tiny picture of your life. God sees the whole picture. He's seen every step of your path since you were a tiny baby in your mother's womb. God can see right up to the day you will die. If this young man is the one for you, do you not think God will make a way for you two to be together?"

"I believe He's already done that, sir." A familiar voice spoke from the middle of the shop, and Kate spun around to find Gabe standing there, a grin on his face.

"Gabe?" How had he come in without her hearing him? Wonder and confusion filled her. "What are you doing here?"

"You know this young man?" Uncle Rudy slid his arm from around Kate as she straightened.

"Yes, I do." Kate tugged Uncle Rudy around the counter toward the man that made her heart pound. "Gabe, this is my Uncle Rudy whom I told you about. Uncle Rudy, this is Gabe Flanagan."

"Flanagan?" Uncle Rudy held out a hand. Gabe gave it a hearty shake. "Sounds Irish."

"Yes, sir." Gabe's smile grew.

Uncle Rudy turned toward Kate. "Is this the young man you were just telling me about?"

Kate's eyes skittered away as warmth rolled over her. Sure her cheeks must be red, she managed a nod. "Umm, yeah."

Gabe chuckled. "Good. That means you didn't forget me."

Uncle Rudy squeezed Kate's shoulder. "Oh, I can assure you, that didn't happen. It's a pleasure to meet you, Gabe." He started to turn away. "Katarina, I will mind the shop. Why don't you and your young man take a walk? It's a lovely day out. Go. Enjoy the afternoon."

Kate wrapped her arms around her uncle in a quick hug and handed him her apron. "I'll return shortly," she called as they headed out the door."

Gabe shifted something thin and black from one hand to the other and took Kate's elbow as they strolled down the sidewalk.

"What's that?" she asked

"I'll show you in a bit," he evaded. "Your uncle's a nice man."

"He's the best. He picked up the father role after my grandfather passed. As you're well aware, since I never knew my father, my grandfather filled that role. Both of them have been amazing at it. Uncle Rudy and Auntie Anna never had children. As a result, they always tried to spoil me." Kate chuckled.

"I can see it didn't work." Gabe guided their steps toward a nearby park.

Kate's eyes wandered about the familiar street of her beloved town. "Mother put the kibosh on a lot of their shenanigans, but being the only child in a house full of older people didn't make it easy for her to raise me."

Gabe paused for a moment. "I have some news you might be interested in hearing."

Kate's eyes lit up. "Matt broke up with Gina and decided Skylar's a better choice for him."

"Are you a mind reader?"

Kate released a laugh. "No, Matt called a couple days ago and filled me in. I couldn't be happier for both of them."

"Yeah, they're doing great. Skylar's been working out at the ranch on the article for Megan. I read some of it. She's going to make your mom look like the heroine she truly was."

Kate's eyes brimmed. "I'm glad. She deserves to be recognized for her part in the war. I left my photos with

Skylar to use in the article, and she's going to use Matt's copy of the one Herr Becker gave us from the newspaper office in Munich. I have mine hanging in the living room for all to see."

"It's a beautiful photograph." Gabe gently pulled Kate's elbow, drawing her to a halt. "That's where this comes in." He held up what looked like a leather-bound document folio.

Kate sought his eyes. "What is it?"

Gabe opened the folio to display a two-page document with photos and written paragraphs. "Megan sent this for you. It's the rough draft of the article that will come out in the *Casper Gazette* next month featuring your mother and her service to her country."

He held it out to Kate, and she accepted the folio, holding it so she could look closer. The photos of Mother and Mark, Mother and Major Jäger, the young Megan, Matt and Kate as well as the one of Mother from the National Theater were all there. Skylar had included a few photos from the National Theater and other Munich sights. Kate quickly scanned through the article to find the story of Mother's spying days. Her marriage to a Nazi in order to glean information from high Third-Reich officials. The information about how Mother and Mark had escaped with Matt and Kate to prevent them from being handed over for possible experimentation at the hands of a madman appeared in the article too. Skylar had presented Mother as the heroine she truly was.

A finger touched Kate's cheek, and she lifted her eyes to Gabe. With his thumb he wiped away the tears she hadn't realized wet her cheeks.

"It's all right," he whispered.

Kate drew in a deep breath. "I know. I'm simply touched at how Megan and Skylar honored Mother and her service. They did an amazing job on the article."

"Yes, they did." He swiped a tendril of hair behind her

ear. "I'm happy you like it, and they will be too."

Kate slowly closed the folio and tucked it close to her chest. "What's the other piece of news?"

"Well, it's not as happy and heartwarming as that bit of news, I'm afraid. Major Jäger's trial took place last week, and he was sentenced to death for his war crimes. He'll be hanged like so many of his predecessors."

Kate remained silent for a few moments. "That's sad. I hope he thought about what I said to him. I've been praying for him. Either way, I'm sure he's regretting leaving Argentina to pursue the deed to the schloss. It's not doing him any good now."

"No, it's not."

Kate paused as she stared at the ground for a few moments. Tilting her head to the side, she met Gabe's eyes. "You could've called and told me that, and Megan could've sent the article to me. Why are you here? Did I leave something undone when I flew home from Wyoming? Mark said you and he would take care of arranging things as far as the schloss. I love the idea of opening it up as a hotel. It's an amazing idea, in fact. There's a lot of work to be done first, but Friedrich and his son offered to oversee it. Mark will find an Austrian contractor to do the work, and when it's ready, we'll make a trip back to check—"

Gabe silenced her with a light finger on her lips. Wrapping his arms around her, he gathered her close. Kate's breath caught as Gabe's lips settled against hers. This kiss was firmer, deeper, and even more wonderful than their first. She forgot completely what she had been saying. Her arms slid up around his shoulders, slipping her fingers into his hair and drawing his head closer. She rested the folio against his back. She stood on tip-toe and felt his arms cradling her against his chest. Kate began to grasp just how cherished she was. When Gabe withdrew his lips and leaned his forehead against hers, she opened her eyes to find love written plain and simple within his.

"Kate, the last time I kissed you, I told you I loved you, yet you walked away. You saw an obstacle in our path to a future together and didn't even respond whether you loved me or not. Sweetheart, I've been praying about…us." A half-grin lifted a corner of his handsome lips. "I tend to agree with what your uncle said."

Kate blinked. "You heard all that? How long were you standing there?"

"Long enough to hear him tell you that God sees your path and has since before you were born. He sees the big picture and can make a way past any obstacle you can't see around." Gabe reached up to stroke her cheek. "I'm here to tell you, there is a way. That is depending on your heart's status." His head tilted, as he waggled his eyebrows. "The way you kissed me back tells me you have feelings for me. Unless it's all physical, of course."

Heat warmed Kate's cheeks again. "Oh, of…of course, it's…it's *not*." She stammered before huffing out an indignant breath. "Stop teasing me, Gabriel Flanagan. I love you too."

His grin faded. "Do you?"

Kate met the query in his eyes. "With my whole heart."

He began to smile again and dropped a kiss on her lips. "Want to hear how we can be together?"

"More than you know." Kate ran the tip of her finger across his bottom lip eliciting a groan.

He grasped her hand in his and held it against his chest. "If you keep that up, there won't be any more talking." He swallowed hard. "Now, for your information, I'm moving to Ohio. Dogwood Station, to be exact. I thought I'd ask your lawyer if he could use a partner. Before you ask, yes, I'll remain ranch partners with Mark and Matt, and I'll fly back when they need me, but this will be my new home. Mark suggested this idea when he found me moping around. He knew I fell in love with you on our journey. The night I declared my love to you, I was ready to give up, but he told me not to."

Kate leaned her forehead against his chest and shook her head, tears stinging her eyes.

"Please tell me you aren't going to throw another obstacle in our path." Gabe tucked a finger beneath her chin and lifted Kate's face up to meet his eyes.

"No, I'm simply in awe that you would change your home and do all this for…for me."

A gentle smile settled on Gabe's lips. "Then you don't understand just how much I love you. I'll do whatever it takes to be with you."

As he lowered to one knee, he tugged a little burgundy velvet box from his jacket pocket and opened it. "I know we haven't known each other for only a couple of months, but I know all I need to, and my heart's settled on you. I'm at perfect peace. Will you marry me? Soon?"

Kate's hands covered her mouth as she dropped to her knees in front of Gabe. She gazed at the large solitaire diamond on a golden band before lifting her eyes to stare into his with all the love she had. "It's…amazing. More beautiful than anything. Yes, I'll marry you. I love you, Gabe."

He removed the ring from the box and slid it onto her finger. Gabe gathered Kate close. "I love you. You are my world. Life's going to change soon. We're going to have our ups and downs. There's a schloss to manage, of all things. And I want to have a family with you."

Kate smiled. "I'd like that. More help in the bakery since my elderly loved ones won't be there forever."

With a raised brow, Gabe whispered, "We'll get right on that as soon as we're married."

Kate eyed him with a side-eyed glance. "I had a feeling you'd say that."

He lowered his head. "We can begin by practicing the kissing part now."

Kate lifted her head to receive his kiss. With God at their side no matter what obstacles littered their path, life would be an incredible adventure with this man. She could hardly wait.

The End

Dear Reader,

If you enjoyed reading this book and want to help me to continue writing and publishing more books for your enjoyment, please take a moment to leave a review. They are very important to authors. We depend on them to let other readers know what they think about our books so they in turn will know whether or not to purchase and read them. Should you not care for it, I would appreciate an email to me rather than a negative review. And remember, the author has no control over prices, so please keep that in mind if you're not happy with the cost. You can find me at Amazon, Goodreads and BookBub should you choose to leave a review. Thank you again for reading my story. I hope you enjoyed it.

For His glory,
J. Carol Nemeth

I hope you enjoyed reading *Discovering Elena: My Mother's Secret*. Keep watching for the sequel, M*y Father's Secret*. Check out my other books on my website at https://www.jcarolnemeth.com/books.

Here's a sample chapter from *Mountain of Peril, Faith in the Parks Book One*:

Chapter One

Wwith a whistle on his lips, Jake Stuart rounded the corner of the ranger station. He pulled his keys from his pants pocket, prepared to flip the Closed sign by the door to Open as he did every morning. As he approached the front stoop, he froze. The whistle hung in his throat. He jerked back, a gasp slipping out. The decapitated head of a black bear perched on the floor of the porch stoop, a pair of severed paws positioned on either side of the head. Blood seeped from beneath the black fur of the head and ran across the cement stoop dripping into the grass. Jake tasted bile as his gut knotted. He clenched his fists and shook his head. Who would do such an awful thing? And why? The glazed eyes of the bear were haunting. This bear had died needlessly.

Avoiding the horrible mess, Jake stepped onto the stoop from the side and unlocked the station office. Grabbing the phone, he called his supervisor, Cal Bishop. He'd come out and assist in the processing of the crime scene. Because that's exactly what it was. He pulled his digital camera from the desk drawer. Photo-documenting the evidence was an important part of any investigation. After searching carefully, no vehicle tire tracks or footprints could be found. Too much grass and gravel and not enough dirt to hold a print.

By the time Cal arrived, the spring morning had warmed considerably and flies had found the bear head.

"Now that's not a pretty sight to greet you in the morning." Cal climbed out of his National Park SUV.

"We're getting more and more reports of poaching lately, and out of season too. They took the carcass and left the head. Pretty disgusting."

"Yeah, well, this is different." Jake squatted down, pulled out his pocketknife and probed the fur for possible gunshot wounds. "This is more than just poaching. Someone's left us a strong message." But for what? A warning, maybe? Or a threat?

~

"What'd she say, Burt?" The elderly man turned to his companion where they sat on a bench in front of the old service station.

"I dunno, George. Can't understand her." Burt cupped his ear with his hand and leaned forward. "What'd ya say, young woman?"

Molly Walker stepped closer and raised her voice. "Sir, I asked for directions to Deep Creek Ranger Station." This was the first business she'd found open on this road and somehow she thought she'd gotten turned around. The two elderly gentlemen sitting on the bench in front of the station were why she'd stopped, but she wasn't getting very far with them.

"Sounds like gibberish to me, George. Can't make out a word." He turned his head toward the screen door beside him. "Hey, Bertha!" he called, hand cupped around his mouth like a megaphone. "Come out here a minute, would ya!"

Molly sighed as a large lady in a bright print blouse, orange-red curly hair and large dangly earrings propped open the screen door. "What ya bellowin' about, Burt? Oh, hello there," she added with a congenial smile upon spotting Molly.

"This here young woman wants something, and I can't understand her." Burt and George both shook their heads.

The woman rolled her eyes, "What can I do for ya, sweetie? You need help with the gas pump? It's not one of those newfangled ones, but it works. Some of the young folks can't figure it out."

Molly smiled wide. "No, thanks. I just need directions out to Deep Creek Ranger Station. I seem to have gotten turned around somehow."

"Oh, sure. Take this road into town then turn right at the courthouse. It's the big building with the gold dome." A touch of pride edged her words. She gave Molly detailed directions all the way to Deep Creek.

"Thanks! You've been a big help." Molly waved at Burt and George. "Thanks, fellows!"

"Who's Hank Bellows, Bertha?" George raised his bushy eyebrows.

"Never mind, George." Bertha huffed as the screen door banged shut behind her.

Molly followed Bertha's directions, liking the laid-back quaintness of the little town. It had that certain "Mayberry" feel to it. She half expected an old black and white to cruise past with Andy or Barney at the wheel. Turning right at the courthouse, she spotted two more elderly men sitting on a park bench, a checkerboard between them. Remembering Burt and George, she grinned. Laid back, indeed!

Small storefronts, a hardware store and an old drugstore lined the street. Taking another right at the old train depot, Molly left the town behind, passing small mountain homes along the green hillsides, a country store and the occasional mobile home. The North Carolina Smoky Mountains rose up from the valley she drove through, their smoky blue color beautiful against the brilliant blue sky. Spring had arrived in the Smokies, and the vibrant pink and white Laurel bushes were in full bloom. Redbuds and dogwoods peeked between the new green leaves sprouting on the poplar, maple and oak trees.

Molly spotted the sign for Deep Creek Campground and a surge of exhilaration knotted her stomach. She'd waited a long time for this. It was her first position with the National

Park Service, and she was certain great-grandpa Murphy would've been pleased. Having trained for this very day, she was ready to begin her new career. Gratitude for how circumstances had worked out swelled in her heart. *Thank you, Lord.*

Turning right, she crossed a bridge that spanned a swiftly flowing creek then entered a large clearing in the woods. A small brown building sat near the center with a sign beside it that read Office. The early afternoon breeze stirred an American flag at the top of a flagpole.

Molly parked across from the office and exited her SUV, stretching stiff muscles and glancing around the quiet clearing. Strolling over to the little office, she opened the squeaky screen door, hoping Cal Bishop was in. As head ranger over the campground and this part of the park district, he was meeting her here to explain her duties.

The small front office was split by a wooden counter along the front, a desk holding a base station radio and a file cabinet positioned behind it. Mountain scenes and maps graced the walls while a tattered and torn backpack hung by the front door. An old coffee pot and tin can, both punctured and bent, hung from the backpack. Beneath, a sign read, Campers: Please Store Food Properly. A partition to the left of the counter indicated more office space.

A young auburn-haired man dressed in a National Park Service uniform leaned on the counter, grinning as Molly glanced around. His hair was short and freckles spattered across his nose. His name badge read "Craig Wilson."

"Can I help you?" A bright smile crossed his lips.

"I hope so." Molly returned his smile. "I'm looking for Cal Bishop. Is he in?"

"No, he's out in the campground somewhere. I can call him if you'd like."

"I'd appreciate that. My name's Molly Walker. I believe he's expecting me."

"Molly Walker!" He extended his hand to Molly. "You

bet he is. He'll be glad to know you're here. I'm Craig Wilson. It's nice to meet you."

"I'm happy to meet you, Craig." Molly shook his outstretched hand.

"Hang on a minute. I'll call Cal." Craig reached for the base radio microphone on the desk, depressed the button and called out some numbers followed by Cal's name. "Guess who's here? Yeah, she made it. Come back?"

A deep male voice responded he was on his way.

"He'll be here shortly. I just made some coffee a little while ago. Would you like a cup?"

"I'd love some." Molly glanced around the office. The coffee maker sat on a small table near the desk. "May I help myself?"

"Sure. May as well. You'll be working here so make yourself at home."

"Thanks." Molly chuckled, filling an insulated cup. "Where are you from, Craig?"

"Montana."

"Wow! You're a long way from home. Been in the park service long?"

"This is my first season." He perched on the barstool behind the counter. "You're coming in a little late, I suppose."

Molly settled onto the rolling chair at the desk, sipping the hot brew. "I understand I'm replacing someone that didn't work out."

"Yeah, that was Howard, Cal's assistant ranger for the past two seasons. He took seriously ill. Don't know the whole story, but I don't think he's returning to the park service. Early retirement, I think." He shrugged his shoulders.

"So what do you do?"

"I'm a summer seasonal park aide. I'm still in college and working my way through, but I'll graduate next spring. The experience here will be good."

The screen door opened and a man of stocky build strolled in. He wore the gray shirt and dark green pants of the National Park Service uniform, and when he removed a dark green NPS ball cap and sunglasses, Molly noticed his sandy colored crew cut and bright blue eyes surrounded by laugh lines. Determining he was in his mid-forties, she stood as he approached with outstretched hand.

"I'm Cal Bishop," his voice deep and gravely. "Welcome to Deep Creek, Miss Walker."

"Please, call me Molly."

"Certainly, but you have to call me Cal. We don't stand on formalities around here. Come on back and have a seat. I have some things to go over with you." He led Molly behind the partition where another desk and file cabinet made up Cal's office. Through an open door to the left, Molly spotted what passed for a bathroom. It would be a tight fit, but certainly better than nothing.

"Did you have a good trip?" Cal motioned her to sit in a chair beside the desk while he took the rolling chair behind it. "Where'd you drive from?"

"From Charlottesville, Virginia. Except for a couple really bad storms that kept me alert, it was uneventful."

"They're predicting storms this evening. We need it. It's been a dry spring so far." As he chatted he drew a file folder from the desk drawer, removing several pages. "Here's a list of required uniform items and you'll get a uniform allowance, so that'll help you out."

He removed a small plastic bag stapled to the list then handed the list to her. "You can order by mail or online, but it takes a week or so to get your items. However, if you don't mind taking a drive, there's a store in Maryville, Tennessee that carries the NPS uniform shirts, pants and leather belt. You can also pick up the ball cap."

Cal pointed to his on the side of the desk.

Molly glanced at it. "What about the "Smoky-Bear" hat?"

He tapped the list in her hand. "It has to be ordered. Pick up some good hiking boots too. You'll need 'em."

Dumping the contents of the little plastic bag onto the desk, he picked up a little brass bar. "I took the liberty of ordering your name tag so you'd have it when you arrived." He handed her the name tag and a metal, shield-shaped badge. "This gives you your authority."

"When do I start?" Eagerness threatened to overwhelm Molly. Had he noticed her wiping her palms on her pant legs? It was hard to tone down her beaming smile.

Cal glanced at his wristwatch, a broad grin on his lips. Yeah, he'd noticed. "If you want to drive over to Maryville for your uniforms, go today. Then you can start in the morning. On your way, if you don't mind, you can deliver something to the remote Twentymile Ranger Station for me. I have some paperwork for Ranger Jake Stuart."

"I don't mind. Is it on the way?"

"Yep. You drive right past it to get to Maryville. Before you go, I'll take you up to the duplex where you'll lodge temporarily until you find a place." Grabbing a notepad, Cal drew a rudimentary map and handed it to Molly along with a manila envelope. "Here are directions to Maryville with Twentymile marked on it. This is the packet for Jake." Unlocking a drawer in his desk, he opened it and pulled out a Glock 19 9mm and a brown leather holster.

"This is your sidearm." He peered closely at Molly. "From your weapon scores, I see you know how to handle one of these."

"I didn't do too badly." Pleasure warmed Molly at his compliment. "Besides, my father made sure my brothers and I knew how to protect ourselves."

Cal nodded and handed her another form. "That's what I like to hear. Sign on the dotted line. This says you were issued the weapon. Just make sure the serial number matches the paper before you sign."

Comparing the numbers, Molly signed the form and

returned it to Cal.

"Follow me and I'll show you to your quarters." Clapping his cap on his head, he led the way out the door.

~

After Molly and Cal dropped off her suitcases, bags and boxes at the little duplex up the hill from the office, Molly grabbed lunch at the drugstore in town then headed west toward Twentymile Ranger Station. The drive was pleasant with the road winding just past the edge of a huge lake and around hairpin curves. According to Cal's map, the lake was Fontana Lake. The scenery was gorgeous. Molly's family had visited the Great Smoky Mountains in her childhood, and she'd always loved the gentle yet mysterious smoky-blue mountains. Not nearly as tall as the Rockies or some of the other western mountain ranges, the Smokies had a quiet, peaceful beauty all their own.

Molly spotted a sign for Fontana Dam and another for Fontana Village. Having read up on the area before coming, she knew the dam, one of many in the area, was built by the Tennessee Valley Authority during WWII. The village was a summer resort with a lodge, swimming pools and hiking. It was located south of Fontana Lake, while the boundary to Great Smoky Mountains National Park lay along the northern shore.

With no time to explore the area today, Molly vowed to return on a day off to investigate further. Passing the entrance to the village, she descended a winding, wooded mountain road to the bottom where a bridge crossed a wide river. To her right, the sheer wall of Fontana Dam rose far above. A power generating station sat to one side. On the left of the bridge, the river flowed into another lake. Here in the valley below the dam, the road wound along the lake's edge on the left while on the right the wooded foot of the mountains rose up into the park.

Turning into a gravel driveway by a sign for Twentymile Ranger Station, she parked in the small lot in front of the building. Climbing out, she stretched, listening to the peace and quiet that enveloped her. A creek flowing merrily alongside the station, a gentle breeze rustling the trees and birds singing were the only sounds. Bright sunshine belied any sign of a predicted storm.

Molly stepped onto the small front porch and found a large wooden clock face with movable hands indicating the ranger would return in an hour. She glanced at her wristwatch. She couldn't wait that long. Not with an hour drive to Maryville.

Exploring the grounds, she hoped to find Jake Stuart. A long, dark green garage stood fifty feet behind the station. A light green NPS Jeep was parked in front beside a blue Ford Ranger. The gravel and dirt driveway wound past the station, the garage and on up the hill. It curved past a little brown shanty before disappearing around the bend.

Well, now what should she do? A faint sound came from up the hill. Was that a metallic ringing noise? Following it, she stopped at the little shanty only to find it locked. Twenty-five feet further an iron gate blocked the road that meandered into the woods. Ducking beneath the gate, Molly followed the road toward the sound of a faint voice, an occasional metallic ring and a horse nickering. Ahead she spotted a barn surrounded by corrals.

Shoving open one of the barn doors, she glanced around for the owner of the voice. Two horses and a mule stood in their stalls, softly nickering at her appearance. As they stirred, motes of dust danced in the sunbeams that slipped through the cracks above the rafters. The scent of hay and horses filled her nose.

"Hello?" she called in a soft voice. Frightening the horses would be a bad idea. "Anyone here?"

Molly approached one of the horses and stroked its head, crooning softly to it. "Easy, fellow. Where's the ranger, huh?"

The voice spoke again, louder this time. The owner

switched back and forth between talking and humming in a deep baritone. Striding to the double doors leading to a corral, Molly found a man working beside a horse. Bent from the waist, he held the horse's back hoof between his knees, a hoof pick in his hand. With his back to her, he hadn't heard her approach. The horse noticed her and nickered, shifting his weight.

"Whoa, Billy!" A deep voice soothed. "Stand still, boy. We'll be done shortly."

"Excuse me," Molly said quietly. "Sorry to interrupt your work, but I'm looking for Jake Stuart."

Glancing over his shoulder in surprise, the man accidentally allowed the weight of the horse's leg to slip from his grasp. Suddenly off balance, he fell forward, landing on his shoulder and knees.

"Oh, no!" Molly gasped, covering her mouth with her hands. "I'm so sorry. I didn't mean to startle you."

Picking himself up, he dusted off his pants and grinned. Molly wasn't sure if the red in his cheeks was from embarrassment or from leaning over too long. She had a pretty good idea which it was. Her hands still covering her mouth, she tried not to laugh, but found one working its way out.

~

Jake Stuart noted the woman was trying unsuccessfully not to laugh at him. "You know, seeing as how we've never met, I don't think it's very polite to laugh at me." His voice and face were stern, but his dark sapphire eyes shone with laughter. "Especially since *you're* the one who startled *me*."

"I truly am sorry, but if I'd shouted, would I have startled you any less?" The pretty woman chuckled again.

He shook his head. "I suppose you have a point. Did you say you're looking for Jake Stuart?"

"Yes, I am."

He surveyed her thoroughly, taking in the long brown braid hanging carelessly over her shoulder. The soft curve of her cheeks, and the dark chocolate eyes. Her lips were a delicate shade of pink, slightly compressed at the moment and compressing more and more as he observed her appearance. She wore a pair of blue jeans and a white button-down shirt with flowers embroidered on the collar.

"Do you know where he is or don't you?"

Uh-oh. A frown was forming between her delicate eyebrows.

Jake couldn't take his eyes from her. She blushed, and the pink color delighted him. Was that a Virginian accent he detected? Whatever it was, it sounded great coming from her.

"What do you need him for?"

Eyes narrowing, she lifted her chin defiantly. "That's none of your concern. I have something for him, and I need to give it directly to him."

He crossed his arms over his chest. "Well now, he never mentioned expecting you. I'm sure if he knew you were coming, he would've made sure he was here to meet you."

Boy, this was fun. He checked his grin as she crossed her arms as well and tilted her chin upward.

"Be that as it may, I'm still looking for him."

~

Molly jumped as the walkie-talkie propped on a nearby stump crackled to life. After the usual call numbers, a deep voice said, "Come in, Jake, this is Cal."

Whoever this man was, he glanced at the walkie-talkie then back at her. Was the call for *him*? "Come in, Jake. This is Cal. Do you read me?"

Molly watched with dismay as the man hesitated momentarily before reaching for the instrument and pressing the button, responding. "Cal, this is Jake. What's up?"

"Just wanted to let you know that Molly Walker will be by sometime this afternoon to drop off those papers you wanted. She's the new ranger over here. Should be getting there soon, I expect. Was going to call sooner, but got caught up in a situation here."

Jake's gaze flicked back to hers. "Thanks Cal but she beat you to it. She's already here." He shrugged, never removing his eyes from her face.

"Roger that, Jake. Talk with you later. Cal out."

"Jake out."

Molly spun on her heels and headed back through the barn. Glancing over her shoulder, she saw Jake yank off the leather apron covering his uniform and nametag. He tossed it on the stump, slipped the walkie-talkie into its belt holster, and hurried after her.

"Hey, wait up," he called.

She sped toward the station, wanting to put some distance between them.

Jake caught up with her just before the gate. Catching hold of her arm, he gently tugged her around. "You're quick, you know that?"

Molly turned her best blank expression on him and pulled her arm away. "Thanks."

"Look, I'm sorry. I shouldn't have led you on like that, but I guess I was a little sore at being caught off guard and having fallen flat on my face. I think they call it male ego or something like that. Anyway, I know you didn't surprise me on purpose." One side of his mouth lifted in a crooked grin as his eyebrows rose. "Am I forgiven?"

Molly grinned at the "male ego" comment and knew she couldn't stay mad. She'd have to work with him some time or other. Best to get things squared and make life a little easier. Besides, she *had* laughed at him. She held out her hand. "You're forgiven, if you'll forgive me for laughing at you."

His large calloused hand engulfed hers then released it. "Done. Now let's start over. Hi, I'm Jake Stuart."

"Molly Walker. I have an envelope for you in my car. The one Cal referred to when he gave you away."

As Jake strode on long legs back toward the station, Molly tried to keep up.

He shortened his stride. To match hers? "Right. Needless to say, I wasn't expecting you. I knew someone was replacing Howard, but I didn't know who. It's been awhile since I've been over to Deep Creek." As they stopped by her car, Molly retrieved the envelope.

"When did you get to town?"

"Today. I checked in with Cal, dropped my things at my temporary quarters then headed here. He suggested purchasing my uniforms in Maryville so that's where I'm heading. He asked me to drop this off to save him a trip."

"You're heading to Maryville, huh?" Jake's eyes gleamed with interest. "Could I impose on you to pick up something for me?"

"Sure. What do you need?" Another errand for another ranger? Was she going to be a ranger or a courier?

Jake pulled out his wallet and handed her a few bills then removed a notepad from his shirt pocket. "I'll jot down what I need." As he wrote, Molly took the opportunity to observe him unnoticed. His thick black hair was cut short and neat. A very handsome man in spite of the faint scar marring the right side of his chin. When she'd first seen him at the barn she'd noticed his broad shoulders and his dark sapphire eyes beneath black brows.

She suddenly realized those same eyes were gazing at her now. Uh oh. She'd been caught staring. Looking down at the paper he was holding out, she willed herself not to blush.

"R...right," she stammered. "I'll pick these up for you and drop them off on my way past. Will you be here?"

Jake's smile was bright against his tanned face. "I'll be here. When you live in the backcountry, there aren't too many places to go. If I'm not here at the station, I'll be up at the barn. I still have two more horses to shoe."

As Molly drove away, she was still embarrassed that

she'd stared, much less been caught at it. What had come over her? Staring at a man wasn't her style. She shook her head and concentrated on the winding road.

Here's another sample chapter from *Death Goes to School*, the second sequel to *Mountain of Peril, Faith in the Parks Book One*:

End of May
Current Year

Prologue

Kaitlyn stepped out of the women's bathroom and stopped. The late afternoon sun had edged behind the top of the mountains and dusk threatened. Searching for any sign of her friends, she wished she hadn't needed to rush ahead to the restroom and leave them behind. As her eyes darted along the side of the small building housing the restrooms, the hair sprang up on the back of her neck, her skin crawling.

A man in a black hoodie leaned against the building, the hood drawn low, his hands jammed into the pockets. Glancing about, Kaitlyn realized they were the only two people in sight. Where were Jenny, Allyson, and Kelly? The only sounds were a slight breeze rustling the trees and the sound of her own heartbeat hammering in her ears. She circled around behind the building and again searched the road for her friends. They were nowhere in sight. She couldn't even hear their usual chatter.

As Kaitlyn stepped toward the road, a hard, gloved hand clamped over her mouth and a steel band of an arm yanked her against a solid frame. The man by the bathroom? Who else? She attempted a scream but only a muffled sound emitted past the hand clamped over her mouth. With little effort he dragged her toward the parking lot beyond the bathrooms. No matter how hard she kicked, it was to no avail.

When they reached a car, he shoved her against it and held her there with his hard body. Still covering her mouth, he popped open the trunk and forced her inside. Ripping duct tape from a roll in his pocket, he slapped it over her mouth before she could utter a sound. Tearing long strips, he yanked her arms behind her and wrapped the tape around her wrists so tightly it hurt. He did the same with her ankles.

Kaitlyn endeavored to catch a glimpse of his face but the black hood hid it. Did it matter? The situation appeared as bleak as it possibly could. Lifting her head, she struggled to see if Jenny, Allyson and Kelly might be approaching. Kaitlyn's car was parked a mere twenty feet away. When they found it, and not her, they'd know she hadn't left on her own. They'd know she was kidnapped. She didn't see them and dropped her head back to the trunk floor. Her captor slammed the trunk lid and darkness filled the space. *Oh, dear God, what am I going to do? Help me.*

The car's engine revved and, as it took off, Kaitlyn rolled against the rear of the trunk, smashing her face. Tears sprang to her eyes, and she scooched back. Her back banged against something hard and angular. A tool box, perhaps. After several right turns, the driver took a curvy road way too fast. Kaitlyn thumped back and forth between the tool-box-like-item and the rear of the trunk.

The further they drove the more Kaitlyn was certain where they were headed. The Road to Nowhere. That didn't bode well for her. Kaitlyn's heart pounded. She probably wasn't going home. Not tonight. Not ever. Who was this man? What did he want with her? Why was he doing this?

The car stopped and the engine died. The car door slammed, and Kaitlyn heard scuffing footsteps headed toward the rear of the car. *Give me grace, Lord.* Were prayers worth praying? *God, are You listening?* Of course, He was. God always listens. If this was to be her end, then so be it.

The trunk popped open. It was nearly pitch black out except for the zillion twinkling stars filling the inky sky. *Those are for me tonight, aren't they, God? I need them right now as a reminder that You're here with me.*

He yanked her from the trunk, tossed her over his shoulder and started walking. Kaitlyn couldn't see where they were going until he walked past a set of cement barrier posts set in the pavement to prevent cars from passing. She recognized them. Glancing over his shoulder, she could barely make out the stone tunnel entrance up ahead. She'd been right. They were at the end of the Road to Nowhere at the tunnel that went nowhere, and Kaitlyn was sure she would be going nowhere. Except inside. Her heart raced as fear threatened to overwhelm her. *God, are You still with me?*

At the entrance to the tunnel, he tugged a flashlight from his pocket and flipped on the light, never breaking his pace. Born and raised in Bryson City, Kaitlyn had been to this place many times. How many? As a child with her family. With her teen friends. Hiking with her friends Jenny, Allyson and Kelly. And now? She was going to die here. It was a long walk to the other end of the tunnel. Would he go all the way? Or stop somewhere in between?

Except for the flashlight, which she only caught glimpses of, it was pitch black inside the hollow space. The pavement had long ago broken up and dirt filled in. Water seeped through the rounded dome roof making the tunnel floor wet and leaving puddles. He walked right through them.

Kaitlyn's head swam from being slung over his shoulder for so long, and her heart pounded with fear. It was hard to breathe. *Lord, help me.*

At the end of the tunnel, he dropped Kaitlyn onto the

damp, grassy ground. She lay gasping in the precious spring mountain air. Landing on her arms and hands behind her back was excruciating. She'd heard a pop and pain shot through her wrist. Was it broken? Kaitlyn bit the inside of her lip to keep from crying out, she eyed her tormentor. He stood over her, his face still hidden beneath the hood. He aimed the flashlight in her face and laughed--the first sound he'd made since kidnapping her. It was a malevolent sound that sent a chill down Kaitlyn's spine. He knelt beside her and clasped the lower half of her face in his gloved hand.

His voice was soft and raspy. "So pretty, Kaitlyn. So pretty. But not enough. You can't be around anymore. She won't like it, but you have to go. Kaitlyn. Is. Dead."

Kaitlyn's heart froze. *No. Please.*

Even as the thought rang in her mind, his hand slipped from her face to her throat and his other one joined it. Both increased pressure, squeezing, and blocking off her air supply. Kaitlyn couldn't breathe. The duct tape blocked her mouth. No air came. With her hands behind her back, she couldn't even claw at his hands in an attempt to pull them away. She couldn't fight for her life. She couldn't even gasp.

"Oh, poor Kaitlyn." He rasped as he slipped the hoodie back. An evil smile curled familiar lips. "Recognize me now?"

Darkness threatened her vision as Kaitlyn identified her killer, but it was too late. No one would know. She'd be dead, and no one would...Darkness swallowed Kaitlyn as her lungs failed and her heart stopped.

End of August
Current Year

Chapter One

Jenny glanced around at the twenty-two squirming first graders coloring at their desks then at her wristwatch. Five more minutes. Time to clean up. "All right, class. Put your crayons away and gather your backpacks and lunch bags. Take your pretty, colorful pictures home to show your parents. They'll love them. Now, in an orderly manner."

Within minutes, the class was ready and the bell rang. "Make two lines, class. Let's go."

Jenny led one line out to meet their parents, who picked up their little angels, and the other line to catch their buses.

Jenny had bus and child duty today, and when everyone was delivered, only two children remained: Cassie Hunter from her class, and a little boy from another class. With school only in session for three days, she hoped this wasn't a portent of things to come.

It wasn't long before the little boy's parent arrived to pick him up. Five minutes passed. Then ten. Jenny glanced at her wristwatch, her toe tapping on the cement sidewalk. All the buses had left, and she and Cassie were the only ones left in front of the school building. Whoever her parents were, they packed a load of inconsideration. Jenny hoped they also had a great reason for leaving Cassie waiting so long.

"Excuse me." A deep voice sounded behind Jenny.

She spun around to find a tall man in a National Park Service uniform striding toward them. His broad shoulders, muscular arms and lean waist indicated his fitness. A crooked smile lit his handsome features beneath clean-cut dark brown hair, and his chocolate brown eyes held an apology. He twisted a national park ball cap between his fingers. How had she not heard him approaching?

His gaze moved to Cassie, and he winked.

"Uncle Flint. You're here." The little girl beside Jenny dove toward him, and he lifted her into his arms.

"I'm here, peanut. Sorry I'm late."

She leaned back. "I don't mind," she lowered her voice to a loud whisper, "but you might have to apologize to her." She tossed her thumb over her shoulder toward Jenny.

His eyes met Jenny's, and his lips twisted into a wry grin. "You might be right."

Jenny stood silently waiting. She would not make this easy for him.

He held out his hand. "Flint Stockman. I'm Cassie's uncle and guardian."

Jenny reluctantly shook the outstretched hand. No matter how handsome and fit this man was, he was extremely late, and he needed to understand that wasn't acceptable. "I'm Jenny Mitchell, Cassie's teacher. Mr. Stockman, I hope you understand how late you are. School has only been in session three days, and we can't allow tardiness to be a precedent. You must pick Cassie up on time. We have a schedule for a reason." Had she gotten her message across? He certainly looked contrite.

Cassie wrapped her arms around her uncle's neck and gave him a hug. He patted her little arm, his gaze never straying from Jenny's.

"I apologize for my tardiness, Miss Mitchell. Unfortunately, there was an unforeseen circumstance that prevented me from being here sooner. I can't guarantee it won't happen again. Since I'm Cassie's only guardian, and I work in the park at Deep Creek, unforeseen things happen. I'll try to be here on time, or send someone to get her if I can't."

That idea appalled Jenny, and her brows rose. "Well, you can't just send anyone. They have to be on a pick-up list that you've registered with the school. We won't release her to someone not on a pre-approved list for safety's sake. Her safety, you understand."

He nodded. "Well, of course. I understand that. I'll make arrangements."

Jenny crossed her arms over her chest and lifted her chin, narrowing her gaze. "You're new here, aren't you, Ranger Stockman?"

He nodded again, a wry smile lifting one side of his handsome lips. "Yeah, and I'm new at being a guardian, too, so you might give me a little leeway here. I'm doing the best I can."

Cassie squeezed his neck again. "He's doing great."

Jenny couldn't prevent the smile that worked its way to her lips. "I'm sure he is, sweetie." She returned her eyes to his. "Work on that list of folks who can pick Cassie up when you can't. It's the best option."

He set Cassie on the ground and took her hand, then seated his cap on his head. "I'll do that. Have a good evening, Miss Mitchell. See you around."

He gave her a wink then turned and led Cassie away. Jenny had a funny feeling his last three words were more a promise than a goodbye.

~

Flint buckled Cassie into her car seat and glanced back to where Miss Mitchell had been standing. She'd returned inside the building, of course, but he couldn't forget the ire that flashed from her gorgeous hazel eyes. Not a great start with Cassie's teacher. He'd have to do better. Something about the beautiful teacher made him want to improve her opinion of him. Not sure why that was important, but deep down, he didn't want anyone to have a sour opinion of him.

He closed the back wing door of the extended pickup truck, walked around and climbed in. Starting the engine, he met Cassie's innocent eyes in the rear-view mirror. "Do you like your teacher?"

"Oh yeah. Lots and lots." Her head bobbed up and

down several times. "She makes class fun, and she's pretty too. Don't you think she's pretty, Uncle Flint?"

Turning the truck out of the school parking lot, Flint kept his eyes on the road and thought about his niece's question. Did he? With hazel eyes and delectable lips set in an oval face surrounded by what looked like soft wavy blond hair, yeah, he did. She was more than pretty. She was beautiful. And he'd spotted a tiny mole beside her lips that begged to be.... *What the heck, Stockman? You just met her.*

"Uncle Flint? Don't you think she's pretty?" A frown tipped Cassie's brows downward.

He met the concern in her gaze then looked back at the road. "Sure, I suppose she is. As long as she's a good teacher, and you have fun while you're learning, that's the important thing, sweetheart."

A smile returned to the little girl's lips. "Yep. She's a great teacher."

They discussed what Cassie had learned in class that day, all the while Flint attempted to shove the image of Jenny Mitchell from his mind. With a heavy sigh, he realized it might be a hard task to accomplish.

~

"How are you doing, now that you're back?" Allyson sidled up beside Jenny in the school lunchroom as their students went through the lunch line. "Sorry we haven't had a chance to chat. Things have come up. You know how it is."

Jenny gave her friend and fellow teacher a side hug. "Of course I do. No problem, but now that you're back, too, we'll have to catch up from our summer away."

"Yes we will." Allyson moved her students along in the line. "There's so much to catch up on, but you were on a mission trip to Romania and Ukraine, for goodness sake. I can't wait to hear about that."

Jenny smiled and urged her own students forward,

seating them at a table. "It was amazing. Just what I needed to…well, to help me through the difficulty of losing Kaitlyn. How about you? Did your time away give you any peace?"

Allyson nodded as she seated her class at a table and helped them open their milk cartons. "Yes it did." She lifted eyes that held a sparkle and her lips tilted upward. "It most certainly did."

"Uh-huh. You met someone, didn't you?" Jenny finished helping her students and stood at the end of the table, one eye on her students and one on her friend. "So when do we get together?"

Allyson eyed her cautiously. "Are you ready to walk again? Or is it too soon?"

Jenny clasped her hands in front of her and dropped her gaze to her hands. The mere thought of heading back out to Deep Creek and walking where their friend had vanished…. She tried to swallow but her throat was like sandpaper.

"Excuse me." She retreated to the water fountain near the exit and took a long drink, all the while thoughts of Kaitlyn swirling through her mind. Missing. She'd disappeared months ago. No one knew how. Simply gone. Her car left behind.

Jenny straightened. She had to get back to her class. Allyson still stood where Jenny had left her.

"I'm sorry, Allyson. I shouldn't have taken off like that."

Allyson placed a gentle hand on her arm. "It's fine. I watched both classes. Are you okay?"

"Yeah, I am. I just needed some water." Jenny swiped her hair behind her ear. "I'm not sure I'm ready to go back out there."

"I know it's hard, but we have to try. Even if we simply drive out and sit in the parking lot or walk up to the first waterfall. That's not far."

Jenny wasn't sure she was ready to take that walk. Not yet. But sitting in the parking lot? Maybe. "Let me think about it."

Allyson nodded. "Let me know. If you decide to, we can get Kelly and do it together."

Jenny gave her friend's arm a little squeeze. "Thanks, my friend. This has to be just as hard on you as it is on me. And we should check on Kelly to see how she's doing too."

"For sure." Allyson glanced at the first-grade tables. "I think our little angels are finished and getting restless. What do you think?"

Jenny smirked. "Without a doubt. Let's move them to the playground and dissipate some of this energy before attempting to teach them."

~

Walter and Agnes Barnes parked their car in the parking lot at the end of the Road to Nowhere. They climbed out and stretched their septuagenarian bodies in the morning sunlight filtering through the branches of the trees. A light breeze tickled the branches, inducing the dappling light on the pavement to dance about.

"What a gorgeous drive, Walter." Agnes glanced around. "This road may be a dead end, but it sure is beautiful and peaceful out here. And look. We're the first ones to arrive this morning."

"Sure thing, my love." Walter bent and placed a kiss on his sweetheart's cheek. "But I read that there's a tunnel down that road." He pointed past the end of the parking lot. "I don't know about you, but I'm feeling adventurous this morning. And I'm taking my flashlight." He waved the flashlight he'd brought from the car."

Agnes lifted a hand. "Well, if you are, I suppose I am too. As long as I'm with you, sweetheart."

They walked in the direction of the tunnel. "What kind of tunnel do you think it is, Walter?"

"Well, my dear, we'll soon find out."

235

They passed barrier posts used to prevent vehicles from entering the road and walked along the pavement. Before long they rounded a slight bend and the tunnel came into view.

"Oh my. That's a large one," Agnes pressed a hand to her breast, "and it's so dark inside. I can barely see the light at the other end."

Walter chuckled and squeezed her shoulder. "Never you mind, my love. Stick close to me and my flashlight. Remember, we're adventurers today."

Agnes tittered a nervous laugh. "Well, of course we are, dear."

The gaping mouth of the tunnel grew wider as they approached, and Agnes began to doubt the wisdom of this adventure. She clung to her husband's arm as he flipped on the flashlight. They stepped into the tunnel and began their trek inside. The morning light only lit the first fifty feet or so then it began to fade as the darkness enveloped them. The pavement, laid long ago, had broken up and the dirt had become muddy from the water seeping from the rounded cement ceiling. Walter shined the flashlight around in the darkness and they spotted graffiti on the walls and rounded ceiling. Black spots indicated places where campfires had been built along the lower edges of the rounded ceiling.

"Interesting place, don't you think?" Walter chuckled.

"Hmm." Agnes clung tighter to his arm. Her eyes focused on the light at the end of the tunnel. They couldn't get there fast enough for her liking. What about this had been a good idea? And to think they still had to return the same way.

What seemed like an eternity finally brought them to the other end where sunny morning light filled the mouth of the tunnel and welcomed them to a serene and beautiful scene. The broken pavement ended and a small grassy clearing surrounded by trees and lovely vegetation stirred with the cool early September morning breeze.

"Well, it was worth walking through that to see this, don't you think?" Walter strolled around and Agnes did the same.

"Oh, it is lovely here. Too bad they didn't install benches for visitors to sit and enjoy the scenery before having to trek back through that horrid tunnel." Agnes moved around the perimeter of the small clearing. "Oh my, look at these blue gentian flowers. And the yarrow. My, my, aren't they lovely?"

Walter chuckled. "My love, you'll find flowers anywhere, and you know all their names too."

"What in the world? What is this? Why it looks like...."

Agnes screamed and Walter hurried to her side. "Agnes, what...?"

Then he saw it and gasped.

~

Flint jammed the SUV into park and climbed out leaving the blue lights on top flashing. Slamming the door, he clicked the lock button on the fob and took off at a jog toward the tunnel. Retrieving his flashlight from his utility belt, he entered the darkness and ran all the way to the other end where he found a couple in their seventies waiting for him.

Sucking in a few deep breaths before speaking, he tucked the flashlight back in its place and held out a hand. "I'm Ranger Flint Stockman. I take it you're Walter and Agnes Barnes?"

They nodded, their features pale and twisted in horror. The man held his wife close, his arm supporting her. Flint hoped she wouldn't faint. He had nothing for her to sit on out here.

"I'm terribly sorry for the shock you've experienced." He planted a hand on his utility belt. "We have EMT's coming to check you out in case you need them."

"Oh, I don't think that's necessary." Walter waved a hand.

Flint eyed the man's wife and wasn't so sure about that. Her features held a green pallor around the edges. Her gaze fixed on his face, and she didn't blink. Agnes wavered on her feet, and Walter held her tighter.

"Well, maybe that would be a good idea." He cast a worried glance at his wife.

Flint placed a gentle hand on Agnes's arm. "Hang on, ma'am. Help is on the way, and you can lay down for a bit."

She gave a brief nod, her eyes never leaving his face.

Flint eased next to Walter and lowered his voice. "Can you tell me where you found...it?" The subject was difficult to avoid when he needed to get to the investigation, but he didn't want to upset Agnes any further. He hoped the ambulance would arrive soon.

"At the back of the clearing behind those blue flowers. Believe me, you can't miss it." Walter shuddered then closed his eyes as if attempting to purge the image from his mind.

Flint clapped his shoulder. "Hang tight. I'll be back."

"Oh, I don't think we're going anywhere, are we?" Walter heaved a heavy sigh.

"Afraid not." Flint strode to the area Walter had indicated and searched until he found a patch of ground in the weeds and high flowers that had been freshly gouged. He stepped closer, but not too close. This was now a possible murder scene. He squatted for a closer look. The ground had been dug up recently, possibly by a fox or coyote. No claw marks from a bear. The disturbing thing was what had been unearthed. The side of a decomposing face and dark brown hair.

"What've you got there, Flint?" The deep voice of his supervisor, Cal Bishop, came from behind him.

Flint glanced over his shoulder. "Nothing good, that's

for sure. Looks like a female with dark brown hair. Her ear is missing. Likely whatever dug the hole took care of that. I'm sure the coroner can identify her."

Cal stepped closer and eyed the grisly contents in the hole. He huffed a heavy sigh. "Yep, but I think I know who that is. Of course, I'll wait for the coroner's findings to be sure." He held out a hand to help Flint up and back to the clearing.

"Thanks." Flint eyed his supervisor. In the short time he'd worked at Deep Creek, he'd come to admire and respect the man with the sandy-haired crew cut. Flint had worked in a couple of parks and with a few supervisors, but Cal Bishop was by far the best.

A siren echoed in the distance through the tunnel. Poor Agnes looked as if she were about to pass out. Walter was her stalwart wall to lean on.

"The coroner is on the way." Cal turned back to Flint. "Let's start investigating. Here." He handed Flint a 35mm camera. "Start snapping pictures of the scene. I'll look around."

Flint accepted the camera and moved in on the burial site of the unknown female. At least she was unknown to him. Cal had an inkling of her identity. Flint would sure like to know how. He aimed, focused and snapped shots from every possible angle, then he moved around the clearing, searching. Searching for anything out of the ordinary. Searching for clues. Searching for...yes, that. He spotted something shiny near the edge of the clearing tucked in the grass. It shone in the morning sunlight. Stepping closer, he snapped a few photos then called Cal over.

"What'd you find?" his supervisor bent over.

"Do you have tweezers in your investigative kit? We've got something shiny."

"Sure thing." Cal grabbed his kit and returned, retrieving a pair of long metal tweezers and a small evidence bag. He handed the tweezers to Flint.

Separating the blades of grass, Flint grasped the shiny object and lifted it for them to observe. A small, gold flat oval with a loop on one end rotated between the tweezer tips. Bits of dirt encrusted areas of the surface on both sides.

Cal zoomed in and snapped a few photos while Flint held the object still.

"Drop it in here." Cal held the small evidence bag open. "We'll have it cleaned and see if there's anything on it that may give us a clue. Good eye." He clapped Flint on the shoulder.

"Thanks." Flint stood. "Did you find anything else?"

"Not yet."

The EMTs had arrived with a gurney for Agnes and were treating her for shock. Walter stood by, her hand held securely in his. A few minutes later, the ambulance backed through the tunnel and parked. The barrier had been opened by the park cop on duty, allowing the ambulance in.

Flint stepped to Walter's side as the attendants loaded his wife inside the ambulance. "Is she all right?"

The older man turned, the wrinkles on his face deep with his concern. "I hope so. Agnes has a heart condition, and this was a terrible shock for her. They're taking her to the ER, and I'll follow in my car. I'm sure they'll admit her, for observation, you know. This is all my fault." He ran a shaky hand down his angular face. "I shouldn't have forced her to come through that tunnel. I thought it would be a fun adventure."

"Walter, you had no idea you'd find a body." Flint laid a hand on the man's shoulder. "You can't blame yourself. Simply walking through the tunnel and back to your car would've been a fun adventure. Are you a praying man, sir?"

Walter's sad eyes met Flint's. He shook his head. "I haven't prayed in a long time, son."

Flint gave him a gentle grin. "Maybe now is a good time to start again."

"Sir," the EMT at the back of the ambulance waved Walter forward.

He nodded then eyed Flint. "You're probably right." Walter walked over and talked with the EMT, then climbed aboard where he'd catch a ride to his car.

Flint gave Walter a two-fingered salute when he looked out the back window before he settled into his seat, and the ambulance drove into the darkness of the tunnel.

"Poor fellow." Cal stepped beside Flint, investigative kit in hand. A set of headlights passed the ambulance then the coroner's van appeared in the entrance. It parked at the edge of the grass and a woman in her fifties climbed out accompanied by her young assistant. It was a good thing he was young. It was likely he would be the one doing the digging to remove the body.

"Doc Peters." Cal approached the red-haired woman. She wore wire-framed glasses and her hair was held back in a ponytail. She and her young dark-haired assistant wore navy coveralls and ball caps with the word Coroner printed on the caps and the left breast and back of the coveralls.

"Cal." She waved as she opened the side panel of the van and extracted cases of equipment. Her assistant pulled out a shovel and a small hand broom. "It's good to see you. We haven't been out to the park in a while."

"Nope. We've been fortunate that we haven't needed you." Cal chuckled. He waved a hand in Flint's direction. "This is Flint Stockman, our new ranger. Flint, this is the best coroner east of the Mississippi. And she'll tell you so too. That's her assistant, Wilson Carter, or Will for short."

The silent Will waved a hand and returned to the van for a body bag and the gurney.

"Nice to meet you, Flint. Welcome to the Smokies. I take it you're not from around here." Doc Peters eyed him over the rim of her glasses. "Where are you from?"

"Silver Springs, Florida."

"Oh, I've visited there." She set down her cases and shoved her glasses up. "Beautiful place. I love the glass bottom boats. They filmed the old Tarzan movies there. I'm an old movie buff."

Cal chuckled. "You and my wife, Pam. Come on over here." He led the way to the burial spot. "It's not pretty, but I'm sure you've seen worse."

"Honey, there's not much I haven't seen. I could write a book only nobody would want to read it." Doc bent over and scanned the unearthed partial face and hair. "Uh-huh. From what I can see, we've got ourselves a female missing an ear, but that's all I can tell. Will, bring that shovel and let's get to work."

Author's Notes

If you've read many of my books, you've discovered that I enjoy doing research to add authenticity to them. There are generally facts sprinkled amongst the fiction. *Discovering Elena* is no exception. I passed through Frankfurt twice during my US Army tour of duty in Pisa, Italy, but saw nothing but the airport and the train station. Anything in the story I gathered solely from my research. The same is true of my trip to Munich. A friend of mine and I took a tour from Italy to Bavaria and we visited several places including Neuschwanstein Castle (not in Munich,) and the tour ventured into Munich to the Oktoberfest. That was interesting and about the extent of my visit to Munch. I don't recall much else from the city, but I did extensive research for this book and found a lot:

The hotels in the story, the Steigenberger Icon Frankfurter Hof in Frankfurt and the Hotel Bayerischer Hof in Munich are actual hotels, and I kept the descriptions as close to the pictures as I could. I did the best with the interiors and left the rest to writer's license.

The Czechoslovakian aspect of the story is a nod to my husband's mom's side of the family. Her mother's parents came from there. Auntie Anna, Auntie Genevieve and Uncle Rudy are named after Mark's great-aunts and great-uncle. Their personalities are similar, especially Auntie Genevieve (or Auntie Genny.) They're all passed now. I've attempted to find the proper Czech words, but there's no one to ask anymore. Mark's grandmother is no longer around. If anyone reads this and finds I've blundered, please forgive me.

The food is as authentic as I've been able to make it. If

you find a mistake, help a girl out.

The apartment building and the B&B were built from my imagination. Strictly writer's license there. The schloss's exterior came from a picture. The interior from my imagination. I hope you enjoyed the visit.

As most folks know Dachau Concentration Camp is an actual place. It is less than a half-hour drive from Munich. Martin Gottfried Weiss was the actual commandant of Dachau at the time of the liberation of the camp by US forces in 1945. I was unable to find who the real-life Nazi in charge of executions was. Dachau was originally intended to house Hitler's political opponents such as communists, social democrats and other dissidents. Heinrich Himmler changed that purpose to include the imprisonment of Jews, Romanians, Germans and Austrian Criminals. As mentioned in the story, over 32,000 documented executions took place here and thousands of undocumented executions. At the time of liberation on April 29, 1945, about 10,000 of the 30,000 prisoners were sick. I won't go into the brutal treatment and terror the inmates lived under.

The Viktualienmarkt that Mark Scott took their group to was an actual market that stood for over two hundred years and is still in use today.

I enjoyed researching the National Theater on Max-Joseph-Platz and would dearly have loved visiting this landmark. I found as many pictures as possible and kept my description as true to them as possible with a few exceptions. The building was nearly destroyed during World War Two, and it was planned to simply tear it down. Munich citizens pleaded for it to be rebuilt, and it was approved. It took many years and finally reopened on

November 21, 1963.

Do you recall Mark mentioning Viscardigasse? This street became known as Drueckebergerasse or Shirkers Alley. A shrine to Hitler and his thugs and to a night back in 1923 when they attempted to overthrow the German government had been built just down the street by the Nazis. Nazi guards stood forcing Germans to salute the shrine as they passed. People didn't want to salute it and began slipping down narrow Viscardigasse to avoid it. It wasn't long before the Nazis caught on, and they started shooting and killing the German shirkers. Today the small alleyway is only for pedestrians. A trail of meandering bronzed paving bricks commemorates the brave Germans who stood up and refused to salute Hitler and lost their lives for it.

There are two sets of life-sized dancers in the Rathaus-Glockenspiel at the Munich Town Hall Tower. One plays to music at 11 am and the second plays at noon. The first tells the history of the marriage of Duke Willhelm V in honor of his marriage. A joust of life-sized horses and knights were made for the glockenspiel. The colors of blue and white represents the region of Bavaria and win the joust every time they play. The second set of figures are coopers' dancers. They dance to celebrate the end of a severe plague that happened in 1517.

The US military group, Supreme Headquarters Allied Expeditionary Force, or SHAEF, led the invasion on D-Day headed up by Gen. Dwight Eisenhower and was located in London, England. The invasion was executed on June 6, 1944. To my knowledge a lady named Elena Cigler or Elena Jäger never spied for this cause. This was all writer's license.

The Nuremburg Trials took place in Nuremburg, Germany between Nov. 20, 1945 and Oct 1, 1946. The International Military Tribunal tried twenty-one of the most important surviving Nazi leaders. They were from Nazi political, military and economic groups. They were indicted on four counts: crimes against peace, crimes against humanity, war crimes and conspiracy to commit the first three crimes. During the Third Reich's reign of terror they killed more than 27 million in the Soviet Union alone. That's only one country. Their war machine spread across Europe swallowing up Poland, Denmark, Norway, the Netherlands, Belgium, Luxembourg, France, Yugoslavia, Greece, Czechoslovakia and the Soviet Union. They imprisoned, murdered, exterminated and more across every country they acquired. The trials dealt with every aspect of these crimes.

Twelve subsequent trials were held between 1946 and 1949. The Holocaust and the deaths of millions of Jews played a huge part in the trials and led to the Universal Declaration of Human Rights.

When the final trials ended, that did not mean the hunt for Nazis ended. The US military as well as organizations such as Israel's Mossad and various private groups searched through the years to bring Nazis to justice. Many were found, tried for the above crimes and executed depending on their place in the Nazi war machine. One example is Adolf Eichmann, one of the major organizers of the Holocaust. He was discovered by Mossad in Argentina in 1960. He was tried in Jerusalem, Israel, and hanged. Dr. Joseph Mengele, the "Angel of Death" fled to Brazil. Israel's Mossad searched for him for years but never caught up with him.

Author Bio

A native North Carolinian, Carol always loved reading and making up stories since childhood. She began writing in junior high school. As a young adult, she worked in the National Park Service and served in the US Army where she was stationed in Pisa, Italy. While there she met the love of her live, Mark Nemeth, who also served in the Army. They've lived in various locations including North Yorkshire, England. Now living in West Virginia, in their spare time they enjoy RVing and traveling to research for Carol's books. They have two grown children, Matt and Jennifer, a son-in-law, Flint, a daughter-in-law, Holly, and three amazing grandchildren, Martin, Ava and Gage.

A multi-published author of fourteen books and multiple short stories, Carol is blessed to be an Amazon #1 bestselling author and an ACFW Carol Award Semi-finalist, an American Bookfest finalist, and a Selah Award finalist. She's a member of American Christian Fiction Writers and Faith, Hope & Love Christian Writers. She writes romantic suspense, both historical and contemporary. Her goal is to write stories that will be entertaining and enjoyable while at the same time uplifting and faith-building. May Christ always be glorified.

Connect with me on FaceBook
Twitter

Sign up for my newsletter and receive a free short

story

www.JCarolNemeth.com

Follow me on Amazon
Goodreads and Bookbub

Enjoy other books by J. Carol Nemeth

Christmas Historical Romantic Suspense

Yorkshire Lass

Faith in the Park Series

Dedication to Love: Prequel to Mountain of Peril
Mountain of Peril, Faith in the Parks Book 1
Canyon of Death, Faith in the Parks Book 2
A Beacon of Love, Prequel to Ocean of Fear
Ocean of Fear, Faith in the Parks Book 3
Glacier of Secrets, Faith in the Parks Book 4
Battlefield of Deceit, Faith in the Parks Book 5

Small Town

Death Goes to School
Courage on the Run

Christmas Novella

Parade of Hearts

Hearts of the Manhattan Project
Short Story Collection

The Secretary
The Nurse
The Chemist

Collections

The Peaceful Valley Wounded Soldiers Anthology

Collections with Other Authors

Run Faster

Made in the USA
Middletown, DE
27 March 2025

73349972R00144